Little Ricky

Little Ricky
Copyright © 2023 by Luis Zaensi

Published in the United States of America

Library of Congress Control Number: 2023923397
ISBN   Paperback: 979-8-89091-373-9
ISBN   eBook: 979-8-89091-374-6

All rights reserved. No part of this publication may be reproduced, stored in a retrieval system or transmitted in any way by any means, electronic, mechanical, photocopy, recording or otherwise without the prior permission of the author except as provided by USA copyright law.

The opinions expressed by the author are not necessarily those of ReadersMagnet, LLC.

ReadersMagnet, LLC
10620 Treena Street, Suite 230 | San Diego, California, 92131 USA
1.619. 354. 2643 | www.readersmagnet.com

Book design copyright © 2023 by ReadersMagnet, LLC. All rights reserved.

Cover design by Jhiee Oraiz
Interior design by Don De Guzman

Little Ricky

Luis Zaensi

Chapter 1

It was a hot night in July 2015, but it is even hotter inside the Disco Forever nightclub. The music of KC and the Sunshine Band is deafening. The song "That's the way I like It" seems to have a narcotic effect on Ricardo and his wife Dorothy. They have been married for almost five years, but they are still living the crazy life, as if they are still teenagers. Ricardo is very handsome, tall, with straight black hair, while Dorothy is equally beautiful, with long blond hair and blue eyes. And even though they do not exercise, they have enviable bodies.

They dance as if they are professional dancers. They are the life of the party, known to all, and they all chant their names in the center of the dance floor. They steal the show with their erotic way of dancing. Between the dances come the drinks, accompanied by some marijuana cigarettes to complete their routine.

The doorman does not charge them entrance to the premises; their presence animates the nightclub, and that is good for the business.

At four thirty in the morning, they say goodbye to the owner and the security guards. Once again, they get into their car, a blue Toyota Corolla that only sees the water when it rains and has the registration expired for more than three months.

The owner of the nightclub asks Ricardo.

"Do you want me to call you a taxi? You are a little more drunk than usual."

"No, thank you, the car knows the way and always takes us home." Ricardo responds.

Everyone just laughs, perhaps a bit irresponsibly, not thinking about the danger this presents. Ricardo tries to start the car, but after several attempts, the car's battery runs out of charge.

Ricardo asks his wife. "Dorothy, did you put gas in the car today?"

She sighs. "No, love. I thought you did it this morning?"

Ricardo hits the steering wheel and screams. "Shit, not only do we have no gas, but we also killed the battery!"

The security guard approaches him, asking. "What happened? You do not want to go home today?"

Ricardo gets out of the car and answers him. "You will not believe this, John. The gas gauge is broken, so we ran out of gas without realizing it, and now we killed the battery!"

"I have a container with gasoline for the generator. I also have cables to jump your battery. But remember, you owe me one."

Ricardo shakes his hand and responds, "Thanks, John, but you have been paid more than enough by looking at my wife's ass when she is dancing, instead of guarding the door. Or do you think I have not noticed?" He chuckles. "I do not care if you look, though, as long as you don't touch."

Dorothy gets out of the car and asks. "Rick, what are we going to do?"

"All good, love. Our guardian angel, Johnny, has everything under control." Ricardo answers.

Ricardo and Dorothy live in a mixed lower-middle-class area in Miami. Upon arriving home, Ricardo sees that he has a car blocking the entrance to his house.

"Shit, there is no respect in this neighborhood. This is the second time this vehicle blocks our entrance. I'm going to puncture the tires!" He hisses.

"No, please! We don't know whom that vehicle belongs to, and they might retaliate against us!" Dorothy responds nervously.

"Okay, just so you don't worry. Now, let's see where the hell I can find parking."

After ten minutes of searching for parking, they find a space one block from their house. Ricardo keeps cursing all the way home, and his wife tries to calm him down.

Once at home, the two sit on the bed in their nightclothes. Dorothy gives Ricardo the phone and tells him.

"It's 5:40 AM, time for you to call work."

Ricardo takes the phone and makes a face, raising his eyebrows to indicate he is uncertain. "My god, what do I say?"

Dorothy answers him. "Tell him we went to my parents' house and ate seafood. It apparently was not good, and we both got food poisoning. I will talk to Mom just in case."

Ricardo kisses her and tells her. "You are not only beautiful, but you are also intelligent. That is why you are with me."

Dorothy pushes him back and responds. "Cocky! You are the one who is lucky to be with me."

Ricardo calls his work, and the supervisor answers.

"Hi, Peter, it's me, Ricardo."

"Oh my god, what story do you bring me this time?" The supervisor responds.

"No story, Peter. I went to my in-laws' house, and we got food poisoning with some shellfish. Dorothy and I are both in bed. You can come in and convince yourself if you want."

"Fuck off, Rick," Peter responds. "You are irresponsible! It's time for you to grow up. I'm not going to put my job in danger for you. I have a family, and I'm not going to cover for you anymore. What's more, I will give you some advice. You better say you are a Seventh Day Adventist and for religious reasons, you do not work on Saturdays. It will be a more credible lie. The next time you call absent again on a Saturday, make sure it is to quit!" Peter then hangs up the phone angrily.

Ricardo makes a surprised face when he hears the screams of his supervisor. Dorothy laughs and tells him. "If it were him, I would have fired you a long time ago."

"Very funny." Ricardo answers. He then gives the phone to his wife and tells her. "It is your turn now."

Dorothy calls her work, and her supervisor answers.

"Hi, Hellen. It's me, Dorothy."

"Yes, I know," Hellen says. "You are not coming to work, as usual. You cannot even walk because of your menstrual pain."

"Do not mock me. I do not see the humor in it. I think it is a cruel and inappropriate comment." Dorothy responds.

"None of that. Only that you are the only woman who menstruates on Saturdays. You are worthy of a medical study!" The supervisor responds sarcastically.

"Well, you are wrong. My husband is very ill with food poisoning from seafood. I warned him not to eat it, but he was stupid and ignored me. Now, if he does not improve, I will have to take him to the hospital before he dehydrates."

Dorothy hears a prolonged silence. She looks at her husband, who opens his hands and shrugs Dorothy hears a prolonged silence. She looks at her husband, who opens his hands and shrugs since he does not know what is happening either.

Suddenly, the supervisor responds. "I have to give you credit. You have been original this time. But next Saturday you do not come to work, do not worry about calling or coming in on Sunday. We will send the check to your home." The supervisor throws down the phone angrily and tells her assistant, "I'm going to get rid of this garbage, I swear."

Dorothy looks at her husband and says.

"What a temper this old woman has. I swear, one of these days, I'm going to have a collection at the supermarket to buy her a vibrator!"

The two laugh and begin to roll in bed, making wild love, and then later fall asleep, exhausted.

******

Dorothy wakes up at eleven in the morning when the sun hits her face through the vertical blinds, which are missing two strips.

"Damn! When are you going to fix that curtain? If you are not going to fix it, then sleep on my side, so it will wake you up instead of me," Dorothy says, somewhat irked.

Ricardo sits on the bed, looks at her, then gets up, takes a towel that is on a chair, and puts it on the curtain, blocking the sunlight.

"Satisfied?" He asks.

"Yes, as long as it doesn't fall." Dorothy smiles sheepishly. "Now, come and snuggle me. I'm cold."

Ricardo goes back to bed.

Both are still sleeping when they are awakened by a loud knock on the door.

"Rick, someone is knocking on the door. Please go see who it is." Dorothy tells her husband.

He responds, annoyed. "I am not waiting for anyone. If you care so much, you go see who it is."

Neither of them gets up, but the blows do not stop and only get stronger. Dorothy then decides to get up. She puts on a robe and goes to answer the door. She is surprised when she sees that it is the postman bringing a certified mail.

"You look like you are in a hurry to deliver this letter. You almost knocked down the door!" Dorothy says, exasperated.

"I got tired of ringing the bell, and you didn't open the door."

"The doorbell does not work," Dorothy responds.

"I was leaving, but the boy next door told me to knock hard, that you were at home." The postman points to Tamian, Dorothy's little neighbor. "I need a signature. It is a certified letter for Mr. Ricardo Suarez."

Dorothy takes the letter and responds. "I am his wife. Where do I sign?"

"Here, please."

After handing the letter, the postman leaves, and Dorothy stares at the letter. She does not know the sender's name. Dorothy looks to her right and sees Kenya with her two children. Tamian is eight years old, and Tamima is seventeen years old. They are all cleaning around the front of the house.

Tamian tells her. "Hello, Mrs. Dorothy. I told him to knock louder!"

"Thank you, Tamian. You are very kind."

Dorothy closes the door and says to herself.

"What a gossipy child!"

Dorothy enters the kitchen and puts the letter on the table. Ricardo enters the kitchen, still in his underwear, and asks her.

"Who was it, love?"

"The postman brought a registered letter for you."

Ricardo, surprised, asks, "For me? From whom?"

"I don't know. Read it and you will know."

Ricardo takes the letter, looks at the sender, and exclaims.

"My God! This woman again?"

Ricardo throws the letter without opening it, and his wife asks him.

"What do you mean that woman again? Who is that woman?"

"She is a crazy woman with whom I spent a night on a cruise in the Bahamas nine years ago. About three months later, she invited me to her house to tell me she was expecting my child."

"Why didn't you ever tell me?" Dorothy asks.

Ricardo takes her by the hand and sits her on his legs. "That was a year before we met. I was reborn the day I met you. I only have eyes for you now, and our pasts don't count."

"Yes, but we are talking about a son!" Dorothy responds.

"The fact I have been with her does not mean that he is my son," Ricardo, irritated, tells his wife. "They are people with a lot of money. Her father is a judge, and if the child were mine, they would have hit me with the full weight of the law. It is obvious that, to avoid a scandal in their high society, they looked for an asshole to blame."

"Well, in that case, read the letter to see what it says." Dorothy responds.

"No, read it yourself if you want."

Dorothy opens the letter and begins to read it, then she says.

"Interesting."

"What's interesting about it? Read it out loud, please." Ricardo asks, curious.

Dorothy says. "Well, it goes like this."

LITTLE RICKY

Mr. Ricardo Suarez

I hereby inform you that I will be leaving soon and you, as Ricky's biological father, must take care of him. My departure is early, but I don't know when. I do not hold a grudge against you, because with the many problems and anguish that you caused me, you gave me the most beautiful thing that I have had in life. To make an appointment, please call 954-603-8011.

Sincerely,
Virginia Clark

Ricardo, indignant, says. "That woman is a son of a bitch! First, she wanted to blame me for the boy, and since that didn't work, she calmed down for a while. Now she gets tangled up with another rich man who doesn't accept her son and tries to give him to me again so she could go live her happy life!"

Ricardo rips the letter into tiny pieces and angrily says.

"I may be poor, but I am not the asshole that woman thinks I am. She will not ruin my life. She cannot buy me, and neither can she intimidate me!"

Dorothy tells him.

"I believe you, and I am on your side, but what are you going to do?"

"First, that is not a court order, and that tells you that she knows she is lying. Second, I am not going to do a damn thing to convince her she is barking up the wrong tree. If I want a child, it will be with you."

Ricardo suddenly sweeps Dorothy off her feet and takes her to bed, where they make love again like a pair of juveniles.

******

Three months pass. Ricardo and Dorothy had forgotten about the letter. After all, they are convinced that it is a plot to force Ricardo to recognize a son who does not belong to him.

Ricardo and Dorothy are preparing to celebrate their fifth anniversary. They will be going on a cruise through Mexico and the Caribbean. It will be a whole week to celebrate and not have to call in sick the next day. Their luggage is ready, and the ship will sail from the port of Miami at two o'clock.

For Dorothy, it is a dream. She will not only celebrate her fifth anniversary with her husband, but it is also the first time that she takes a cruise and will be leaving the country.

Dorothy asks her husband. "Did you call the taxi?"

"Yes, love, remember that we must be there three hours in advance to pass all the security checks without having to rush."

Ricardo hugs his wife and kisses her passionately.

"On this trip, we are going to make a request to the stork. If it resembles you, it will be a beauty, and if it resembles me, it will be double the beauty!"

Dorothy pushes him, telling him.

"You will not contribute anything to this. I will do it myself, because everything you touch, you damage it!"

Someone knocks on the door, and Ricardo says.

"Strange. Taxi drivers usually sound the horn, but this one gets out of the taxi. If he thinks by doing that, he will receive a big tip, he will be sorely disappointed."

Dorothy looks through the torn curtain and sees a luxury limousine in front of the house, but she doesn't see anyone in it.

"My love, you earned 100 points with me today. That detail of asking for a limousine, I never expected. This is going in style!"

Ricardo thinks his wife is joking, and so he decides to play along.

"That is so you see I do not skimp when it comes to celebrating. I told you this anniversary will be unforgettable, and I doubt that with a baby next year, we can go anywhere."

Each one takes their suitcase and begins to leave the room, heading toward the door. Dorothy hears the knock on the door again, and Ricardo screams.

"Wait! Don't be so desperate, for God's sake!"

LITTLE RICKY

Ricardo opens the door, thinking he will see the taxi driver, but he is rendered speechless when he sees two men impeccably dressed in suits, one holding a black briefcase in his right hand.

"I'm sorry, gentlemen, but you have the wrong address—obviously the wrong neighborhood, or maybe even the wrong planet."

Dorothy, who is standing with her suitcase behind Ricardo, laughs.

"No wonder it seems strange to me that you had asked for a limousine to go to the port."

Ricardo proceeds to close the door, but the taller man puts his foot on the doorframe, preventing Ricardo from closing it. Ricardo gets upset and opens the door and stands in front of the man, telling him.

"Look, penguin, who the hell do you think you are, coming to my house with gangster attitudes? Get out of here before I kick you and your puppet out of here!"

The man, undeterred, replies.

"I am Tony Clark. I represent Virginia Clark, mother of Ricardo Clark, your son."

"What the fuck are you talking about?" Ricardo shouts. "This has gone too far! Get that hell out of my house before I lose my patience!"

An enraged Dorothy pushes Ricardo and stands in front of Tony, pointing her finger at Tony's face, screaming at him.

"This is harassment, and I am going to sue you!"

Everyone turns their heads when they hear the sound of a car horn, which seems to not stop.

It is the taxi driver, who has come to take them to the port and is waving.

Ricardo yells at the taxi driver.

"Wait, Haitian, and stop that shit!"

The taxi driver, who is Black but not Haitian, angrily replies in perfect English.

"Haitian will be your mother, and I'm going to start the meter!"

The taxi driver gets into the taxi and starts the meter, saying.

"Take all the time you want, asshole!"

Tony asks Ricardo. "Are you Ricardo Suarez?"

"Yes, I am, and I have nothing to talk to you about."

The two men step aside, and Ricardo sees a blond boy with blue eyes, impeccably dressed in a suit, with a suitcase next to him. Ricardo and Dorothy are speechless for a moment. The child's gaze is cold as ice, and there is no expression on his face; he looks like an ornament doll.

"But who the fuck is this boy?" Dorothy asks.

Tony responds. "I already told you; he is his son. The mother died, and unfortunately, he has no blood family other than him, so I am bringing him to you. It is in the mother's will."

Tony almost loses control, pushes Ricardo, opens his portfolio, and takes out some papers, almost squeezing them in Ricardo's face.

"Look, asshole, if you don't stay with him, I'll take him, but I want you to know that I will sue you for the sum of sixty thousand dollars for not having paid child support for eight years, and I will make your life miserable. So, tell me now if you won't accept him, so I can call the police to file a report to use it against you in court."

The taxi driver lays on the taxi's horn again, further making the situation more straining. Tony, who is angry enough, turns around and yells at him to shut up with that stupid shit.

The enraged taxi driver gets out of the taxi. He is a very fat man, and his face is sweaty because, to save on gas, he does not turn on the air-conditioning unless he has a passenger.

Tony sees the taxi driver approaching, so he takes out his wallet, taking two one-hundred-dollar bills. Tony keeps his eyes fixed on Ricardo, who, confused, does not know what to say and looks at his wife as if asking for help. The taxi driver comes up and says.

"You called me, and here I am. You can argue, you can kill each other, you can make love, but with my time you don't play."

Tony, without taking his eyes off Ricardo, stretches his arm back with the two one-hundred-dollar bills, hitting the taxi driver in the chest. The surprised taxi driver opens his eyes, thinking that Tony has attacked him, but he notices the money and his eyes widen even more. The taxi driver takes the money and, in a very friendly voice, says to Tony.

"Sir don't bother. I just wanted to tell you that it doesn't bother me to wait a little longer."

Tony, without looking at the taxi driver and with his eyes still fixed on Ricardo, as if it were a duel from the Old West, he answers.

"No, that's all. You can go."

The taxi driver, almost dancing, leaves in a hurry; after all, he has earned two hundred dollars for waiting about ten minutes. He now wears a happy face that is worthy of a TV commercial.

Ricardo takes the papers and begins to examine them. Dorothy breaks down in tears and hugs husband, who caresses her with his left hand while he holds the document with his right hand and continues reading. After a minute, Ricardo is still reading and caressing his wife, and not a single word has been said. The silence is broken by Ricky, who, like a robot, without showing any emotion, takes his suitcase and says in an authoritative voice,

"Excuse me"

Ricky enters the residence, passes them, and then looks back. He sees Ricardo and Dorothy, who are looking at him as if he were a ghost.

"My name is Ricardo Clark. I am eight years old. Where is my room?"

Dorothy puts both her hands on Ricardo's shoulders and shakes him hard as she tells him.

"Tell me this is a bad joke. Please tell me that it is a lie!"

Ricardo tries to hug her. "Love, I am as surprised as you are. We had already talked about this, but I never thought it was true."

Dorothy, in a fit of rage and helplessness, slaps Ricardo, then she turns and kicks the suitcases and locks herself in the room. Ricardo looks like a mummy; his world has changed in a second, and he doesn't know what to do or say. But his greatest fear is losing his wife.

Tony breaks the silence and asks Ricardo.

"Can you show me Ricky's room?"

Ricardo, still stunned and without saying a word, points his finger toward the door. Ricardo's house is a two-bedroom, one-bath house built in the 1950s, and what is not broken is about to break. Tony takes the suitcase from Ricky and carries it to the room. When he opens the room, he sees it is full of junk and dirty clothes. In one corner there is a small sofa bed with many dirty clothes on it. Tony tries to turn on the light, but the bulb explodes. He closes the door and kneels in front of Ricky, hugging him tightly, and tells him.

"You don't have to do this. I'm sure your mother would understand. I can't be calm knowing that you are living in these conditions."

Ricky hugs Tony and responds to him, saying.

"Uncle, I'll be fine. Mom asked me, and I promised her to do what she wanted."

Tony takes a phone out of his pocket and hands it to Ricky.

"This is for your personal use. You cannot give it to anyone. Every night I will call you and you will tell me if you are okay."

Tony embraces the boy again. He can't stop the tears from running down his cheeks. Ricky is his nephew, but he has to respect his sister's will. Drawing strength from the depths within him, he gets up and leaves the room. Tony looks at Ricardo, who is standing, leaning against the wall. Tony approaches him and asks him.

"Do you need anything?"

"Yes. I need you to get out of my house."

"I mean for the child." Tony responds.

"If he is my son, then he is my problem not yours. I do not need your help."

Tony, about to lose control again, stands in front of Ricardo.

"Listen, you idiot, if something happens to that child, you will not only go to jail, but also, when you get out, you will be going to the cemetery next."

Ricardo pushes Tony and responds.

"What do you think? Because you're with a briefcase and dressed like a penguin you're going to intimidate me? I will kick you and your penguin ass if you don't get out of my house right away!"

Tony understands that this is not the time for a fight, and it will further aggravate Ricky's situation, so he decides not to respond and just leave.

As Tony is sitting in the limo, all the time he is remembering how he had asked his sister many times to leave Ricky with him. In his opinion, there is no one better than him to take care of the boy. He remembers the conversation he had with her the night before Ricky's mother died.

"I need you to reconsider your position." Tony had said.

"I can't. I want a father for my son, not an uncle." Virginia had answered.

"I know I'm adopted, but we've been closer than if we were family by blood. I lost Father and Grandfather in the accident, and now I'm losing you and you want to take Ricky from me before you go? That's not fair!"

Virginia, squeezing his hand, replied.

"I am not taking him away from you. I am going in peace knowing that you will be looking over him. I just want him to have his father. I know you will not abandon him, but if he did not get to know his father and you are missing, then he would not have anyone in this world."

"You are being pessimistic and unfair." Tony had responded.

"No, I'm being realistic. Mom died of breast cancer when I was thirteen. Dad and Grandpa died in a car accident two years ago, and I've been fighting the same breast cancer that killed Mom for three years. It's not pessimism, it is realism. Just promise me you will do what I asked you, brother."

"Against my will, but I will. I promise you." Tony had answered.

******

Ricky has been left alone in the room. He sits on the sofa and gives his emotions free rein. He begins to cry, sitting on the sofa with both hands covering his face and his elbows on his knees. He stays like that for a while, until he suddenly stops and looks around. On his face there is a great fury. Ricky begins to take out the toolbox and put it in a corner of the kitchen, all while Ricardo tries to comfort Dorothy, who has stopped crying but is still refusing to accept Ricky.

"I can't believe he doesn't have anyone else in the world. That's impossible!" Dorothy says angrily.

"Love, I will find out, but if the mother died, even if he has family, I am responsible for him. I doubt they will make such a mistake, because with a DNA test, the truth will come out, and then would be millionaires!"

Dorothy points her finger at his face and flushes with her rage. She answers him.

"Well, take the DNA test tomorrow, because I doubt, he is yours—he doesn't even look like you!"

A sound is heard in the kitchen as if something has fallen and smashed.

"Damn! What the hell was that?" Ricardo yells, scared.

Ricardo and Dorothy, both scared, ran out of the room toward the kitchen. They see Ricky on the floor, still holding the handle of the toolbox, with all the tools scattered all around the floor.

"What did you do, boy?" Dorothy says, exasperated.

Ricky answers from the ground without looking at her.

"You don't care if I hit myself, if I am hurt, if I can stand up, or if I broke my soul? You just want to know what I did when it is obvious that I am taking out these things to have a little space in my room."

Dorothy did not expect such a response from the boy and takes it as lack of respect, but deep down she knows that the boy is right. Dorothy closes her eyes and takes a deep breath. She looks at her husband, who is standing next to her. Ricardo is petrified. He is afraid to speak or do something that can further enrage his wife.

Dorothy shakes her head from side to side and tells her husband.

"This is the last straw. Now I must put up with a disrespectful brat!"

Ricky, sitting on the floor with his gaze fixed on Dorothy, answers.

"I have not disrespected you. I only answered your insensitive question."

Ricardo understands that if he does not intervene, things will get a lot worse. He tells Dorothy.

"Go back to the room, love. I'll take care of this."

Ricardo is about to put his hand on Dorothy's shoulder, but she abruptly dodges him.

"Do not touch me!" Dorothy yells at him and leaves the kitchen.

Ricardo, without looking at Ricky, kneels and begins to pick up the tools from the floor. Then he finally looks at Ricky and asks him. "Are you okay, boy?"

Ricky, who until now has been sitting on the floor, gets up and, looking at his father, answers,

"If you are going to call me boy, then it's better if you don't ask me if I am okay. I understand that I am a child to you, a nuisance, an intruder, but Mom told me that you would be Dad for me, and that's what I'm going to call you, even if you don't like it."

Those words hit Ricardo hard, and he feels regretful, even though Ricky has no physical resemblance to him. He felt paternal love at first sight. Under other conditions, he might have hugged and kissed him but was afraid of his wife's reaction. Ricardo looks at Ricky and says.

"Excuse me, son. It was not my intention to make you feel bad. It's a matter of habit. This is all new to me, and I do not want you to misinterpret me. I am your dad. We can be the best of friends, but I need your help."

Ricky, still sitting on the floor, answers.

"What do you need from me? I do not have money."

Ricardo laughs, he did not expect such an answer.

"No, son, it is not money. It is something more difficult."

"What do you want, then?" Ricky responds.

"I need us to be a family, and for that, we have to win over Mom, who is very angry with us."

"That lady doesn't love me. I haven't even done anything to her. Maybe you did something to her, but I didn't."

Ricardo shakes his head from side to side.

"Well, it's a difficult thing to explain, but she has her reasons to be upset."

"What reasons have I given her to get upset with me?" Ricky asks him.

"None, son."

"So, you gave her the reason to be upset, then you're the one who must fix it."

Ricardo rubs his hand on Ricky's head.

"Just join us as a member of the family, change that serious face, smile, and be friendly. You will see that everything will change."

Ricky answers him.

"She is the one with the problem. She has been screaming and fighting the whole time. She kicked the suitcases and left us here alone. I think that's not very friendly."

Ricardo responds in a soft voice.

"No, son, that's because you don't know her. She is good, friendly, loving, and always has very good feelings for everyone. She always has a sweet smile on her lips."

Ricky makes a puzzled face, squints, and asks.

"Are you sure we are talking about the same woman?"

Ricardo understands that he has a long and tortuous road ahead of him. He imagines himself walking on a tightrope, holding a long stick, with Ricky at one end and Dorothy at the other. He will have to fight to maintain the perfect balance, because if one falls, then they all fall.

Ricardo helps Ricky pick up the tools and then changes the burned-out light bulb in the room. Realizing that he has been with Ricky for about twenty minutes, he quickly goes to their room to see Dorothy.

Ricardo finds the door locked. He knocks on the door, and Dorothy doesn't answer him. Ricardo knocks again and speaks.

"Love, open, please. We have to talk."

Dorothy opens the door and says sarcastically.

"You took so long I thought you'd stay over to sleep with him."

Ricardo does not respond; he just enters and sits on the bed. Dorothy bolts the door again.

Ricardo tells her. "Sit next to me, love."

Dorothy does not respond and just continues to remove clothes from the suitcase and place them back in the drawers.

Ricardo repeats to her.

"Please, love, it is important that we talk." He then takes her by the hand.

Dorothy sits on the bed next to her husband, holding in her hands the bikini she had bought for the trip.

Ricardo puts his arm around her shoulders and tells her.

"That boy—"

Those words are like putting gasoline on a fire. Dorothy jumps up, picks up the scissors from dresser, and cuts the swimsuit to pieces. She intensely responds.

"That's what that child has done to our lives—he smashed it to pieces!"

Ricardo stands up and, without shouting, but very firmly, asks her.

"What do you want me to do? Throw out an eight-year-old to the streets? Can you do it? Do you have the heart to throw him out as if he were a dog? Whether or not he is my son, I cannot throw him out! We will get to the bottom of this. I want you to know that if he is mine, I will not abandon him. Is that clear to you?"

Ricardo's words are so firm Dorothy understands that her husband will not back down on what he's said. She also understands the boy is not to blame for what is happening and that he is one more victim of circumstances. Dorothy sits on the bed, taking three deep breaths, then answers.

"You are right in what you say. Forgive me for losing control but promise me that we will do a DNA test to make sure he is your son, which I highly doubt because he looks more like me than you."

Ricardo feels great relief, the fear of losing his wife had led him to the point of madness.

"Of course, love. I am the most interested in clarifying all this, and I also noticed that."

"Notice what?" Dorothy asks.

"He looks more like you than me."

Dorothy responds angrily.

"He looks like me, but he is not mine! We cannot hide a child like you men do."

Ricardo has tried all means to calm his wife, and he has almost succeeded. But time has passed so quickly that it is five in the afternoon, and neither of them has any notion of time. Eventually, Ricardo manages to calm his wife down. Ricardo is sitting in bed with his wife sitting on his lap when suddenly Ricky tries to open the door. The two of them look at each other in amazement. For a moment, they've had the notion they are alone.

Dorothy angrily says. "You don't see the door is closed? Privacy is respected in this house."

Ricky knocks on the door and says. "Dad, I'm hungry."

Ricardo answers. "Just go to the fridge and looks for something to eat."

"There are only beers in the fridge."

Ricardo looks at Dorothy, asking her. "Don't we have anything to eat in the house?"

"Did you forget that we were going on a cruise for a week? Why should we have food in the fridge?" Dorothy responds, slightly infuriated.

Ricardo tries to remedy the situation by telling him. "All right, we'll all go to Burger King. It'll be our first family dinner."

"That's junk food. My mom never let me eat it. She says it's not good for your health."

Dorothy angrily yells at him. "And what delicacy does Your Majesty want to eat?"

Ricardo looks at his wife, and opening his hands as a sign of patience, he tells her.

"Please, love, let's try a little on our part. It's late, and we haven't eaten. Let's all just eat together."

"Go ahead. I'm not hungry." Dorothy answers without looking at her husband.

Ricardo decides not to argue and leaves with Ricky. It is Ricky's first time visiting a fast-food restaurant. An elderly couple who are at the cash register adjacent to Ricky's tells Ricardo.

"Your child reminds me of my grandson. Every Saturday we had to bring him to eat here."

Ricky asks him. "And why isn't he here today?"

The man laughs and responds. "He is already a married man. He hardly has time for himself."

Ricardo makes the order and sits with Ricky in a corner. Ricky is observing everything as if he were in a museum.

"What strikes you so much, son?" Ricardo asks.

"My mom said that this food is bad for the health, but that old man has been eating the same junk for years, and they are healthy and happy. However, Mommy died young."

"This is life, son. We have to live in the present since we do not know when the end will come. Look what a change life has given us today. We did not know each other, and today we are eating junk food together as father and son." Ricardo answers, smiling.

"That's because of you. You never wanted to see me." Ricky answers sharply.

Ricardo can't keep his eyes from watering. He looks at his son and responds.

"I would give my life to be able to go back in time, but that is impossible. I can only promise you and your mother, who is looking at us from heaven right now, that I will not disappoint you or her. I want your mom to be proud of our relationship as father and son, from heaven. I hope she forgives me for how stupid and irresponsible I have been all this time."

Ricky says mockingly. "We'll see what happens. And by the way, this junk isn't as bad as I thought, especially the fries."

Ricardo laughs, rubs his hand on Ricky's head, and tells him.

"I'm glad you liked it. Now, let's go home."

Ricky responds. "No, Dad, you have to bring the lady something to eat. There is nothing at home."

Ricardo likes the idea that Ricky cares about Dorothy, but at the same time, he's called her lady, as if putting distance between him and her.

"Sure, son. Thanks for reminding me, although I would have liked you to call her mother. You think you can try?"

Ricky, with a very serious face, answers him.

"That lady doesn't love me. She considers me an intruder in her life. The day she calls me her son, I will call her mother, and the day she loves me like a son, I will love her like a mother. I am not the one with the problem."

Ricardo and Ricky arrive at the house and find Dorothy in the kitchen. Ricky has the Burger King bag in his hand, holding it out toward her.

"We brought you junk food. It's not as bad as I thought, especially the fries." He tells her.

Dorothy stares at Ricky with a blank face. Ricardo, who is standing behind Ricky, fearing that Dorothy is going to snub him, puts his hands together as if in prayer, begging Dorothy to accept it. Dorothy looks at Ricardo, takes the bag, turns around, and sits at the table.

Ricky, seeing that Dorothy has ignored him, tells her.

"You're welcome, ma'am, and have a good night." He turns around, goes into his room, and closes the door.

Ricardo, seeing the putdown Dorothy has done to Ricky, tells her.

"I understand this is very difficult for you, but if you really love me, this is the time to show it. Our parents never accepted us. Together we fought against them, and we have been fighting against winds and tides for more than five years. I cannot believe that you would quit now."

Ricardo then leaves the kitchen and goes to his room, lying down on a corner of the bed.

The three of them are separated at extreme points of the house, each one thinking about what fate has in store for them. Ricardo usually will turn on the wall air conditioner and the television before going to bed, but this time he just turns on the air. He lies down on the corner of the bed, thinking about how he can save his marriage.

After two hours, Dorothy decides to return to the room. She enters and locks the door, then lies on the opposite side of the bed. For the first time they are sleeping apart like two strangers sharing a room. Ricardo tries to get closer, but Dorothy immediately tells him. "Please stay by your side. I need to be alone."

Ricardo understands that it is better to distance himself and turns over, leaving the two of them at opposite ends of the bed.

LITTLE RICKY

An hour and a half later, when the two have almost fallen asleep, Ricky knocks on the door. Dorothy jumps up on the bed and screams.

"Now, what the fuck do you want?"

"I can't sleep. It's very hot in my room, and the wall air does not work. You do not feel how hot it is, but I do. I am not going to sleep in that room!"

Dorothy gets up and opens the door while Ricardo turns on the light. Dorothy sees Ricky in his pajamas, holding his pillow with one hand and his blanket on the other.

"Do you want to sleep in my bed or for me to sleep in your room?" she asks.

"As you wish, but I will not sleep in that room." Ricky answers sharply.

Dorothy angrily replies. "Listen, you brat—"

Ricardo intervenes immediately, and this time shouting. He has never raised his voice to his wife before, so Dorothy is totally surprised.

"That is enough, damnit! Can you stop it?"

He turns to his son. "Come in here, boy."

Ricky doesn't wait a second and tells Dorothy, who is in front of the door. "Excuse me, lady." He enters the room and stands in a corner.

Ricardo takes out an inflatable mattress he has in a box, prepares it, puts it in a corner, and tells Ricky.

"Go to bed once and for all. If you are not going to sleep, at least let the others sleep." Ricardo then looks at his wife and asks her.

"Are you going to bed or not?"

Dorothy responds angrily. "I prefer to sleep in the room that the prince will not tolerate. Have a good night."

She slams the door and locks herself in Ricky's room. Ricardo thinks about going after her but decides to stay in the room and go to bed.

It is a hot summer night. Ricky's room has reached an almost-irrepressible temperature, and the lack of insulation on the roof is not helping at all. Dorothy is bathed in sweat and understands that it will be a torture to spend the night in that room, but she does not want to return to her room. She takes an armchair out to the patio and tries to sleep. Ricardo and Dorothy did not bother to clean the patio, and due to the rain, several objects have become breeding grounds for mosquitoes, which begin to attack Dorothy without mercy. After only ten minutes outside, Dorothy gets up and goes into the house, walks into the bedroom, and lies down at the far corner of the bed.

Ricardo, happy to see that his wife has returned.

"Thank you, love, for coming back. You don't know how much I appreciate it."

Dorothy angrily replies. "You and him, fuck off. Yes, I mean it—fuck off!"

CHAPTER 2

They all fall asleep. Dorothy, knowing that the sun will penetrate through the broken curtain, covers her face before the sun enters. Ricardo is sleeping pleasantly on his side of the bed.

It is ten thirty in the morning when Ricky wakes up due to sunrays hitting his face. Ricky, after scowling several times, gets up and tries to stand up, not making any noise. Ricky puts a chair in front of the window and tries to cover the opening of the curtain with a towel. In his attempt to place the towel on the top of the curtain, however, Ricky falls from the chair, making a great noise, which awakens Dorothy and Ricardo. Dorothy looks at Ricky, who is still scared, sitting on the floor with the towel in his hand.

"Are you okay, kid?" Dorothy asks him.

"Yes, thanks. I was trying to block the sun coming through the window."

Ricardo gets up, looks at the curtain. "Today I'll fix this curtain."

"Bravo, Ricky. I have been asking him for five months to fix the curtain. You arrived yesterday and today he is going to fix the curtain!" sarcastically says Dorothy.

Ricardo stares at his wife. Dorothy also stares at him, waiting for him to answer, but Ricardo does not respond to her. Instead, he helps Ricky get up. "Lie down, son. I'll cover the curtain."

Ricky answers. "I am no longer sleepy, but I'm hungry."

Ricardo closes his eyes, moves his head from side to side, and responds. "Son, we will eat soon. You will not starve here."

Dorothy laughs, mocking Ricardo. "And you never let me have a dog because they are troublesome a lot!"

Ricky instantly says. "Are you calling me a dog?"

"Not in any way. Dogs don't fuck up that much." Dorothy replies, laughing.

Ricky, offended, takes his bedspread and pillow, and goes to his room. Dorothy stands up and tells her husband in a tone as if ordering him.

"Get ready. There are a million things to do today."

"Like what?" Ricardo asks.

Dorothy responds. "First, we must go to the supermarket. I need to return to work tomorrow.

"Second, we will have lunch in the supermarket cafeteria because there is nothing to eat here, and then we will shop for groceries.

"Third, we should go to your parents' house and ask your mother for money to buy a wall air conditioner for the kid's room, and you will buy a new curtain for our room."

At another time, Ricardo would have protested the way Dorothy had spoken to him, but for her to just ask for an air conditioner for Ricky is a victory from his point of view.

"Of course, my love. You are right. I will also go back to work, and on Monday, we will go to the school to register him in the third grade."

Dorothy's face changes when she hears that they should register Ricky at school, that will mean he is staying, at least for now.

Thirty minutes later, everyone prepares to leave. Ricardo and Dorothy sit in front, but Ricky does not enter the vehicle. He opens the car door and just stands there, looking into the car.

Dorothy asks him. "Do you need a special invitation, or is it that I have to come down to close the door for you, Your Majesty?"

"No…I just need a rag to clean this seat." Ricky responds.

Ricardo and Dorothy only use the back seat to transport all kinds of items and throw away the garbage. Ricardo gets out of the car, reluctantly looking for a cloth to clean one side of the back seat.

"You can sit down now." He says once he's done.

"Thank you." Ricky responds. "But this car must be cleaned. It is very dirty."

Dorothy takes the opportunity to answer him. "I agree with you. As soon as you have a chance, wash it. We would really appreciate it."

"I will. Since you do not mind or feel ashamed about it."

Dorothy and Ricardo look at each other. Dorothy tells Ricardo.

"His answer is always insulting and scrupulous. What a beauty of a fucking kid!"

Upon their arrival at the supermarket, Dorothy tells Ricardo.

"You go straight to the cafeteria. I'll catch up with you later. I must go to the office first."

Dorothy walks into the office, and Hellen, her supervisor, looks at her in amazement.

"What happened? You didn't go on a cruise?"

"At the end, it was not possible, so I prefer to return to work, if possible," Dorothy responds.

Hellen has wanted so much to get rid of Dorothy; she has even told Mr. Bob, the supermarket owner, that Dorothy is a troublemaker, irresponsible, and an untrustworthy employee. Hellen is thinking of what to answer, but an employee is sick, and she is short of cashiers, so she decides to accept Dorothy back to work.

"Magdalena is sick, and we don't know when she will come back. You can return tomorrow if you want, but remember, if you miss the weekend again, make sure it is because you are dead."

Dorothy bites her lip in order not to reply. She doesn't like Hellen either.

"I do not think that will be a problem. I feel very healthy, and I am not like I was before."

Dorothy, leaving the office, cannot contain the anger any longer and says. "I can't stand that fricking bitch!"

Dorothy does not realize that Mr. Bob, the owner of the supermarket, is coming in as she mutters with, but Mr. Bob is at a close enough distance for him to hear her.

"Good morning, Dorothy. I thought you were on a cruise?"

"Yes, I should be, but I couldn't." Dorothy responds.

"What old freaking bitch were you talking about so contemptuously?" Mr. Bob asks sarcastically.

Dorothy goes pale; she didn't know Mr. Bob had heard her.

"I meant the damn old woman who gave us the wrong cruise tickets, and because of her, we couldn't take our vacations."

Mr. Bob stares at her and smiles sarcastically. It is obvious that Mr. Bob doesn't believe her at all.

"Yeah, sure. It must be frustrating." He answers, then walks into the office.

Dorothy takes a deep breath. She had a serious scare, but thanks to her great mental agility, she was able to get out of the predicament. Dorothy decides to continue and sees Ines coming toward the office.

"Hello, Dorothy. I saw your husband at the cafeteria. I did not know that you have a secret son. He is just like you! How did you get your husband to accept him without any problems?"

Dorothy wants to grab her by the neck. Ines is a cashier better known as Mini Snooper because she is small and will stick her nose everywhere.

"He is not my son!" Dorothy angrily replies.

"Well, you should not feel ashamed. The child is very cute and is a picture of you. You should be proud of him instead!"

"He is not my fucking son. He's Ricardo's son!" Dorothy angrily replies.

Ines opens her eyes and covers her mouth.

"My god, that is news! You meant to say they blamed the boy on him? He can't be the father of that child, but I can see he doesn't even care. Are you going to put up with that?"

"That's not your problem. You are being fucking gossipy, and nobody asked your opinion!" Dorothy responds, almost yelling.

Dorothy walks away and goes to the cafeteria. She sees Ricardo and Ricky waiting for her with food on the table. Dorothy sits down to eat, and Ricardo asks her.

"What's wrong with you? I see you are a little upset."

"It is old lady Hellen and the mini snooper of Ines. Everyone looks at me strangely. I know they talk about me behind my back." Dorothy responds.

Ricky takes a sip of his drink and speaks.

"If they talk about you, it is because they envy you, love you or hate you. However, it is better than being ignored."

"Good! Not only are you a pain in the ass, but you are also a philosopher." Dorothy replies sarcastically.

"That's what my mother used to tell me, so I wouldn't worry." Ricky responds.

Ricardo takes his wife's hand, trying to calm her down.

"Ricky is right, it's envy. They just can't help it."

Dorothy looks at Ricardo and Ricky, saying.

"Fuck off, the two of you! Let me eat in peace!"

******

Ricardo parks the car in front of his parents' house. Before getting out of the car, he tells Dorothy.

"Remember the less you talk, the better it is. Your parents don't approve of me, and mine feel the same about you. I have to convince the old lady into lending me four hundred dollars, and I know Dad is going to object. So crosse your fingers and wish me luck."

Ricardo looks at Ricky and says.

"Come on, let's meet your grandparents."

Ricardo rings the doorbell, and Ricky hides behind Dorothy. Ricardo's father opens the door and is surprised to see him.

"What happened? Weren't you going on a cruise?"

Ricardo hugs his father and responds. "It is a complicated story, but with its positive side."

Roberto stands aside and says. "Go ahead. Your mother is in the kitchen."

Ricardo walks by, and Dorothy tells her father-in-law.

"Good afternoon, Mr. Roberto. Your son has a surprise for you."

Dorothy walks in, and Roberto sees Ricky. Roberto, confused, says.

"This is a surprise! I did not know that you took care of children. Only a madman would give you a child to take care of!"

Ricardo puts his hand on his father's shoulder and tells him.

"This child you see there, is your grandson."

Roberto is speechless. He reddens, moving his mustache from side to side. He wants to speak, but he cannot. He feels that he is short of breath and only said. "Come in, kid."

Ricky remains standing without moving, and Ricardo tells him.

"Come in, son, so you can meet your grandmother."

When Roberto hears Ricardo say those words, he is convinced it is not a joke. He could hardly catch his breath; he is about to have a heart attack but manages to come down.

"Go to the kitchen. I have to go to the bathroom."

Ricardo's mother hears that her son has arrived and goes out to greet him.

"Hello, Rick. What a joy to see you!"

She gives him a big hug and a kiss. Then she looks at Dorothy and says coldly. "How are you, Dorothy?"

Dorothy, almost without looking at her, replies. "Well, ma'am, thank you."

Lora looks at Ricky and asks Ricard.

"Rick, this beauty, where did he come from?"

"He is your grandson, Mom."

Lora looks at the boy and then looks at Dorothy, swallows hard, but doesn't say anything so as not to hurt the boy.

"Good, one more grandson. Come boy, I have some cookies for you. You are going to love them!"

Ricky, with a suspicious look on his face, looks all around, says nothing. He just follows his grandmother.

Meanwhile, Roberto has taken some pills for his tachycardia and has recovered a bit. He comes out of the bathroom and, with a harsh voice, calls his son.

"Rick, come to my room for a minute."

When they heard Roberto's tone, they knew it would not be a friendly conversation. Ricardo looks at his mother.

"It seems that Daddy is not in a good mood."

"What do you think, Rick? Just go and find out what he wants."

Ricardo goes to the room, and Lora gives Ricky some cookies, and tells him.

"Go to the patio so you can see the pool. You will like it."

Ricky doesn't move. He looks at Dorothy, waiting for permission. Dorothy tells him. "Go, Ricky. You'll like it."

Ricky steps out onto the patio, and the two women are left alone.

Lora stares at Dorothy.

"You cannot deny it. He is just like you."

"I do not deny that. Everyone says it." Dorothy responds.

Lora angrily replies. "You know that I never approved of your relationship with my son. I always had suspicions about you. But I would never have thought that you had a hidden son. Now you bring him in as if it was not a big deal. What kind of snake are you that you charm a man that way?"

"You offend me, Mrs. Lora."

"To be offended, you have to be ashamed. You and my son have no shame. I have always tried to support Rick, but this has gone beyond what I can bear! I feel sorry for that child, who is the victim of a mother who abandoned him. Now she picks him up after bewitching her husband and gives the boy an immature and irresponsible stepfather. That's the only thing that really hurts me."

Dorothy bites her lip so as not to respond to Lora. She only tells her.

"So, you don't want your grandson, even though you said that you were glad to have one more grandson?"

Meanwhile, in the room, Roberto, visibly angry, tells his son.

"It is very true that a pair of tits can make you do things without thinking, but to let yourself get a boy so easily. This is more than I expected from you! Did you know that your wife had that child, or did you just find out now?"

"No, Dad, he is my son." Ricardo answers.

"Look, don't disrespect me. If you want to be a happy cuckold, that's your problem, but don't disrespect me!" Roberto responds.

"I swear to you, Dad. He is mine. I had never told you because I did not recognize him as my child. I was irresponsible."

Roberto takes a while to assimilate his son's words, then he responds.

"What you want to tell me is that you had a child with her, and her parents had it. Now they are tired of the child, and they gave it back to her."

"No, and a thousand times no. He is mine alone."

Roberto, to the point of slapping his son, tells him.

"Get out of my presence! I don't want to speak to you, you stupid fag. You are a shame!"

Ricardo takes the opportunity to leave the room and go talk to his mother. When he arrives in the kitchen, he finds his mother and Dorothy both standing on opposite corners of the kitchen as if they had finished a boxing round. Ricardo, without wasting time, tells his mother.

"Mom, I have to ask you a big favor."

"What do you want? Or better yet, what does she want?" Lora responds.

Dorothy puts her hand on her forehead and lowers her head. She's about to burst, but she restrains herself.

"The wall air conditioner in the second room has been broken for a long time. I never changed it because that room was not used, but the child cannot sleep in that room. The heat is irresistible. Can you lend me four hundred dollars for an air conditioner? I will pay you as soon as I can."

Ricardo hadn't realized that his father had come out after him and was listening.

Lora, angry, responds. "The same way you pay me back the three hundred from last year or the two hundred and fifty from the year before last?"

Ricardo doesn't know what to say.

"But, Mom, this time it is different. It is the child who needs it."

"Well, let his mother buy it." Lora says, pointing to Dorothy.

"Or to the father of that child. Just because you are an asshole doesn't mean that I have to be one."

Lora realizes that Ricky is behind the sliding glass door that goes to the patio. She lowers her voice, so Ricky does not hear them fighting. Lora opens the door, and Ricky walks in. Nobody says a word. Ricky stands next to Dorothy with his hands behind his back. Ricardo's father, who had left, returns to the kitchen, and gives four hundred dollars to Dorothy, whose jaw drops.

"I know Rick is not going to pay back his mother. I will give it to you, and you are the one that must pay me back. I do this because that kid does not deserve such torture."

Dorothy says nothing. She did not expect such a surprise.

LITTLE RICKY

Ricardo says. "Let's go. Maybe another day the visit will be more pleasant."

Lora, trying to be nice to Ricky and not knowing that Ricky heard the whole fight, asks him.

"What did you think of the pool? Did you like it?"

Ricky remembered the swimming pool at the mansion in which he used to live and responds.

"No, it is a puddle of stagnant water. It does not have waterfalls or a Jacuzzi."

Ricky returns the cookies to Lora unopened. "Here are your cookies. Thank you very much, lady."

Dorothy cannot believe it; she sees Ricky as an ally. She enjoys all the contempt Ricky shows to Lora, and to stick the knife even deeper into the mother-in-law, she tells Ricky.

"Come on, son, we're late."

Ricky turns around and tells his grandma. "Goodbye, lady."

Then when he walks past his grandpa, he stops and tells him.

"Goodbye, Grandpa."

Ricky grabs Dorothy's hand and says.

"Let's go, Mom."

Dorothy feels like hugging Ricky. She stabbed her mother-in-law with the knife, but now Ricky has moved it from side to side for the final thrust. Lora's and Roberto's faces are worthy of a photograph. Ricardo is petrified. He knows that the relationship between Ricky and Dorothy is not friendly, but apparently, the two of them have agreed to make the life miserable to his parents.

Ricky and Dorothy are leaving, and seeing that Ricardo has not reacted, Ricky tells Dorothy.

"Mom, ask him if he's coming with us or if he's staying."

Dorothy must make an effort not to laugh, but she catches herself and just looks back. Ricardo reacts and looks at his parents, who are looking back at him with an indefinite expression on their faces, between anger, grief, and pity.

Ricardo tells his parents.

"I know it is difficult for you to understand, but it is not what you are thinking."

Roberto, in a choppy tone, almost as if he wants to cry, answers.

"Go away, son. You have already explained enough to us. If you are happy like this, then enjoy it."

Once they are all in the car, an annoyed Ricardo asks Ricky.

"Can you explain to me why you behaved so badly with your grandmother?"

"I did what you asked me to do." Ricky responds.

"That's not true! I didn't ask you to be rude to her."

"No, you asked me to be family."

Ricardo, annoyed, now responds.

"What the hell does being rude to your grandmother have to do with being family?"

Ricky shrugs his shoulders and replies.

"My grandfather told me that the family must be defended with reason or without it. Your mother offended her, and you know it, but you remained silent. So, I had to do what you did not do."

Ricardo is speechless; he just looks at his wife, who tells him.

"You should be ashamed of yourself."

Dorothy curiously turns around and asks him.

"Why did you call Lora lady, Mr. Roberto Grandfather, and call me Mother?"

Ricky shrugs his shoulders again and answers.

"Because Mrs. Lora was unfair to you and hypocritical to me. Mr. Roberto, despite not recognizing me as his grandson, showed human feelings about me. And you called me son."

Dorothy asks him again. "So, if I call you son, will you call me Mom?"

Ricky looks serious, scowls, extends his hand, and moves his index finger from side to side.

"I only respond to how you treat me. If you call me son, I will call you mother. My mother is irreplaceable, but I can accept you as second mother if you show me that you love me as a son."

Dorothy looks at her husband and shakes her head in bewilderment. Ricardo responds.

"There is no doubt we have problems."

"You will have the problems, not me. This is not my problem!" Dorothy, angrily, replies.

Ricky responds immediately. "With that attitude I see it difficult for you to become my mother."

Dorothy turns and angrily tells him. "Look, brat—"

Ricardo doesn't let her finish and screams. "Enough, damn it! You are going to drive me crazy! Is that what you want?"

They stayed silent. Dorothy felt sad. In two years of dating and five years of marriage her husband had never yelled at her, but with Ricky's arrival, he had yelled at her twice. Ricardo was desperate. As much as he tries, everything goes wrong. He feels sorry for having yelled at his wife. Ricardo parks the car in the hardware store parking lot, and before getting out, he looks at his wife and sees that Dorothy has watery eyes and that she has cried silently. Ricardo feels so bad tears also flow. They both looked at each other and understood that they were hurting the one that they loved the most. Ricardo hugs Dorothy and tells her.

"Forgive me, love. I did not mean to hurt you; much less make you cry."

"Forgive me for making you lose patience and for making you cry." Dorothy responds.

The two are hugging, comforting each other, when they hear Ricky's voice.

"Noooo! Are you crying, Dad?"

At the sound of those words, they both part. Ricardo puts his open hands upward like when one asks God for forgiveness or help. Dorothy puts her right hand on her forehead while she shakes her head from side to side as if to say.

"I give up, I can't take it anymore."

"My grandfather used to say that men only cry out of impotence before injustices, but never out of cowardice before things that can be fixed. That one must be strong and never give up."

Ricky continues giving a speech. Ricardo looks at his wife and says with a desperate look.

"I can't take this anymore. Help me, please."

Dorothy sees her husband's face, and she can't help but laugh. It is such a spontaneous and contagious laugh that they both end up laughing out loud.

Ricky keeps delivering his sermon in the back of the car.

"You think it is a lie, but in difficult moments, you do not cry—what is there...there it is, there it is!"

Ricky's scream is heartbreaking, as if he has been bitten by a snake. He jumps out of the back seat to the front seat.

Ricardo, scared, asks him. "What happened?"

Ricky, still yelling, answers. "A cockroach!"

Ricky hasn't even finished saying a cockroach when Dorothy joins in the screaming and they both run out of the car.

Ricardo gets out of the car, walks up to them.

"It is not so bad. I'll fix it."

Dorothy yells at him. "I have told you a thousand times not to leave bags with food residue in the car, but you are a pig!"

Dorothy has Ricky grabbed by one hand. Ricky lets go, takes two steps forward, raises his right hand, points his finger at him, and says three times as if he were shooting him.

"Yes, pig, pig, pig." Then he turns around, looks at Dorothy, and says in a low voice. "But you are also a good little pig."

Ricardo says. "I will fix that problem right now. I will buy a bug bomb, put it inside the car, and close the windows. Then we can go buy the air conditioner and vertical blinds. When we return, the car will be free of insects."

The three of them go into the hardware store and Ricardo buys the smoke bomb to kill insects. He parks his car in an empty spot in the parking lot, closes the windows, and starts the smoke bomb. Then three of them go back to the hardware store since they have to wait at least thirty minutes for the smoke bomb to work and clear out.

Ricardo never thought the smoke would come out through the cracks in the door and through the rusted floor. A store worker collecting the carts for the hardware store sees the car parked in a secluded corner of the parking lot. He observes that smoke is coming out of the car and is scared. The employee, without thinking twice, calls the police and the fire department. The employee communicates the situation to the supervisor, who orders to seal off the parking area. He does not say anything over the store's loudspeakers to avoid panic among customers. The firefighters and the police arrive in record time.

Ricardo hears the emergency sirens in the parking lot and tells Dorothy. "Something serious is happening outside in the parking lot. We better stay in here to be safe."

"You're right. Curiosity killed the cat." Dorothy answers him.

Ricky joins them and says. "It is the first time that the three of us agree."

After a while, the sirens stop sounding and calm returns. Ricardo leaves the store with his cart carrying the air conditioner and the vertical blinds for the room. Dorothy looks to the back of the parking lot and sees the red lights of the fire department.

"Love, isn't that the place where you parked our car?"

Ricardo was pushing the cart and reading the store's advertising magazine. He lifts his head, looks toward the back of the parking lot, and screams.

"No, my god, no!" They run toward the vehicle, but are soon stopped by the police, who are keeping that part of the parking lot closed.

"Stop! You can't pass."

Ricardo, with his hands on his head and kicking the ground, says.

"My god, it's not fair! Don't charge me all at once. Let me breathe a little!"

Dorothy begins to cry uncontrollably, both thinking that the smoke bomb has caused a fire and now they will not have a vehicle to go to work with. Only Ricky is calm and looks like a small statue.

A police officer approaches them and asks. "Is that your car?"

"Yes, Officer, that was our car. I put a bug bomb in it to disinfect it, but I never thought it would start a fire." Ricardo answers.

The officer tells Dorothy. "Calm down, please. It's nothing serious."

Dorothy, between sobs, answers.

"That is our only mode of transportation. We had an ant problem in the car, and we wanted to disinfect it."

Ricky says. "That is not true."

The policeman, Ricardo, and Dorothy turn and look at Ricky, who is standing behind them. The police officer immediately suspects it could be a case of auto insurance fraud or perhaps to cause chaos for another crime to be committed. Ricardo and Dorothy don't know what to think what Ricky would come out with this time."

The officer looks at Ricardo and Dorothy suspiciously and tells them.

"Children and drunk people always tell the truth."

The policeman stands in front of Ricky and tells him.

"Tell me the truth, son. What happened here?"

Ricky responds with all authority.

"My grandfather was a captain in the Palm Beach Police, and he always told me that lying to the police is a crime that is paid with jail."

The policeman looks at Ricardo suspiciously and tells Ricky.

"I assure you they won't get away with it."

The officer then takes his radio and calls the supervisor. He separates Ricky from his parents, so that they will not intimidate him.

Miami police Sergeant Torres and Miami firefighter Lieutenant Garry immediately report to the scene. Ricardo and Dorothy are very nervous. They have no idea what is happening. The sergeant is very careful not to influence or intimidate the boy's confession.

"Tell me what happened to the car, if you know."

Ricky says firmly.

"Yes, I know. They were not trying to kill any ants. They were cockroaches, as big as turtles. That's the truth!"

The officers explode into out-of-control laughter.

Ricardo and Dorothy, upon hearing the laughter, look at each other in astonishment.

"What the hell did that boy do now? He is going to give me a heart attack!" Ricardo exclaims.

The owner of the hardware store has joined the group of police and firefighters by then. He is the only one who is not amused by what happened.

The sergeant calls Ricardo and Dorothy, who approach concerned.

"So, you lied to us. They weren't ants, they were cockroaches." Mockingly says the sergeant.

Dorothy looks at Ricky, shaking her head in bewilderment.

"You are going to kill us."

Dorothy's soul returns to her body. She takes a deep breath and responds to the officer.

"Well, there were ants too."

The fire department lieutenant tells them.

"When a closed vehicle begins to catch fire, only smoke can be seen due to the lack of oxygen. When the doors are opened and there is plenty of oxygen, an explosion can occur, so we had to break the windows and immediately pour water on it. I'm sorry your car suffered all this damage. We thought the vehicle was catching fire."

Dorothy breaks down in tears again.

Ricky stands in front of the lieutenant and, pointing his finger at him, in a mature, adult character.

"You broke our car. How am I going to go to school tomorrow? How can they get to work? It's very easy to say, I'm sorry.'"

The business owner is moved by Ricky's stance.

"I am sorry for what happened. We will bear the cost to have the windows fixed and rent a car for you while yours is serviced. We will return your car in good condition. You'll be able to go to school tomorrow, I promise."

The owner of the hardware store passes his hand over Ricky's head. He turns to Dorothy, saying.

"Madam, you have a beautiful son, and, apparently, very responsible too. God bless him. I am actually not obliged to do this, because this is technically all your fault, but your son stole my heart."

The business owner then tells Ricardo. "We are going to take your car now. If you need to take something out of it, do it now."

Ricardo responds. "We only have canned food in the trunk and other things inside the car."

Ricky intervenes. "No, sir, only the canned ones. The rest is garbage."

Ricardo, embarrassed, says. "No, son, that's not true. I have things I need there."

Dorothy, meanwhile, angrily replies. "It is not true. The child is right—throw away everything that is inside the car."

The sergeant looks at Ricardo, shakes his head, and tells him.

"If I were you, I will remain silent."

Two hours later, Ricardo parks the rented car in his garage, and when he gets out of the car, his wife says.

"The day has not gone so bad, after all. Don't you think? Your parents loaned us the money, and we bought what we needed. The businessman is going to have our car washed, and we have a new car for a week!"

Ricardo answers her. "Love sometimes is not all negative and things happen for a reason."

Dorothy responds without looking at him. "I prefer to be on the cruise, though, and not here."

Ricardo enters the house and goes into his room. Dorothy and Ricky are left taking the groceries out of the car. When Ricky and Dorothy finish, they go to their rooms. Ricardo is in his room, dressed only in his underwear, watching the television. Dorothy enters the room and sees her husband lying down, watching television, and reproaches him.

"Your Majesty, do you feel comfortable?"

Ricardo looks at her and extends his arms.

"Come here, my love. I was waiting for you."

"Do you want me that much?" Says Dorothy.

"You know very well the answer to that question."

"Then you should have helped us unload the car."

Ricardo stands with open arms, embraces her, and tells her.

"Don't fight me, love. We don't do that in our house."

"You're right, but so much has changed this weekend that I could not get used to it." Dorothy answers, hugging her husband.

The two of them sit on the bed and start kissing. When they are right in the middle of the most passionate moment, Ricky knocks on the bedroom door loudly.

"Dad, you have to install the air conditioner in the room before it is late." He remembers that tomorrow I must go to school early.

Ricardo and Dorothy lie on the bed on their backs, looking up at the ceiling.

Ricky knocks on the door again. "Papa, Papa, don't pretend to be asleep. You have to install the air conditioner in my room!"

Ricardo raises his arms upward, moving his hands as if asking for help.

"My god, I need help! I'm losing the strength to put up with this!"

Ricky answers. "My mom read me the Bible before bed instead of reading me stories."

Ricardo and Dorothy look at each other, confused. Ricardo opens the door and sees Ricky standing like a robot, looking at him. They both look at each other. Ricky, like a soldier looking up at attention, and Ricardo, in his underwear, with his hands on his waist, looking down. Dorothy carefully observes the scene, sitting on the bed. It is comical to see her husband and the child standing face-to-face in a challenging way. They are so different physically and culturally she thinks to herself. *"If these are father and son, then I am Chinese!"*

Ricardo tells Ricky. "Can you explain to me what the hell the Bible has to do with this?"

Ricky says. "I'm asking you to install the air conditioner, and you asked God to help you. The Bible does not say anything about God knowing about air-conditioning."

Ricardo bends over and puts his face on Ricky's level.

"Tell me, son, do you see everything in black-and-white? What do you have inside that little head? Don't you know what a metaphor is?"

"Dad, I do know what a metaphor is." Ricky responds. "If you want, I will explain it to you, and for your information, seeing in black-and-white has its name. It is called achromatopsia."

Ricardo stares at Ricky, pretending to knock on Ricky's head.

"Hey, is there anybody there? I think you need to grease up your brain a little to see if you relax. You look like a robot."

Ricky doesn't answer but turns around and says. "I'll wait for you in the room."

Ricardo enters their room to put on his pants, and before he leaves the room, Dorothy tells him. "Remember that we have to do a DNA test, because if there is one thing, I am sure of, it is that this child is more my child than yours."

Ricardo answers her. "Tomorrow we will take a sample of the hair, and after I leave you at work, I will take it to a lab."

Ricardo pulls the old air conditioner out of the wall and is starting to install the new one back in when Ricky stands in front of him.

"How are you going to install it if you didn't read the instructions?"

Ricardo, a little angry, answers him, "Do you think that I am useless and cannot change a wall air unit?"

Ricky, surprised, shakes his head. "I didn't say that! My grandfather always told me—"

But Ricardo won't let him finish.

"Enough already! Always the same 'My grandfather used to say,' 'My mother said.' I won't be as perfect as they are, but I am your father."

Ricky tells him in a conciliatory way.

"Don't be angry. My grandfather used to say that nobody is perfect, that we all make mistakes."

Ricardo, working in the air unit and without looking at Ricky, tells him.

"He must have said I was the biggest mistake your mother made."

Ricky, in a firm tone, answers. "No, he never referred to you as my mother's mistake."

Ricardo is surprised, he did not expect such an answer. He turns around and looks at Ricky, who, sitting on the sofa bed with both hands on his knees, is staring at him.

"If I was not a mistake in your mother's life, then according to him, what was I?"

Ricky responds with the same firm tone.

"A big fuckup! And Grandpa didn't say bad words, only when he mentioned you."

Ricardo closes his eyes, shakes his head, takes a deep breath, and asks him.

"And do you think he was right?" Ricardo looks at his son and sees that Ricky's face is like a stone and that he is thinking about the answer.

Ricky shrugs his shoulders and says. "I don't know. Grandpa was always right."

Ricardo, almost losing control, tells him. "So, I'm a piece of shit?"

Ricky looks at him with a puzzled face. "Are you asking me that, or are you telling me?"

Ricardo turns around and continues working.

"Forget it, son. Tell me about something else. How was your life before?"

Ricky crosses his fingers, puts his hands behind his neck, leans back on the sofa, and begins to count. "My papa grandpa looked after me in the mornings. He was a retired police captain, and then he became a businessman. He taught me many things. My grandfather was a judge. He was always with me when he could, especially on weekends. My mom would wake me up in the morning, and at night she would send me off to bed, read the Bible to me before going to sleep, and I slept with her until she got sick."

Ricardo feels that the boy's voice has changed, that he sounds sad. He turns around and sees that Ricky is squinting his eyes. Ricardo runs to him and hugs him, kissing him with love.

"I'm sorry, son. I didn't mean to hurt you."

Chapter 3

Monday is Ricky's third day with his father. He sets the alarm on his cell phone and gets up early to go to school. When he sees that his father has not gotten up, Ricky knocks on their door.

"Dad, get up or we'll be late for school!"

Ricky hears no response, and so he knocks again, harder.

"Dad, it's getting late! I don't like being late for school!"

Ricardo heard the first time and opened his eyes but stayed lying down. Dorothy wakes up too, but she had to start work at eleven in the morning. When they hear the second knock, they both look at each other and realize that Ricky will not stop until they get up. Ricardo sits on the bed, shaking his head from side to side when he hears the third call, but this time much louder.

"Dad, you're going to have to explain to the teacher why we're late, and I'm not going to lie for you!"

Ricardo hits the mattress.

"Hell, I'm paying for all my sins at once! This is not a boy. He is a robot programmed to fuck with me!"

Ricardo screams. "I'm coming! I'll be out in a minute!"

Dorothy sits on the bed. "I will wait for you to come back to take me to work."

Ricardo thinks for a moment and answers her.

"It would be better if we all go, because I don't know how long it might take. That way, you can take the car and leave. Anyway, I don't have to report to work today."

Dorothy opens the door and sees Ricky impeccably dressed, carrying a backpack full of books.

"Apparently, you took an early shower and are pumped to go to school."

"Yes, it is good to bathe early, and one must bathe at least once a day. Not like Dad, who did not bathe yesterday and is now dressing without bathing."

******

The school is only three blocks from the house, so they decide to walk to show Ricky the way. When they get to the principal's office, they wait to be attended to by the principal, Ms. Black.

Ricky, the whole time, has been looking around as if he had been taking in a movie. One of the assistants comes over and asks.

Are you Mr. Suarez?"

"Yes, we are the Suarez family." Ricardo answers.

"Follow me, please."

Everyone walks into the office, and the school principal tells them. "Have a seat, please."

Ricardo and Dorothy sit down, but Ricky remains standing. They all look at one another, trying to understand the child. The principal turns to Dorothy.

"Madam, the situation of your son is not clear to me."

"You mean my husband's son?"

The principal keeps silent. She looks at the child and then looks at Dorothy.

"Excuse me, I thought he was your son."

"What led you to that conclusion? Would you share that with me, please, if you can?" Dorothy is annoyed. She is tired of everyone saying that the child is her son.

The principal shakes her head and responds.

"Because he looks so much like you that if he was not your son, I would say that he is your younger brother. Also, the child's last name is Clark, which may indicate that he is from your first marriage, since your husband's last name is Suarez."

"Well, you are wrong about everything, and since we are in a school, let's say don't judge the book by the cover." Dorothy replies sarcastically.

Ricardo intervenes. "I don't think that's the important issue at the moment. The important thing here is to enroll the child."

The principal reads the papers that give Ricky's custody to Ricardo and understands that the situation is different.

"Okay, Mr. Suarez, it's just that I hadn't read to the end of the documents that you gave me, for which I apologize. We will enroll your child immediately."

The principal gives the papers to her assistant.

"Please make copies of this documents and put it in his folder."

The principal gets up and tells them. "Come with me. I will show you the classroom and your child's teacher." Then she goes to Ricky, puts her hand on his shoulder and tells him.

"By the way, tomorrow you have an activity I am sure you will like. All third graders are going to the zoo!"

Ricky takes a step back, as if the principal's hand has burned him.

"Wait, Ms. Black, I'm not in third grade. I'm in fourth."

The confused principal asks his father. "How old is your son?"

"Eight years." Ricardo answers.

"So, he must be in third grade, not fourth." Responds the principal.

"Are you sure you are right?" Ricardo asks Ricky.

Ricky turns red, and enraged, he raises his right arm and, moving his index finger from side to side, says.

"No, no, no, you are wrong. I am in fourth grade. I am not going to come to this school to be delayed or waste my time. If you want, call my previous school, and find out, but I'm not going to repeat third grade. It's boring enough as it is."

The totally confused principal asks Dorothy.

"Can you explain to me what your child is saying?"

Dorothy responds sharply. "I saw that child for the first time in my life two days ago. Unfortunately, I have no idea what he's saying."

The principal looks at Ricardo and asks him. "Are you the father, yes, or no?"

"Yes, I am."

"Then tell me what's going on here."

Ricardo raises his eyebrows and then shrugs his shoulders in a sign of utter bewilderment. "The truth is that I also saw him for the first time two days ago too, and I have no idea about his academic record, but I promise you I will find out."

The principal looks at Ricky, who has crossed his arms and has a determined face. Trying to appease him, she says.

"Let's do something, Ricardito."

"My name is Ricardo Clark. You can call me Ricky, but not Ricardito. It sounds ugly, it is not my name, and it is not okay." Ricky answers sharply.

Ricardo tells him. "Ricky, don't be disrespectful and rude to the principal."

"I have not disrespected the principal. I just clarified that my name is not Ricardito, nor do I like to be called that. My grandfather used to tell me that you shouldn't keep quiet about things you don't like. You should communicate so they don't happen again. That's all I did, and I did it without disrespecting Ms. Black."

The principal is amazed at Ricky's response. "You speak like a lawyer, Ricky. That's very good. You have character."

Ricky responds like a robot. "My grandfather was a judge, and many lawyers visited him. He said that they are all cheaters but that they are a necessary evil."

The principal laughs out loud. "My god, this child is a tremendous gem! I congratulate you!"

Dorothy and Ricardo are so serious they don't even say a thank-you.

"Well, you will go to third grade for now, and when the verification comes, if it says you should be in fourth grade, then we will transfer you."

Ricky stares at her and asks. "And that can be done?"

"Sure, Ricky," responds the principal. "I give you, my word."

Ricky opens his arms and tells her. "In that case, take me to the fourth grade, and when you verify that it is true, I will not have to be transferred. I also give you, my word."

"Look, young man, the rules are not set by you. It will be done as I told you." The principal responds with character.

Ricky looks at his father, runs to him, and takes him by the arm.

"Dad, help me, please. Don't allow this. I'm not lying, I'm in fourth grade."

Ricardo kneels and sees that Ricky is crying, so he hugs him and responds.

"But, son, how can I help you if I have no idea where you studied?"

"I studied at San Francisco which is a private school in West Palm Beach. Please call there!" Ricky pleads to his father.

"I don't know where that school is, nor do I know the phone number, go to class for now and then I'll find out."

Ricky lets Ricardo go, then he hugs Dorothy and, crying, tells her. "Help me, please! He never cares. Please do not allow this!"

Dorothy is moved. She reciprocates with a kiss on his forehead and tells the principal. "I am taking the child home."

The principal responds. "You cannot do that. The child must attend classes."

Dorothy angrily tells her. "Where is your pedagogy? Do you think this child can learn anything in this state of mind? His father will get the documents at the school where the boy previously studied, and we will bring them tomorrow."

The principal, not too friendly now, responds.

"Very well, but if you don't bring him in tomorrow, I'm going to report you to the children and family's department."

Ricardo, Dorothy, and Ricky leave the office, and the principal tells her assistant.

"I believe this child has problems. He acts like a robot and expresses himself like an old man. That outburst that he gave us is not normal. If they do not bring him in tomorrow, it would be better. We have a lot of problems here with ours already."

As they sit in the car, Dorothy says. "I hope they take a long time returning the car to us."

Ricky tells Dorothy. "Thanks for helping me. Dad doesn't care what that old woman wanted to do to me. He was going to leave me there."

Ricardo answers him. "That is not true! Nobody was going to leave you there. We take you to school, and they have their rules. It is as simple as that. What did you say the name of the school was?"

Ricky angrily replies. "See! You didn't even pay attention! The name is Saint Francis."

"Where is it?"

"In West Palm Beach. I said that too. You don't really pay attention." Ricky repeats.

"I meant the address of the school, son, please."

"I don't know. The bus picked me up in front of the house and brought me back after school."

Ricardo turns around, looks at Ricky.

"Calm down, please. I have to take Dorothy to work. After that, I will take you to Grandma's house. You will stay with her until I pick you up in the afternoon."

"But I don't want to go to Grandma's house! She doesn't like me! Let me stay with you instead."

Ricardo responds. "You can't. I have to go to my job to see if I can return to work. Children are not allowed there. I will try to find out the address of your old school so I could go there to get your documents."

Ricky answers. "It's okay. I'll go to Grandma if you promise to go to my school and bring the documents."

"Done deal son! No more talk about it." Ricardo says.

Dorothy looks at him sideways. "If you don't bring those documents today, I'm the one leaving the house, and tomorrow you'll take him to school yourself!"

Ricky instantly says. "If you don't go with me tomorrow, I'm not going either. That old woman doesn't like me, and Dad does not care. He is afraid of her!"

Ricardo leaves his wife at work and goes to his parents' house. Ricky tells him before getting out of the car.

"I can stay in the car and wait for you to finish."

"No, Ricky, it can't be. You'll stay here, and that's it, finito. It's over. Comprende?"

Ricardo rings the bell, and his mother opens the door.

"Hello, Rick," she says. "I did not expect to see you so soon. What do you need?"

"Mom, do you think I only come when I need something?" Ricardo answers.

Lora sees that Ricky is with him, and she doesn't know what to say, but then asks.

"Are you stopping by to say hello to your father?"

Ricardo does not want to see his father; he knows the relationship between them is not the best, so he responds.

"I'm in a big hurry, and I need you to do me a big favor."

Lora puts her hands on her waist, stares at him, and says slowly.

"Really! You don't change. If you weren't my son, I would slam the door in your face!"

Ricardo hugs her. He knows it is Lora's weakness, and he tells her.

"If you slam the door in my face, I keep knocking until my knuckles wear out."

Lora pushes him to separate him from her.

"You have no shame! Your father is right, you are a lost case. What do you want now?"

"Thanks, Mom. I need you to take care of Ricky until I come to pick him up in the afternoon. I have to go to work and then to the school where he previously studied."

Lora reluctantly responds. "Why doesn't your wife take care of him?"

"She started working today, and the school would not accept him without the papers from the previous school."

Lora takes a deep breath and responds.

"Okay, for today, but make it clear I'm not going to be your babysitter."

Ricardo hugs her again. "No, Mom, I swear this is an emergency."

LITTLE RICKY

After that, Ricardo leaves in a hurry before his father comes out. He leaves so fast he doesn't even say goodbye to Ricky. Lora looks at Ricky, who has not said a word and holds his backpack with both hands, as if his life depended on it.

"Come inside, kid."

Ricky walks past his grandmother and says.

"Good morning, Mrs. Lora. Excuse me."

Lora sees him go by and follows him with her eyes. She feels like telling Ricardo to take him back, but Ricardo is leaving.

Ricky sees his grandfather coming out of the room and tells him. "Good morning, Grandpa."

Roberto is surprised to hear Ricky and sees him standing in the hallway, holding his backpack. It's strange to him that Ricky has called him Grandfather. He does not consider him his grandson, but at the same time, he does not want to make the boy feel bad. So, he says.

"Good morning, Ricky. Shouldn't you be at school?"

"Yes, but the principal is a bitter old lady who wanted to put me in third grade, and I am in fourth grade already. Dad promised that he would look for my transcript at the old school so that tomorrow they could enroll me in the correct grade."

Roberto puts his hand on Ricky's shoulder and asks him.

"How old are you?"

"I am eight years old."

"So, you must be in third grade, not fourth grade. My grandson Gabriel is nine years old and in fourth grade!" Roberto responds.

Ricky thinks, then asks. "Do you have more grandchildren?"

"Yes! I have a grandson named Gabriel, who is nine years old, and a granddaughter named Arleen, who is seven years old."

Ricky asks again. "And why is Gabriel in fourth grade and not fifth or sixth?"

Roberto looks at him curiously. "Because it's one grade per year. That's how the school system works."

Ricky scowls. "Well, the system here must not be working. In my school, you learn as much as possible, and you can do two years in one."

The surprised grandfather tells him. "You must be very smart to do two years in one!"

"My grandfather always helped me with my homework. He was very intelligent." Ricky responds.

Lora asks Ricky. "Did you have breakfast?"

"No. Dad told me they would give me breakfast at school, but we left, then he took his wife to work and brought me here."

Roberto looks at Lora and tells her. "Your son is a disaster! He will never change. There is no way to fix him!"

Ricky looks at his grandfather and speaks. "That's what my grandfather used to say. Did you know him?"

Roberto smiles and answers. "No, but we both knew your dad, and came to the same conclusions. By the way, what do you have in that backpack you hold so tight and looks so heavy?"

Ricky responds. "I have the laptop my mom gave me, and the schoolbooks."

Roberto, surprised, asks him. "Do you know about computers?"

"Yes. My grandfather taught me. He had a collection of encyclopedias that took up a whole wall. He said that every year he had to add one more book to it, but now all that information can be found on the internet, through the computer."

Roberto feels some sympathy for the boy.

"That's right, everything changes in this world. Come to the kitchen to have breakfast and then we will come to the living room."

Ricky tells him. "I want to thank you for the air-conditioning unit. It makes a noise that helps me to fall asleep."

Roberto laughs again and responds. "You're welcome, son. Now, go and eat."

Ricky enters the kitchen and sees that his grandmother has put breakfast on the table for him. Lora tells him coldly. "Sit down and eat."

Ricky sits down and begins to eat.

Roberto asks his wife. "Why do you treat the boy that way? He is not guilty of anything—he is just a kid!"

Lora responds, in a bad temper. "I don't know what you're talking about. And leave me alone! I'm not in a good mood."

LITTLE RICKY

When Roberto sees his wife leave and decides to sit in the kitchen so as not to leave Ricky alone.

Ricky eats all his breakfast, gets up, picks up the plate and silverware, and starts washing them. Roberto, surprised, asks him.

"What are you doing? Leave that. Lora scrubs them later."

Ricky responds. "At home, everyone cleaned their dishes. Nana Silvia cooked and maintained the house, but she did not wash—she had arthritis in her hands."

"Did you have a maid?" Roberto asks.

"She started working for my great-grandfather, then she continued with my grandfather. My grandfather retired her, but she stayed with us as part of the family. She raised my mom."

"And where is Nana Silvia now?" Roberto asks.

"She is in heaven with my grandparents and mom. They all left together and left me alone." Ricky responds. He can't help the tears running down his cheeks.

Roberto is moved and changes the conversation.

"Come with me to the living room and give me that backpack. No one is going to touch it, I promise."

Once they are in the living room, Roberto tells him. "Sorry, but I don't have Disney Channel.

Ricky responds. "It doesn't matter. I don't watch that channel, anyway. I only watch the History channel, the National Geographic Channel, and the Discovery Channel. Those are real educational channels. Nana Silvia used to watch romantic soap operas, and my grandfather used to tell her that novels are a waste of time."

Roberto looks at Lora, who watches as many soap operas as she can and responds. "Your grandfather and I had a lot in common, then."

Lora was not amused by her husband's comment, and once again Ricky was the point of controversy. Lora tells her husband.

"Look, old man, wait for your natural death and don't rush it!"

Roberto says. "I'm very sorry, but those are paid channels that I don't have them. I only have the basic channels."

Ricky instantly says.

"Okay, let's play the capitals. I will tell you a country and you tell me its capital. Then you ask me, and whoever fails three times loses."

Roberto, out of curiosity, agrees to play with Ricky, and after half an hour, he had lost three times. He is impressed with the boy's knowledge.

"Okay, you won. You know them all."

Roberto gets up and calls Lora.

'Lora, I have to go to the auto parts store. I need to buy the rear lights for the Volkswagen."

Scared, Ricky says. "I'll go with you."

"I'll be right back." Roberto responds.

"No, please take me with you." Ricky pleads with him.

Roberto understands that Ricky does not want to stay with his grandmother and knows that his wife has no sympathy for Ricky.

"Okay, you're coming with me."

Upon arriving at the auto parts store, Roberto sees the parts man and greets him cordially. He has been a customer for more than twenty years.

"Hello, Roberto. How can I help you?"

"Hi, Martin. I need taillights for a 2010 Volkswagen Jetta, but originals, please."

The clerk comes back after a few minutes, brings a box, and puts it on the counter. "It's sixty dollars total. Need anything else?"

"No, thanks. That's all."

Roberto takes the box and gives it to Ricky, who begins to examine it. They are almost out of the store when Ricky stops and goes back to the counter. Ricardo, surprised, follows him.

"What happened, Ricky? Why are you going back for?"

Ricky doesn't answer and instead calls the clerk.

"Sir, please, this is a mistake."

The clerk looks at Ricky, laughs, and mockingly replies,

"Seriously! Was I wrong? Excuse me, I didn't know that you were an expert in foreign parts?"

"My grandfather asked for originals. These are made in China and says it right here." Ricky shows him with his finger where in tiny letters it says, "Made in China."

Roberto is surprised. He never imagined that Ricky pays attention to those details.

The employee responds. "The fact that this says 'Made in China' does not mean that they are not original. Germany has a factory in China."

"No, sir, those parts are called generic. The originals are made in Germany." Ricky responds emphatically.

The clerk puts his hands on the counter, leans forward, and asks. "I can't distinguish between a Chinese and a German, but you can."

"Yes, sir, I can."

The clerk, still leaning forward, looks at Ricky, who holds the box in his hand, with his finger where it says, "Made in China." Roberto enjoys the scene. He does not expect an eight-year-old to have such character.

The store manager was standing behind Roberto, paying attention to what was happening.

"Tell me the difference between a Chinese and a German."

Ricky places the box on the counter. He puts both index fingers on the sides of his eyes and stretches them back.

"The Chinese have eyes like this, and the Germans do not."

They all laugh out loud.

The clerk says. "You beat me, and you are absolutely right! Chinese are very different from Germans, but we are talking about car parts."

The manager interrupts. Until now, no one has seen him.

"Sorry, Roberto. Martin is not aware that we have the original taillights from Germany that we ordered for you. They arrived yesterday very late, almost at closing."

The employee is confused. "Where are they? I didn't see them."

"You will not find them. I put them in the back of the warehouse. I'll look for them. You will not find it on the computer either, because it is not in the system yet."

The manager comes back after a while and brings another box. They inspect this one, not willing to accept it sight unseen.

Roberto asks. "How much is the difference?"

"These are twenty-five dollars more, but we are going to give them to you for sixty dollars. We value your trust in us."

The manager asks. "Where did you get this kid?"

Roberto, without realizing it and without thinking twice, says. "He is my grandson."

The employee shakes hands with Roberto and tells him.

"I congratulate you, and I envy you. But don't take me the wrong way—it's a healthy envy."

Then he turns to Ricky. "Hey, kid, if you want to work here, you know you have a job."

"Thanks, but I have to study very hard. I promised Mom."

Roberto and Ricky then leave hand in hand as grandfather and grandson. Ricky's face changes and looks more human. He almost stops being the tin soldier he always seems to be. Roberto notices the change in Ricky and asks.

"What should we do with the twenty-five dollars we have to spend thanks to you? I suggest we spend it on ice cream, and you are invited!"

Roberto sees Ricky's eyes sparkle.

"I love the idea! My grandfather always took me to eat ice cream. He liked it more than I did, though, and used me as an excuse to go."

Roberto smiles. "I love ice cream, but nobody at home likes it as well and I don't want to go alone."

Ricky responds mischievously. "Don't worry, Grandpa, you can always count on me."

Roberto looks at Ricky and thinks how much he would really like Ricky to be his grandson. He is still convinced that his son is covering up for his wife, Dorothy, and that they had kept Ricky hidden for eight years. The feeling of Ricky's hand grasping his hand and hearing him speak incessantly gives him great satisfaction. Oh! how much he would have wanted his grandson Gabriel to be like Ricky! Suddenly, he feels a tug on his arm and listens.

"Grandpa, you are not listening to me. That is not polite. When one person speaks, the other must pay attention."

The ice cream parlor is a short distance away and in the same shopping center. Roberto answers him to hide his lack of attention.

"Sorry, I was looking for the ice cream shop. I know it's around here, but I don't quite remember where."

Ricky enters the ice cream shop, and his eyes almost pop out of their socket. He walks from one side of the counter to the other and explains to his grandfather the different flavors like an expert. A middle-aged couple at the ice cream parlor looks at Ricky with great curiosity. The employee of the ice cream shop tells Roberto.

"Sir, your grandson knows more about ice cream than I do!"

Roberto is proud and enjoys the moment.

"Well, Ricky, you already described them all to me. Now, tell me, which one you want?"

Ricky puts his hands together as if begging. "A chocolate scoop and strawberry scoop—those are my favorites!"

Roberto laughs and responds. "Those are my favorites too."

Ricky realizes that the couple in the store is looking at him carefully. Pointing at Roberto with his finger, he says.

"This is my grandfather. He has great taste for ice cream."

The couple laughs, and one of them asks him. "Do you love your grandfather very much?"

Ricky looks thoughtful, looks at his grandfather, then looks at the couple again, responding.

"Yes, I love him, and I'm sure he loves me too. He bought me an air conditioner for my room!"

The man goes to Roberto and tells him. "Your grandson is a beauty! God bless him and take care of him."

After the ice cream shop, Roberto does not want to return home just yet; he is having a great time. So, he decides to take Ricky to a park a few blocks from the house. Ricky has a great time in the park, and at the same time, Roberto feels rejuvenated with Ricky's jokes and laughter.

The hours pass without Roberto noticing. He looks at the watch and sees that it is three thirty in the afternoon.

Roberto asks Ricky. "Are you hungry?"

"A bit." Ricky responds.

"Then let's go back to the house." Roberto responds.

Roberto can see that the idea of returning home is like a bucket of cold water on Ricky. He is not comfortable with his grandmother.

"Would you like to eat elsewhere?"

"Yes, Dad took me to eat junk food. That was the first time I ate it and liked it a lot. I don't want mom to find out. She won't let me eat it."

Roberto is amazed. He knows that Dorothy does not cook, and what she mostly eats is junk food.

"It's strange that your mom won't let you eat junk food because that's what Dorothy eats most of the time."

Ricky reacts instantly. He becomes another child, and it is visible that he is offended.

"Dorothy is not my mother. My mother is in heaven with my grandparents and Nana Silvia."

Ricky's response is so blunt he makes Roberto think. He prefers not to touch on the subject, and they go to eat at the fast-food restaurant.

When they return home, Lora receives them very coldly. She simply opens the door for them, turns her back, goes straight to her room, and slams the door. Roberto stands contemplating Lora's attitude when he hears the door slam. He looks at Ricky, who only raises his eyebrows. "That's why I did not wanted to stay."

Roberto passes his hand over his head and answers him.

"Ignore her. That will pass."

Ricky enters the bathroom, and Roberto takes the opportunity to go talk to his wife.

"What's wrong? Why that face and attitude?"

Lora, visibly annoyed, replies. "Why did you not call and say that you were going to spend the whole day out?"

Roberto shakes his head and responds.

"You're right, but we had such a good time that I didn't even realize it."

"Ah! You had a great time." Lora sarcastically responds and reproaches him. "With your grandchildren, you are a bag of ice, and with this kid you are the grandfather of the Year! Do not get your hopes up. You well know that he is not our grandson and that Ricardo, for fear of losing his wife, will do anything."

Roberto remains silent, so Lora asks him.

"Do you think I'm lying? You will not say anything?"

Roberto responds. "Yes, I have a lot to say. When have you seen my grandson thank me for something I have done for them? Not even the parents say thank you. When have you seen a grandson of mine want to go out with me somewhere? And it's not that I didn't invite them either!"

Roberto points his finger at his wife and tells her.

"If that child is Ricardo's son, I swear to you that I will go to court and take him from them. That kid does not deserve to have a father who never loves him and a stepmother who is a White trash!"

Lora is amazed. "So, it is not just Ricardo—now you have fallen for it too!"

"What do you mean by that? Explain yourself." Roberto, annoyed, answers.

"Simply that Dorothy is as charming as a snake and has captivated Ricardo. Her son has the same gifts as his mother and therefore captivated you. Or did you forget how last time, when they were leaving, he called Dorothy Mom, and he took her hand and Ricardo didn't even look at him?"

Roberto does not answer. He is trying to analyze his wife's words and finds no argument to contradict her.

"Are you going to say anything?" Lora asks.

She sees that her husband is silent and decides to go on with the attack again. But Roberto is literally saved by the bell. Ricardo has arrived and is ringing the doorbell.

"I'm going to open the door. That must be Ricardo." Roberto responds.

Roberto sees Ricky standing behind the door, but the bell continues to ring. "Why don't you open the door?"

"Because my grandfather taught me that children should not open the door without an adult present. It is for everyone's safety."

Roberto stares at him and answers. "Your grandfather is right. I can see you've learned very well."

Roberto opens the door and sees Ricardo.

"Hello, Dad. The traffic is impossible. I almost did not arrive."

Ricky immediately asks him. "Did you get the documents to take to school with me tomorrow?"

Ricardo makes a troubled face. He knows that his son is not going to accept any excuse. He gets on his knee to get on the same level as the boy and responds. "Son, thanks to the internet, they helped me at work to find the school, but traffic was so congested that when I arrived, they had already closed the offices and I could not get them."

Ricky turns his back to him and hugs his grandfather's legs as he cries out in great pain.

"I knew you were going to lie to me. Grandpa, help me! I cannot be in third grade—I'm in fourth grade! But he doesn't care if I lose a year. Please help me!"

The boy's crying moves Roberto.

"Can you explain to me what the hell is going on?"

"Nothing, Dad. The school wanted to enroll him in third grade, and he made a tremendous scene saying he should be in fourth grade. We had to take him out of school because of it. The principal said that if we didn't bring her proof that he should be in fourth grade, she would put him in third grade. That's all."

Lora, hearing Ricky's screams, leaves the room, and sees her husband comforting Ricky and her son on his knees, looking at her husband. That scene does not silence her at all, and she takes it as another poison from Dorothy and Ricky, who have not only stolen her son, it seems, but are now also stealing her husband.

Roberto, visibly angry, tells Ricardo. "Tell me the truth. Is he your son? In what grade should he be?"

"Of course, he is my son. You know I would not play with a thing like that! But I don't know what grade he is in."

Roberto, even more enraged now, answers him. "So, you don't give a damn whether your child is in the third or fourth grade. You don't care if your child suffers a crisis you can avoid just by getting documents from his previous school. You don't give a shit about anything!"

Lora tries to intervene to defend her son and uses Ricky as a pretext.

"Roberto, please don't yell like that in front of the kid!"

"You…don't get involved, because you couldn't care less about the kid either."

Ricky is still hugging Roberto's legs, and the older man is caressing him on the back with his left hand.

"Ricky, tell me the truth. What grade should you be in?"

Ricky just stretches his right arm back, pointing at his father, and responds. "Grandpa, he is the liar, not me."

Roberto separates Ricky from him, puts both hands on his shoulder, and tells him.

"Tomorrow, you go to school. Do not worry what grade they put you in. I promise you that I will go to that stupid school, and I will bring the documents. The next day, you will be in fourth grade. I give you, my word."

Ricky answers. "Thanks, Grandpa, but that's a very good school, and it's not stupid."

"Yes, you're right, though you took it literally. Excuse me."

Roberto realizes he has defended Ricky over his son without thinking twice and so decides to walk away. He goes out to the patio.

Lora, meanwhile, takes the opportunity to add a little poison against Dorothy.

"Your father is very angry, but you know that he adores you. We owe all this to your dear wife."

Ricardo takes Ricky by the hand and answers her. "Please, Mom, Dorothy has nothing to do with this. You blame her for everything."

Ricky tells Lora. "She is not to blame for anything. You are being unfair to her."

Lora answers him. "Does it bother you that I talk about Mom?"

"Yes, injustices bother me."

When Ricardo and Ricky leave, Lora goes straight out to the patio to look for her husband. She finds him sitting on a bench under the shade of a tree.

"I know Ricardo is a little crazy, but I think you were a little hard on him. You are putting that child above your own son. You should see how he defended Dorothy!"

"What are you talking about?" Roberto asks.

"It's just that I told Ricardo that Dorothy is to blame for everything, and the boy defended her at all costs. I understand that he's defending his mother, but it is good that you open your eyes. Remember that whoever gives bread to someone else's dog loses the bread and loses the dog." Roberto does not answer.

******

The next day, Ricky gets to school early. Dorothy and Ricardo look at each other as if they were preparing for another Ricky show in front of the principal, but Ricky is so calm that they decide not to bring it up.

Upon their arrival at the school, the assistant tells them. "Ms. Black wishes to speak to you."

Dorothy tells Ricardo. "If that old woman gets shitty again, I'm going to tell her to go to hell."

Ricardo answers. "Please calm down and leave this to me. We don't want any problems."

When they enter the office, the principal gets up from her desk and, looking at Ricky, says.

"Good, young man. Are you ready to go to class?"

"Yes, ma'am, I am."

"You don't mind if I send you to third grade?"

"No, ma'am."

The principal, surprised by the change in Ricky's attitude, looks at Ricardo and Dorothy. Ricardo says.

"We spoke to him last night, and everything is under control."

"Liar! You don't get tired of telling lies, do you?"

"How dare you say something like that! That's a lack of respect." Ricardo answers.

"Disrespect is lying like that in front of everyone."

Ricardo turns red and is about to reprimand the child, but Dorothy puts her hand on his chest, stopping him.

"Leave him alone. Don't make things worse. We don't need another incident like yesterday."

The principal takes a folder from her desk and says.

"Yesterday, I was concerned about the incident we had, so I contacted your old school, and they verified that you should be in fourth grade and that you are an outstanding student. So, I congratulate you and welcome you to our school."

The principal has been expecting an expression of joy from Ricky, but Ricky shows no emotion.

"After everything that happened yesterday, today you have nothing to say?" The principal asks.

"Yes. I need to make a phone call, please."

They all looked at one another; they did not expect such an answer.

"Is it important?" Asks the principal.

"Yes. I must call my grandfather, who promised to look for those documents today, and I want to save him the trip."

The principal agrees to the call. Ricardo gives her the number, and Ricky calls his grandfather.

"Hello, Grandpa. Good morning."

Roberto is totally surprised by Ricky's call so early.

"Hi, Ricky. Everything is fine?"

"Yes, Grandpa. I just wanted to inform you it is not necessary to go to my old school. The principal of this school got the documents, and everything is in order. Today I start classes in fourth grade. Thank you for your help. Have a good day."

The principal sends Ricky to class with her assistant and tells Dorothy and Ricardo to wait a moment, saying that she needs to talk to them. Ricardo and Dorothy sit down, and the principal tells them,

"In so many years of my working in the school system, I have never seen a child act like Ricky. He expresses himself as a cultured adult, and the way he acts does not match his age. He has a very high IQ, but he lacks the ability to interact with others, shows no feelings, and acts in a robotic way. It is as if he sees the world in black-

and-white. He was studying in a private school that has a system where they can take advanced classes and they learn according to their ability, and that is why he is more advanced than normal. We are a state school, and we cannot step outside of our curriculum, but we do have special programs for gifted children like yours. We'll see how things turn out but pay attention to Ricky because I think he's autistic."

Ricardo feels uncomfortable with the principal's words. He stands up and says defiantly.

"The problem with my son is that all these years he has lived alone with two rich old men who thought they were very intellectual and a resentful and sick mother, without any other children around him. But that's over now. With us he has the family that he really needs. So, while I appreciate your advice, my son has nothing, absolutely nothing. He is absolutely fine."

Chapter 4

At the beginning of class, the teacher points out Ricky and says. "Today we have a new student joining us."

Ricky stands up. "My name is Ricardo Clark. I am eight years old, and I come from Saint Francis Private School in West Palm Beach. I do not like speaking in class. We can speak during the break."

The teacher is surprised. Children usually do not stand up to talk in class, but what catches her attention the most is that he is eight years old.

One of the students tells his classmate.

"My mom says that eating dog food has a lot of side effects. I think he is eating dog's food."

The other students start making fun of Ricky. Ricky turns to the student and responds.

"There is no big difference between the ingredients used to make dog food and hamburgers, which is why everyone, including me, has eaten dog food."

The teacher instantly takes control of the class.

"Silence! Stop. Let's start the class."

Ricky sits next to Tamian, having no idea that Tamian is his neighbor. Tamian whispers to him during class.

"I think you and I are neighbors."

Ricky does not answer him.

Tamian tells him again. "Hey, look, I think we're neighbors."

When Ricky does not respond, Tamian tells him.

"Are you deaf? We are neighbors!"

Ricky does not answer him and writes something on a piece of paper instead, passing it to Tamian. Tamian opens the paper and reads.

"You are the deaf one. I said I don't speak during classes."

Tamian opens his eyes upon reading the paper and says.

"Okay, I'll ask you later."

During the break, Tamian and Ricky have a nice conversation, and that day, after dismissal, Tamian tells Ricky.

"Come on, I'll take you on my bike."

"How much will you charge me for the ride?"

Tamian looks at him and opens his eyes wide.

"What is wrong with you? It is a favor."

Ricky tells him. "My grandfather used to tell me that a favor is more expensive than a high fee."

"Do you mean a high fever?" Tamian replies, amazed.

"I said fee, not fever." Ricky responds.

"How are you in math?" Tamian suddenly asks.

"Love it." Ricky responds.

"Well, you help me with my homework, and I will take you on my bike." Tamian responds.

"Done deal, starting today."

Ricky gets on the back of the bike, and they ride home.

Ricky opens the front door, goes to the refrigerator, opens it, and sees that there is practically nothing to eat. Closing the refrigerator, he then goes to his room and changes clothes. He takes a garbage bag and begins to pick up the papers and other garbage that have been thrown around the front of the house. Ricky fills a large plastic bag with all the garbage, and he is now sweaty and thirsty.

Tamian comes out of his house and yells at Ricky.

"Hey, can you come help me with my homework?"

Ricky puts the garbage bag at the front door and goes to Tamian's house. As Ricky enters Tamian's house, he feels the central air-conditioning and exclaims.

"How nice the AC is! The heat at home was killing me!"

"Don't you have air-conditioning in your house?" Tamian asks.

"No, only a wall unit in the room. The rest of the house is hell."

Tamian, as usual, with wide-open eyes, says. "Good grief! In this heat? My god."

Tamian's sister walks into the house, sees Ricky, and looks at him curiously.

"Who is this boy? Why are you bringing strangers home without Mom's permission?" She dismissively asks Tamian.

Tamian answers her. "He is not a stranger. He is my classmate and our neighbor who lives next door."

Tamima looks Ricky up and down and says in a haughty way.

"We'll see what Mom says about this. You know that she doesn't allow anyone to enter this house without her permission."

Ricky stands up and tells Tamian. "It would be better if we go study at my house. I don't want to cause you any problems."

"That won't be possible either. Mom won't let him go anywhere without her permission." Tamima says bluntly.

Ricky stands up and tells her. "If you want to throw me out of your house, you can just say it up front. No need to beat around the bush about it."

Tamima stands in front of Ricky, trying to intimidate him with her much larger size. "That's your problem if you want to interpret it that way."

Ricky tells Tamian. "I'm sorry, but I have to go. When your mom gets home, if you want, I'll come back over, or you can go to my house."

Tamian is embarrassed by his sister's attitude. He throws the books down hard on the table, points at his sister, and yells. "I will tell Mom everything, you stupid jerk!"

Three hours later, Dorothy hears someone knocking on the door. When she opens it, she sees her neighbor Kenya and her daughter Tamima. Dorothy is surprised, because despite their being neighbors for many years, they have never visited each other.

"Good evening, Kenya. Has something happened?"

Ricardo also enters the room and joins Dorothy.

"Nothing serious, but I want to talk to Ricky." Kenya responds.

Dorothy looks at Ricardo and clenches her fists, as if to signal that she wants to strangle him. "My god, this kid is going to kill us! Tell me what he did."

"Don't worry, just call him please." Kenya responds.

Ricardo invites Kenya to come in the house while Dorothy looks for Ricky. She opens the door to Ricky's room and sees him reading a book.

"Has nobody taught you to knock on the door first before entering?" Ricky asks.

Dorothy, angrily, replies. "And has no one taught you not to screw up so much and look for trouble wherever you can find it? Now even the neighbor comes to complain about you!"

Ricky closes the book. "I haven't done anything. I don't know what you're talking about."

"We'll see about that. Come with me. Mrs. Kenya wants to talk to you."

Kenya has come in with her daughter. She refuses to sit down, and she looks a bit upset. Ricky does not know her. Kenya is an African American lady with an imposing figure, tall and thick. Ricky sees Tamima and thinks that maybe she has made up a story to turn her mother against him.

Ricardo, seeing Ricky scared and Tamima serious, comes to the same conclusion, that Ricky has run into some problems. He tries to apologize to Kenya.

"I don't know what my son has done, but I swear it won't happen again. I give you, my word."

"No," Kenya says. "On the contrary, I want it to happen again, because in my house I am the chief."

Ricardo and Dorothy are concerned. They look at Ricky, who, almost crying, says. "I'm sorry, ma'am. I swear I will not go to your house anymore."

Kenya, seeing that Ricky is about to cry, says lovingly to him.

"No, son, you didn't do anything wrong. I'm here because I want Tamima to apologize to you for what she did this afternoon."

Kenya stands in front of Tamima and orders her. "Apologize to him right now."

Tamima knows that her mother is not playing, and she is in hot water.

"I said," Kenya repeats. "Apologize to him right now."

Tamima steps forward and stands in front of Ricky. "Forgive me. I shouldn't have thrown you out of the house. It was improper and rude."

Ricky stares at her and does not respond. He sees that there is not the slightest remorse on Tamima's face.

"I have nothing to forgive you for because you are not sincere. I can see it in your face. But yes, I am going to come back, if your mother authorizes me."

Ricky then turns toward Kenya.

"Mrs. Kenya, if you allow me, I will go to your house, or Tamian can come here. He needs help with homework. We also have a deal. I will help him with homework, and he will take me on his bike to school. A deal is a deal."

Kenya extends her arm and shakes hands with Ricky.

"Now you have a deal with me. You help Tamian improve his grades and the snacks are on me."

Kenya looks at her daughter and understands that Ricky is right. Her daughter's face is defiant.

"I brought you here to apologize, but your apologies are not sincere. I think a week without television will make you reconsider."

"But Mom!" Tamima says.

"But Mom, nothing! Home!" Kenya yells at her daughter.

From that day on, Ricky and Tamian become great friends. Every afternoon, Ricky religiously helps Tamian do his homework with all the subjects. Ricky enjoys the snacks Kenya keeps for him in the fridge. Tamima stayed away from Ricky and only spoke to him only if it was necessary.

One Saturday morning, Ricardo tells Ricky.

"We are taking Dorothy to work and will have breakfast there in the cafeteria."

Ricky responds with a question. "Then what will we do?"

"I do not know. What do you want to do?" Ricky responds.

"I want us to clean the yard. It is full of trash and there are mosquitoes because of all the standing water in those old tires that are thrown back."

"Can't you think of something more pleasant to do?" Ricardo answers.

"I collected all the garbage that was scattered in the front. Aren't you ashamed to have the ugliest yard on the block?"

"Okay, if that makes you happy." Ricardo responds reluctantly.

Ricky, Dorothy, and Ricardo are preparing to leave when someone knocks on their door. It is the clerk from the hardware store, who has come to return their car and take the rented car.

"Good morning, Mr. Suarez. I brought your car. I need to take the rental you have back to the rental agency."

Ricardo looks back and shakes his head. "I should've known. It lasted too long. Now the charm is over."

Before getting in the car, Ricky opens the door and looks under the seats. "What are you looking for? Don't you see that it is clean?" Dorothy asks.

Ricky looks at her, scowling, and answers. "Remember, you screamed louder than me."

Dorothy gets in the car and asks Ricardo. "Did you ever think you would see this car like this? It even smells good!"

Ricky responds. "The question should not be that."

"What should the question be, then, according to you?" Ricardo asks.

"Well, I think it should be, how long will it last looking like this?"

Dorothy turns to him and responds with character. "I don't dirty the car. It's the one who claims to be your father who is the pig."

"But you don't clean it either. Remember, the one who kills the cow is as guilty as the one who holds its legs," Ricky responds, moving his head forward, weaving it to and for mockingly.

"Please, it's Sunday. I haven't had breakfast, I have to go to work, and you just keep torturing us. Could you let your guard down a bit and give us a break, please?" Dorothy responds.

Ricardo continues driving as if he were alone in the vehicle. Dorothy touches him on the shoulder and asks him. "Aren't you going to say anything about it?"

Ricardo looks at her, and Dorothy sees that his mind is far away.

"Yes, of course, my love. Next month is my parents' fortieth wedding anniversary. You don't understand how bad I would just love to have a valid excuse not to go."

"How bad is your relationship with your parents, anyway?" Dorothy asks.

"It is not going well at all. If you add to that my stupid brother, my sister-in-law, who is known as the Wonder Woman, and the spoiled nephews, it is the perfect storm." Ricardo answers.

"Don't worry, we will have time to train." Dorothy responds.

"What do you mean?" Ricardo asks.

"Obviously, you forgot that Friday is my mom's birthday."

"Oh my god, I forgot about that one! You know that they don't like to be close to me. They would be much happier if I were not going, and maybe not even to know that I exists." Ricardo answers.

Dorothy gives him a little pull of his right ear, telling him. "You also know that I don't give a damn what they want or what you want. If I have to accept your parents, then you will have to accept mine. I also don't want to listen to your dad's negative opinions or the stupid comments of your idiot brother."

Ricky takes advantage of the fact that they are both thoughtful and says sarcastically. "What beautiful families my parents have! Maybe you both are the problem. It can't be that everybody else is wrong?"

Dorothy and Ricardo, in a synchronized and spontaneous movement, turn around and yell at him. "Fuck you, brat!"

"Bravo! Congratulations! What coordination! It cannot be denied that you are the same. My grandfather taught me a Russian proverb that says, *Durack duracka vidiet iz daleka.*"

"What the fuck does that mean?" Dorothy asks.

"Do you really want to know what it means?"

"Of course! If not, I would not have asked you, Mr. Genius."

Ricky takes a notebook out of his bag, which he religiously carries with him, writes down the proverb, and gives it to Dorothy.

"Here you have it!"

"I didn't ask you to write it to me. I asked you to tell me what it means." Dorothy responds with a bad temper.

"I said the same thing to my grandfather, and he told me that if I really wanted to know, I should look it up in a dictionary. I looked for it. It was not easy, but I never forgot it."

Dorothy takes the note and reads it several times. She puts it in her purse, gnashes her teeth angrily, and then says. "Stupid."

Ricky points his finger at her. "Don't you think I didn't hear that? You're disrespectful, and you shouldn't talk about Dad like that."

Dorothy looks at Ricardo, who by then has finished parking the vehicle. Ricardo puts his head on the wheel and says in a desperate tone.

"He acts like an old man, you act like a little girl, and the two of you are going to make me cry like a baby!"

After having breakfast in the cafeteria, Dorothy begins to work at register number five. Ricardo and Ricky start shopping for the items that Dorothy has written on their list. Dorothy's coworker Ines, better known as the Mini Snooper, sees Ricardo and Ricky and walks up to them.

"Hello, beauty. How are you doing?"

"Very well, thank you. And you?" Ricky responds.

Ines is still talking to Ricky, but she is on the lookout for Dorothy's transactions at the cashier. Her supervisor has asked her to watch over Dorothy. Ines sees Dorothy pass a case of beer without scanning it. She says goodbye to them and runs to the office to rat out Dorothy. Ines tries to open the office door, but it is closed. She starts banging on the door loudly while she calls the supervisor's name.

"Hellen, Hellen, open up quick, please."

The supervisor opens the door and asks her.

"What is it? Are you trying to give me a heart attack?"

"It's Dorothy. She let her husband get a case of beer without paying. She did not scan it, and he did not get charged."

Hellen shouts. "Bingo! We have that thief."

Hellen runs up to the security chief, who is sitting in front of the cameras, and tells him. "Give me a copy of the video on register number five."

The chief looks at the monitors. "Damn, I don't have that register covered. I didn't know she was working."

Hellen responds quickly. "It doesn't matter. We can check her receipt against the products she carries. We have them, anyway."

Hellen and the security officer rush out to register number five, but as they get closer, they see that Dorothy is serving another customer.

Hellen exclaims. "Let's run to the parking lot. We'll stop it in the parking lot."

They both run to the parking lot and start looking for them, but they can't see the car. Hellen, furious, says. "You are taller. Look for a beat-up old Toyota. It's easy to distinguish."

"What color is it?"

"It's so dirty I don't know what to tell you. It looks like brown or dark green to me." Hellen answers nervously.

She does not know that Dorothy's car, after the professional, detailed cleaning, does not look like the car she is looking for. The car practically passes by her, and they do not notice it.

Back in their house, Ricky begins checking the store receipt against the products at home.

"What are you doing?" Ricardo asks.

"Nana Silvia always compared the receipt with the merchandise. She said we should not trust the cashiers."

"Do you think Dorothy is going to steal from us? That would be stealing from herself."

"I know, but it is customary."

A few minutes later, Ricky yells. "Dad, hurry! Come and see this."

Frightened, Ricardo runs to Ricky. The boy keeps the receipt in his hand and points to the products on the table.

"Look, she forgot to charge us for the beers. They are not on the receipt. We must go back and return them."

Ricardo sighs deeply, then looks at his son, who is still pointing to the receipt with his finger.

"Look, look, look, it is not there, is not there. We are not thieves! We are poor people, but not thieves!"

Ricardo looks at him, offended.

"Be careful with what you say. You are offending not only her but also me. And anybody can make a mistake. We do not know if the scanner is working well. I will call her on the phone. I will tell her to pay for the beers, and that is it. You don't have to make such a dramatic scene."

Ricky is quiet and thoughtful, but not entirely convinced. His father may be correct.

"You're right but call her right now." Ricky answers, scowling.

Ricardo knows that Ricky won't rest until he calls Dorothy, so he calls Dorothy.

"Hello, love. I am calling to tell you that you made a mistake and did not charge for the beers. Please call your supervisor and pay for them."

Dorothy is thoughtful. She understands that if her husband calls her, it must be for a reason. "Of course, my love. What a shame! I will fix this problem right now. Thanks for letting me know."

Ricardo emphasizes. "It wasn't me. It was Ricky who realized it, thanks to him."

Dorothy understands that her husband is correct. Ricky is a box of surprises and not worth the risk. Dorothy sees the assistant manager and third-in-command pass by and calls out to her.

"Cristina, please, I have a problem, and I don't know how to solve it."

"What is going on?" Cristina asks.

"When I charged for my husband's groceries, something happened that might have caused me not to charge for the beer, and he just called me now to let me know."

"But how did he find out from home?" Cristina asks.

"We are used to checking the receipt against the groceries."

Cristina is astonished. "My god, how honest you all are! I think you people must be from another planet."

"Don't make fun of me, please, and just help me."

"I cannot add a charge to a transaction that is closed on the computer, but we can make a new purchase of just one pack of beer. That way, the inventory will not be short, and the money is recovered."

"Thanks, Cristina. But please look for it before they move me to another register."

Cristina has no idea that Hellen is investigating Dorothy and wants to get rid of her, so she takes the incident as harmless and does not communicate it to Hellen.

That night, Dorothy asks Ricardo.

"Can you explain to me how the hell that brat knew about the beers?"

Ricardo responds, shaking his head. "That child is dangerous and sees everything! The next time, you charge for the beers. I think he did not hear the sound of the scanner when you passed the beer over it, and that was why he started to check the products against the store receipt when we got home."

"My god, you better bring me that DNA test this week. I can't take it anymore!" Dorothy replies, annoyed.

"Don't worry, next time just pass the meat as if it were another product." Ricardo responds, trying to reassure his wife.

******

On Dorothy's mother's birthday, Ricardo tells Ricky.

"Today is Mrs. Sara's birthday."

"Who is Sara?" Ricky asks.

"She is my mother-in-law, Dorothy's mother."

"And what do you want me to do?" Ricky asks.

"That you behave and that you do not cause problems like you did at your grandmother's house." Dorothy responds.

"I didn't do anything. It was that old weed that started—"

Ricardo instantly scolds him. "More respect for your grandmother! You can't talk about her like that!"

Dorothy takes the opportunity to say.

"Well, he didn't say any slander. You don't have to scold him."

Ricardo approaches her and pinches her buttock. "Very funny, young lady. We will see what you say when he throws a bomb of his at your house."

Dorothy jumps, she wasn't expecting the pinch.

"That will not happen. They know that he is not my son and would never treat a child badly."

******

Ricardo parks in front of his wife's parents' house, and Ricky sees a police car parked in front. Ricky, scared, says.

"My god, the neighbors already called the police! That happens when they play the music too loud."

Dorothy answers him. "No, it's not that. They knew that you were coming, and they called the police to control you."

Ricardo rings the doorbell, and Dorothy's brother opens the door.

"Hi, Frank! How are you?" Ricardo says.

Frank hisses and reluctantly answers him. "Well, thanks for coming. Come in, please."

Ricardo passes quickly because he cannot stand to be in the presence of his brother-in-law. Dorothy follows behind him, and her brother Frank whispers to her as they pass. "Now the party is complete!"

Dorothy replies. "Stupid fool."

They are so disgusted by Frank that Ricardo and Dorothy hastily enter the house and forget about Ricky, who is standing behind them. Frank stares at Ricky holding a gift bag with a birthday balloon. Frank is tall and stocky, with blond hair and blue eyes. He is dressed in his police uniform. Frank stands in front of Ricky and looks at him curiously. As Frank is looking down at him, Ricky scowls, looking up at him.

"Who are you?" Frank asks.

"I am Ricky."

"That does not tell me anything."

"But that's the answer to your question, and if the music was too loud for you to hear me, that's not my fault either. I also think that you, Lieutenant, are very far from Miami. You are out of your jurisdiction."

Frank is in uniform because he has to work that night. Ricky's blunt response not only surprises him but also makes him laugh.

Meanwhile, Dorothy and Ricardo are congratulating Sara, Dorothy's mother.

Dorothy tells her. "Congratulations, Mom. We hope that you have many more years of health!"

Ricardo adds. "I hope you like the gift."

That's when they both realize they have forgotten Ricky with the gift outside. They both look at each other, and Dorothy screams. "Shit, he is outside!"

They both have taken a turn to go look for Ricky when they see Frank entering with him.

"Is this what you forgot outside?" Frank asks sarcastically.

Ricardo tells Ricky in the form of a scolding. "You gave us a big scare!"

"I did not stay out, you left me, and that scared me too."

Frank takes the opportunity to start attacking them. "So, you bring a child with you, you leave him outside, and now you blame him. Your irresponsibility really has no limits."

Sara intervenes and tells them. "Not today, please. I don't want fights."

Frank throws his hands up in the air as if he gives up and says.

"Just like your mother. That's why they say that a mother's love is blind."

Frank Sr., Sara's husband, steps in to bring order.

"Enough! You didn't hear their mother." Frank Sr. then asks Dorothy.

"Whose child is this?"

"He is my son." Ricardo responds.

Frank Sr. and Sara laugh. Ricardo is serious and looks at Dorothy, who says in a low voice.

"Don't look at me. You promised me the DNA test, and you never did it."

Ricardo, angry, answers. "It is no laughing matter. He is my son!"

Frank Sr. responds. "Don't be angry, Ricardo. It's just that he looks more Dorothy's son than yours, and we know that he is not hers."

"With all due respect, Mr. Frank, I came to congratulate you and your wife. So please don't offend me. If I bother you, I'll leave and come to pick up your daughter later."

Sara screams. "Shit! I said enough is enough!"

Ricky walks like a robot and gives the bag with the balloon and the gift to Sara, telling her.

"Take your gift, ma'am, because I think this party is going to be over before it even begins."

Ricky's interaction makes Sara and Frank laugh. Only Ricardo, Dorothy, and Frank Jr. keep their very serious faces.

Sara, trying to improve the room's atmosphere, tells Ricky.

"Thanks. You're very kind. What's your name?"

"My name is Ricky, and I want to wish you a happy birthday."

"Thanks! And how old are you?"

"I am eight, and I am in fourth grade."

"That's great! Do you know how old I am today?"

"No. My grandfather said that a man should never ask a woman's age."

Sara and everyone are amazed by that comment.

"Your grandfather was not only wise but also a true gentleman," Sara answers with a smile as she strokes Ricky's hair.

Ricky responds in his robotic way.

"He said you shouldn't ask the age because they all lie about it."

This time, everyone laughs out loud, except Sara, who tells him.

"And I thought I liked you."

Frank Jr. asks Ricky. "Tell me, kid, where do you know the word jurisdiction from?"

"My grandfather was a West Palm Beach police captain, and he taught me many things."

"What else did your grandfather teach you about cops?"

"He told me that policemen are divided into three classes."

Frank looks at him with interest. "I didn't know that, and I'm a lieutenant! Please explain it to me."

"The first one is those officers who do not realize that many women fall in love with the uniform. After they are married and they have to wash their uniform, things change, divorce comes, and with that the loss of half their salary. That mistake is made multiple times, and they end up alone and broke."

"The second one is worse. They think they are Don Juan and they go from one relationship to another, hurting innocents and hurting themselves without realizing that they are losing the best years of their lives as a hummingbird."

"The third is the minority. They are the ones who understand that the uniform does not make them superheroes and that they must do the best they can, knowing that they will not be able to fix the world and put their family above all."

Dorothy wastes no time. "Brother, you are right in the middle."

Frank doesn't answer; his face is as red as a tomato. He realizes his sister is enjoying the moment, so he decides to counterattack.

"You are a brilliant child. What a shame you have a father who dumps you and a stepmother who did not even remember that you came with them."

Ricardo feels like slapping his brother-in-law, but he retrains himself, takes a deep breath, and says.

"Mrs. Sara, I really wish you good health and that you fulfill all your dreams. But I am leaving. I think it will be better."

Ricardo leaves and does not listen to the requests of his wife and mother-in-law asking him to stay. When Ricardo closes the door, Dorothy tells her brother.

"I hope you are satisfied. You really do have a special talent for ruining everything!"

"I have not done or said anything that is not true. The truth hurts, but it is worse not to recognize it."

Sara and Frank say nothing, as they have always been against their daughter's marriage. Ricky sees that Dorothy has tears in her eyes. He stands next to her and takes her hand, telling Frank Jr.

"Listen, Lieutenant. It is clear you do not belong to the third group, because you do not put your family above all. I don't know what your problem with her is, but it seems you prefer to ruin your mother's party, which is only once a year, to satisfy your resentment or frustration."

Frank looks at the boy, his mouth hanging open, but to compensate, he angrily reproaches him.

"Who the hell do you think you are, you little brat, to talk to me like that?"

Ricky ignores him and stands in front of Sara. He tells her.

"Congratulations, Mrs. Sara, but I'll wait outside too."

Ricky turns to Frank Sr. and tells him.

"Have a good afternoon, sir."

Ricky tells Dorothy. "I'll wait outside." Then he turns to her brother. "And to you, Lieutenant, I repeat your own words: *The truth hurts, but it is worse not to recognize it.*'"

Dorothy, seeing that her parents have not said anything and with their silence, in fact supported her brother, tells them between sobs.

"I am not perfect—I do not pretend to be, and I never will be—but family to me is above all, and that includes you. It hurts me a lot to think that the child who does not carry my blood has defended me more than those who carry my blood have. He has accepted me with all my defects and has a much higher concept of family than you, who want me to live the life that you want for me, not the one I choose."

Frank Jr. replies. "You are the one who chose to be a White Trash, and you want Mom and Dad to applaud you?"

Those words reach Dorothy deep down. She stands in front of her brother and slaps him.

Frank does not react; he only tells her. "The truth hurts more than a slap."

Dorothy turns to her parents and pointing at Frank speaks.

"Here you have your hero, the perfect one, the ideal one, your pride. And Ricky described him to the teeth without even knowing him."

Then, Dorothy turns to Frank and tells him.

"And what kind of White Trash are you? I have been happily married to the man I love for five years. We may not have much, but we have not asked anyone for anything. And we have no material ambitions like you, who are not satisfied with anything. You do not have a relationship that lasts more than a year! You play with women's hearts without giving a damn if someone suffers from your deceptions. You have convinced one of your girlfriends to have an abortion, and you even paid another one to have it! And you still have the face to talk about responsibilities? Tell me, who is hiding behind that uniform?"

Dorothy wipes away her tears and walks out, leaving her parents and her brother speechless.

Frank Sr. tells his son. "I think you were very hard on her, and today was not the right day for this show."

"Dad, she started it, and it makes me mad that she does not think about all you have done for her. I am sorry for that child. What will become of him if they bring him to a party and leave him outside?"

Sara says. "That child is more my son than Ricardo's."

Frank Sr. shakes his head and replies. "I do not understand how my daughter puts up with that, because Ricardo's being stupid does not surprise me, but Dorothy is something else."

Chapter 5

The relationships between Dorothy, Ricardo, and Ricky became much more cordial, even though Dorothy has not fully accepted Ricky yet and continues with the suspicions that Ricky is not Ricardo's son. Dorothy has been trying by all means to get pregnant and is beginning to worry. One morning, Dorothy decides to take a DNA sample from Ricky to clear her doubt and takes a glass from which Ricky drank water. She puts it in an airtight plastic bag without noticing Ricky is observing her through the reflection on the glass window.

Before leaving for school, Ricky knocks on Dorothy's room door.

"What do you want? Are you going to be late for school?"

"I have something for you that I want to give you."

Dorothy looks at Ricardo and asks him. "What will your little boy bring up now?"

She opens the door and sees Ricky with his school bag and his hairbrush in his hands.

"What, do you want me to comb your hair? Get that hell out of here! If you think I am going to comb your hair, you are going to be waiting for a long time." Dorothy says, exasperated.

"No. I just want to give you this. Use the hair for your DNA test. Those are the most reliable ones. And for your information, my mom made sure to take Dad's DNA to prove it in court if necessary. She would have never sent me to live in a toilet like this if she weren't sure I am his son."

Dorothy is speechless. She doesn't know what to do. Ricky puts the brush in her hand and says.

"I'm late for school. Tamian is waiting for me."

Dorothy walks into the room with the brush in her hand, still half-stunned. Ricardo, who has seen what happened from a distance, asks her.

"What are you going to do now?"

Dorothy throws the brush at Ricardo, hitting him on the head, and yells at him.

"You told me you would do a DNA test and you never did!"

Ricardo screams and scratches his head, then says.

"I can't do it, love. I am scared."

"What do you mean by that? Explain yourself, asshole."

"It's that…I think I really love him. I no longer care or want to know if I'm really his father. I regret not having recognized him earlier. You and I, would have raised him as a child and not as a robot."

Dorothy angrily yells at him. "You speak as if I do not count here! How do you know if I want to raise someone else's child?"

Ricardo, also a little angry now, answers her.

"For being someone else's son, he has defended you as if he was yours. Who was the one who defended you at my mother's house? When you left your parents' house crying, you hugged him and kissed him, thanking him for defending yourself from your brother before your parents. Even though you have never treated him with affection."

Dorothy cannot answer; she knows Ricardo is right.

"It is that you promised to do the test and you have not done it. I do not want to talk about it anymore. Take me to work. I have to start earlier today."

******

During break, Ricky goes to the fifth-grade classroom and tells the fifth-grade teacher. "Excuse me, can I ask you a question?"

The teacher looks at him in amazement. She does not recognize him, but she responds. "Sure, tell me what you want."

"I need to know how to go on the internet to take your classes."

"What grade are you in?"

"I am in fourth grade, but I brought all the materials to study before I was transferred from my old school, and I am about to finish it."

The teacher stares at him and responds.

"Come and see me tomorrow and I'll give you the answer."

Ricky leaves, and the teacher is left with great curiosity. Later, the teacher bumps into the principal in the hall and tells her.

"Ms. Black, a child came to see me a while ago, and he looks like a tin soldier. He asked me for the fifth-grade materials and said that he is almost finished with the fourth-grade ones."

The principal shakes her head and asks her. "Is he White and blond?"

"Yes, he is."

"That's Ricky. He's eight years old and in fourth grade. That child is a genius. I believe, has some mild type of autism, but his parents refuse to accept it and were offended when I told them. He speaks with the lexicon of an adult, and he is gifted. He should be in another school."

The teacher responds. "What do I say to him? I am sure he will return to ask me again tomorrow."

"We will see. I can't talk now. I have a meeting."

The next day, as the teacher had predicted, Ricky shows up to her classroom and asks her. "Did you bring me the answer?"

The principal hasn't said anything to her, and so she tries to get Ricky off her by telling him. "You have to go to the school's website and look for my class assignments. I will give you a student number so you can enter."

Ricky makes a disgusted face.

"I don't have internet at home. Don't you have books?"

"Sorry, but you need internet."

That afternoon, Ricky can't wait for his father to arrive to ask him to install the internet service. When Ricky sees his father's car park in front of the house, he immediately goes out.

"Dad, why don't we have internet at home?"

"Why will I pay for something if I don't need it? We have lived here for four years, and we've never had it, so I don't see why now."

"It is because I need it for school."

Ricardo sees Tamian outside and asks him.

"Tamian, are you forced to use the internet at school?"

"No, Mr. Ricardo."

Ricardo looks at Ricky. "You, see? That is a whim of yours. It is not necessary."

"But I need it! It is only twenty-five dollars a month!" Ricky says, almost crying.

"Well, pay it yourself." Dorothy says mockingly.

"Is that true, Dad? If I get the money, will you have the internet connected?"

"Sure, son. I give you, my word." Ricardo and Dorothy enter the house laughing at Ricky.

An hour later, Dorothy tells Ricardo. "I am glad Ricky got angry. He has cleaned up the entire garage to burn off his frustration." They both laugh mockingly.

The house has an open garage for a single car.

Ricky knocks on the door of his neighbor from across the street, who is a six-foot-seven Black man with teeth all plated in gold. The neighbor looks at him in amazement and asks.

"What do you want?"

"I want to propose a deal to you."

The neighbor looks him up and down and tries to hold back his laughter. "What deal?"

"You have an antic car, and you do not have a parking garage at home. I see how you take care of your car, so I will rent you my indoor parking for fifty dollars a month."

"You have no authority to rent me the parking garage."

"Yes, I do. My father gave me permission so with that money I will pay for my internet."

"Yes, but that is a lot of money."

Ricky stares at him, takes his time, and responds.

"Have you thought about how much a scratch on your car's paint costs? How about if someone steals your tires? Can you imagine waking up and finding out a drunk driver crashed into your car? I think that is a lot more than fifty dollars. Just sitting in a car that has been in the shade compared to one that has been parked in the sun is worth fifty dollars, I bet."

The man sticks his hand in his pocket and, without thinking twice, gives him fifty dollars, then instantly parks his car in Ricardo's garage.

Ricardo and Dorothy don't hear anything as they are taking a shower together. When they come out of the bathroom, Ricky is waiting for them with money in hand.

"Look, Dad, you can connect the internet tomorrow and put in high speed, which costs fifty dollars."

Ricardo takes the money and replies. "So, you have money, and you don't offer a penny."

"No, Dad, you told me to look for the money, and I did. I rented out our garage to the neighbor across the street. He is very happy, and he already parked his car in the garage."

Ricardo and Dorothy look at each other and don't say a word at first. Ricardo, after sighing deeply, finally says.

"Damn, I can't believe this. You are worse than a pain in the ass! Okay, I'm going to pay for the internet, but you take that car out of the garage."

Ricky stares at him, scowls, points a finger at him, and replies.

"You told me that you could not pay, and now you can. That means you did not want to pay for it! I already gave my word to the man across the street and took his money, so I can't back down now. But when the month is up, I will talk to him and renegotiate or end his contract." Ricky then turns and goes into his room.

Ricardo and Dorothy cannot believe what has happened and the firmness with which Ricky has defended himself.

"I'm going to get that car out of here right now." Ricardo says angrily as he puts on his shirt to go out to talk to the neighbor.

Dorothy sees that her husband is angry, and she doesn't want trouble with the neighbor. She stands up and puts both hands-on Ricardo's chest, stopping him.

"Please leave it like that for now. It's our fault, you know. It's time for us to understand that your son takes everything literally. That neighbor takes more care of his car than he does for his house.

LITTLE RICKY

I remember that he told me that just the paint on the car cost him five thousand dollars. Then he told me that the car is twenty years old and is not worth more than eight hundred dollars. He had it made new and uses it for car shows. He has spent more than fifteen thousand dollars on a car."

Then she adds. "And that neighbor is very violent. Remember that last year he had a fight with his next-door neighbor because his son hit his car with his bicycle, and the police came and took them both to jail!" Dorothy is horrified; she looks as if about to cry.

Ricardo sees that his wife is about to cry and hugs her.

"Okay, love, let us leave it like that now, but the same way he got the garage rented, he will have to get him out of there next month."

Ricky has returned to give his father a message from the teacher, but upon hearing Dorothy tries to convince Ricardo, he stops behind the door. Ricky raises his eyebrows, opens his mouth, and puts his hand on his head, realizing the trouble he has gotten himself into. When he hears his father agree to give him a month, he puts his hand to his mouth like someone trying to hold back laughter and goes to his room on his tippy toes.

******

Dorothy arrives at work about fifteen minutes early. She is sitting in the cafeteria when she sees an employee called Viera, who is from Russia. Dorothy greets her and tells her. "I need to ask you a favor."

Viera responds in her Slavic accent. "Sure, Dorothy. What do you need?"

Dorothy pulls out the Russian proverb Ricky had written on a piece of paper and hands it to her. Viera reads it and laughs, then hands it back to her, telling her.

"In order to give you the exact meaning, I must know what happened before he gave it to you."

Dorothy looks at her somewhat confused, but her curiosity overpowers her, so she decides to tell her.

"My husband and I were talking to Ricky. We both spontaneously called him jerk at the same time. He was amazed because of our timing and told me the proverb, but he did not explain it."

Viera asks with a mischievous smile. "So, the two of you were synchronized?"

"That does not matter. What I want to know is the proverb's translation." Dorothy replies, trying to avoid Viera's response.

"That would translate as, 'The stupid finds each other from far away without anyone's help.'"

Dorothy grits her teeth, flushes, and clenches her fists. Viera has to make an effort to contain her laughter.

******

The fortieth wedding anniversary of Ricardo's parents arrived. Dorothy feels as if she has to go in front of a firing squad. Ricardo does not want to go either, but he has a moral obligation to attend. Their biggest fear is the reaction of Ricardo's brother and his wife when they meet Ricky, because they do not know about Ricky yet. The biggest uncertainty, however, is what kind of trouble Ricky will get into this time, as his responses were unpredictable.

Ricardo is arriving at his parents' house and sees that his brother has arrived before him.

"Isn't that your brother's car?" Dorothy asks reluctantly.

Ricardo looks at his wife and pleads with her. "Yes, the perfects have already arrived, and I'm sure Mom already shared all the gossip with them. Please let us try to make it all go away."

Dorothy turns around and says to Ricky. "You listen to your father. Do not go creating problems as usual., okay?"

Ricky, squinting and moving his finger from side to side, answers. "No, no, no, it's you who starts it all. Don't blame me now."

Ricardo rings the bell and is greeted by his father.

"Hello, Dad. Congratulations!"

Roberto coldly answers him. "Hi, Rick. Go ahead."

Dorothy, trying to ingratiate herself with her father-in-law, tells him.

LITTLE RICKY

"Good afternoon, Roberto. Do I congratulate you or offer my condolences?"

Roberto just responds. "Please continue. Everyone is in the kitchen."

Dorothy passes by, and Roberto sees Ricky, who is standing like a soldier at attention, holding a bouquet of roses as if it were a rifle.

"Hello, Grandpa. Congratulations on your anniversary! I wish you many more with good health together with your beloved wife."

Roberto stares at Ricky, and surprised by his congratulations, he replies.

"How do you know I love my wife?"

"Because in order to be married to someone for forty years, you have to love her very much." Ricky answers, handing him the rose bouquet.

Roberto smiles, leans down, and hugs him affectionately.

"Thanks, Ricky. You really are special."

Ricky also hugs him and kisses him on the cheek.

When Roberto feels Ricky's kiss, he cannot stop his eyes from watering. His two other grandchildren, whom he considers his real grandchildren, did not even greet him upon their arrival. They just entered the house and went directly to play in the yard.

Roberto stands up, taking Ricky by the hand, and says to him.

"Let's go inside so that you can give your grandmother the roses."

Ricky looks at him very seriously and responds.

"I think it would be better if you give it to her. I don't want any problems."

"Do not be afraid; I'm with you. I also want you to meet your cousins." Roberto reassures the child.

"What cousins?" Ricky asks, surprised.

"They are Gabriel and Arleen. They are the children of your uncle Roberto and his wife, Stephany. Gabrielito is nine years old, and Arleen is eight, just like you."

Ricky makes a shocked expression. "Ah! Those are the perfect ones!"

Roberto feels as if he has been hit on the head with a baseball bat. He turns around and asks Ricky.

"Where did you get that from?"

"I did not invent it. That's what my dad said."

"Well, you better not repeat it. That is disrespectful."

"Why, Grandpa? Being perfect? I think that it is impossible, but it is not bad either."

"Listen to me, I only ask you not to repeat it to anyone. Do you promise me?"

"Yes, I promise you."

Roberto enters the kitchen with Ricky, and everyone is silent for the moment. Roberto Jr. and his wife are unaware of Ricky's existence. They both look at Roberto holding Ricky by one hand and Ricky holding the roses in his other hand.

Stephany tells her father-in-law. "This is a big surprise, but please explain it to me. I don't understand."

Roberto does not respond. Ricky is impeccably dressed. He is wearing the clothes he wore the day he went to live with his father. It is a black tuxedo with a black bow on the neck. Ricky looks at everyone like someone who is taking in a movie and doesn't want to lose any details.

"Good afternoon, everyone. Mrs. Lora, congratulations." Ricky reaches out his hand and hands the bouquet of roses to his grandmother.

Lora doesn't know what to do or say. She has also been dreading and avoiding that moment. Lora takes the roses, and just says. "Thanks."

Lora's indifference to Ricky is the first kick in the stomach for Roberto, who looks at his wife and, with his eyes, lets her know that he does not approve of her attitude.

Lora opens the sliding door and tells Ricky. "Please go out to the patio to play with my grandchildren."

Ricky looks at Roberto and Dorothy, who say nothing, then he looks at his grandfather. Roberto tells him.

"Go, Ricky, so you can meet them and play for a while."

Ricky, like a robot, goes out to the patio, but on his face can be seen that he does not like the idea.

Stephany asks one more time. "Are you going to tell me where that child came from or not?"

Roberto, seeing that no one is about to answer, says.

"I don't think it's up to me to say it, but if his supposed father doesn't dare, then I'll say it myself."

Ricardo says sharply then. "He is my son."

Roberto Jr. and his wife, Stephany, burst out laughing. "You would like to be the father, but you don't get to do that."

Then Junior and his wife look at Dorothy, who tries to avoid their gaze.

"Did you have a son and you had him hidden?"

"He is my son. Or did you not hear me?" Roberto says again.

"Well, sorry. Don't be angry. It's just that he is the portrait of Dorothy, and since you have never said anything about him, that gives cause for suspicion." Responds Junior, but his face says that he does not believe his brother at all.

Dorothy tries to change the conversation to avoid conflict.

"Lora, did we arrive too early or too late?"

"Why?" Lora responds, not in a very good mood.

"I just don't see any of your friends."

"No, this time we decided to do something with family only."

Ricardo feels that his mother wants to hide Ricky from her friends.

"I don't think that's the reason. I think Ricky embarrasses you."

Roberto Jr. and Stephany just look at one another. The situation is extremely tense, so Junior intervenes.

"Rick understands that it is not very common for a child of that age to appear out of nowhere. Obviously, something like this will bring up comments and questions. But if you say he is your son, then that is your problem."

That comment adds more gasoline to the fire. Naturally, Ricardo answers furiously.

"Are you accusing me of being stupid?"

"I have not accused you of anything. Only you and Dorothy know the truth."

Dorothy, who has kept quiet before then, finally explodes like a bomb.

"Keep me out of your comments, and if you think that he is my son, then that is your problem. I'm tired of everyone pointing their finger at me."

Roberto, seeing that the situation is getting out of control, yells.

"What the hell is wrong with you? Not one more word on the subject, please. That's enough."

Everyone is quiet for a while, no one brave enough to dare to start a conversation.

Roberto finally understands that the party is ruined, and says.

"What do you think if we cut the cake?"

Roberto has not even finished saying the word cake, when his other grandson, Gabriel, slams the door and enters angrily.

"Ma'am, that child is rude and disrespectful. I do not want to play with him!"

Ricardo looks at Dorothy and tells her.

"And I asked him not to cause any problem, but it seems to be too much to ask."

Lora, who has hardly spoken all afternoon, tells her grandson.

"If he did something bad to you, don't play with him. Just go and watch TV."

Dorothy responds. "But maybe he did not do anything wrong, and it is just a misunderstanding."

Lora, ironically, answers.

"I understand he is your son, and you must therefore defend him, but if he did something wrong, you should correct him and not defend him."

"I understand that Gabriel is your grandson and thus defend him, but we should find out what happened first before pointing fingers."

Roberto shouts again. "Shit! You guys are worse than the kids!"

Roberto approaches the door and orders Ricky and Arleen to enter. Once they are inside, he asks them.

"What happened? Why is Gabriel upset?"

Arleen, almost crying, answers. "Gabriel started it."

"How did he start?" Stephany, a bit worried, asks her daughter.

"Let her talk, and stay out of it." Roberto responds.

"No, but don't yell at me either. Control yourself." Stephany responds.

Roberto closes his eyes. He is about to tell her to go to hell but holds himself back. Roberto looks at his granddaughter and tells her.

"Please continue and start at the beginning."

"When Ricky came, Gabriel told him that he was dressed as a penguin."

Roberto Jr., Stephany, and Lora laugh. "Those are children's games." says Laura.

"What else happened?"

"Ricky did not answer him. Then Gabriel asked him if he had ever gone swimming in a pool like this. He said no. So, Gabriel told him. "That means that you don't know how to swim." He replied that he knew how to swim, that his mother taught him when he was three years old."

"Gabriel asked him. Where is your mom?"

"He replied. No, I don't have a mother."

"Gabriel then asked him. Do you have a pool in your house?"

"I don't have a pool in my house." He answered.

"Then Gabriel told him. You are a liar. You have never gone swimming in a pool like this. You don't have a pool in your house. You say your mom taught you how to swim, and you don't have a mother."

"I asked Gabriel to stop it, but he would not listen. He told me to shut up, that I didn't have a brain."

"He always talks to me like that, and that bothers me a lot. Then Ricky told him that it was not nice to say things like that. Then Gabriel told us that those with blue eyes like me and him do not have a brain because we have seawater inside the head. Then Ricky told him, 'But you have brown eyes."

"Gabriel told him. Yes. So what?'

"That you have brown eyes because you have a dry shit inside your head.'"

Lora covers her mouth. "Oh my god! What a vocabulary!"

Ricardo and Dorothy can't help but laugh.

"I don't see or think anything is funny." Stephany replies.

Roberto sees that each one is pulling to their side, and they are behaving worse than the children.

"I think we should cut the cake and it would be better if you take it and eat it at home to avoid indigestion."

They all look at each other, and Junior says. "I think you are right. Next time, I hope we can have a better time."

Lora cuts the cake without saying a word. Each one takes their piece of the cake and leaves.

Roberto Jr. leaves first. "Goodbye. I will call you tomorrow."

The grandchildren pass their grandfather and do not even say goodbye.

Ricardo takes the cake from his mother and gives her a kiss. He leaves with Dorothy, who doesn't even say goodbye.

Ricky, as if he were on autopilot, tells his grandmother.

"Have a good night." Then, when he passes by Roberto, he gives him a hug and says. "I love you very much."

Roberto leans down and gives him a kiss.

"God bless you, son."

Lora's face changes color. She cannot hide the anger that she has. And once they are alone, Lora tells her husband, "Hugs and kisses with him, and with your grandchildren not even a goodbye."

"My grandchildren passed by me and did not even look at me. Or did you not see it?"

Lora begins to cry. "This is the last straw. That woman not only disgraced my son, but now she also uses her son to try to destroy my marriage!"

Chapter 6

It has been a month since Ricky has rented out the garage. During breakfast, Ricardo tells him to tell the neighbor that the month is over tomorrow and there will be no renewal.

Ricky doesn't answer; he just looks at his father and scowls.

Dorothy looks at him and says.

"Don't make that face. Your dad told you that the same night you rented it out."

Ricky replies, pointing his finger at him.

"Yes, but he is going to pay for the internet. That was the deal."

Ricardo answers mockingly, scowling and pointing his finger at him.

"I'm going to pay for the internet. You get that car out of my garage."

The neighbor rarely goes out in that car. He only uses it on weekends and rents it out for shows. Ricky waits until the neighbor's second vehicle is parked in front of the house before deciding to knock on the door. The imposing neighbor with his gold teeth sees Ricky standing with his arms crossed behind his back and his gaze fixed upward.

"Did you come for the fifty dollars?"

"No, sir, I came to inform you that my father will not allow me to rent the garage any longer, so you must move your car."

The neighbor looks at him seriously, as if trying to intimidate him, and talks in a threatening tone.

"That was not what we agreed on, and I paid you right away."

Ricky is intimidated and takes two steps back. His gaze is fixed on the neighbor's face. The neighbor thinks Ricky will run back to his house, but then Ricky takes the two steps forward again, squints his eyes, points at him with his right finger, and says with his child's voice, but firm and fearless.

"I do not have a signed contract with you. Move it out or it will be towed."

The neighbor, who is used to being a bully, sees that he has failed with Ricky and decides to convince him in another way.

"Please talk to your father again."

"He doesn't want to. He already told me."

The neighbor takes out a hundred-dollar bill and says.

"If you wanted more money, you should have told me from the beginning."

"Why don't you put your vehicle in storage?" Ricky asks him.

"It costs three hundred dollars for that size of vehicle, and since the storage unit is closed and sealed up, the heat will damage the interior."

"Maybe I can convince my dad for $270, but I can't guarantee that."

"If we come to an agreement, I would require a written contract this time." The neighbor says.

Ricky tells him. "I need to know your name so a contract can be written."

The neighbor says. "My name is Deshawn Johnson. Everyone knows me by DJ."

Ricky squints and points at DJ, moving his index finger from side to side.

"No, no, no, you cannot use nicknames or abbreviations on a legal contract. It must have your full legal name."

DJ, confused, looks at him and answers. "I did not mean to say that."

Ricky points at him. "Yes, you did say it. I heard it."

DJ, still confused, tells him. "Don't take everything literally. I said it, but I did not mean it."

"Why would you say something if you do not mean it?" Asks Ricky.

DJ moves his head and tells him. "Forget it, Ricky. Do it the way you want it."

Ricky responds. "No, no, no, it's not the way I want it. It is the right way to do it. My grandfather was a judge. He told me that lawyers could take the same contract and read it with a different intonation and a different meaning. So, the contract must be specific so as not to allow different interpretation."

DJ puts both hands on his head and yells.

"Enough! Ricky, please, I got the point."

Ricardo and Dorothy are looking at Ricky through the window, and when they see that Ricky has not returned, he tells his wife.

"If this big man thinks he is going to leave that shit here, he is going to have to kill me first. I am not afraid of him!"

Dorothy holds him, and almost begging him, she tells him.

"For God's sake, don't go fight with that man. He goes in and out of jail as if it were his house!"

Ricardo, angry, gets away from his wife and tells her.

"I do not care! If I have to go to jail. I will go with pleasure."

Ricardo crosses the street and is prepared to face the neighbor. However, when Ricardo approaches him, he sees Ricky with his arms crossed and that the neighbor has in his hand two one-hundred-dollar bills, another one of fifty dollars, and one of twenty dollars.

Ricky tells his approaching father. "The neighbor is willing to pay two hundred and seventy dollars a month for the parking. If you want, you can accept it, and if not, he will move the car out."

Ricardo is left with his mouth hanging open. He did not expect such a negotiation. Ricky has turned and is already leaving when both Ricardo and the neighbor call him.

"Ricky, come back. Don't go!"

Ricky turns and responds.

"I am finished with this. This is your business from now on. If you accept it, you must tell me so I could write a contract."

Ricardo stares at DJ and asks him. "What happened here?"

DJ answers. "Your son made me feel like a boxer who gets trapped on the ropes and receives so many punches that when the bell rings, instead of running to his corner, he runs home. Anyway, just tell me. Do I move my car or not?"

Ricardo, without thinking twice, responds very kindly.

"It is not necessary. I will park behind you, and please just let me know when I have to move my car."

DJ tells Ricardo. "Ricky told me I can get a written contract. Please get with him as he has all the information."

Ricardo takes the money and returns to his house.

When Ricky walks in, Dorothy tells him.

"Your dad had to go tell the neighbor to get the car out of the garage. As usual, you messed up things and somebody had to fix it for you."

Ricky doesn't answer. Instead, he goes straight to his room and locks the door.

Ricardo enters a moment later, and Dorothy hugs him.

"My god, what a scare you have given me! I thought you were going to fight with him. Your son just brings me a scare one after another. When is he going to get the car out?"

Ricardo answers her. "The car stays."

He gives the money to Dorothy, and she is amazed.

"Love, you do know how to negotiate. This money will help us a lot at this time!"

Ricardo answers her. "It was Ricky who negotiated it. I just had to approve it."

Dorothy opens her eyes and say.

"Shit! Where the hell did that brat come from?"

******

On Saturday morning, the three of them have breakfast in the supermarket cafeteria. Ines approaches them and greets them. "Hello! What a beautiful family! You should be on a magazine cover."

Dorothy and Ricardo only greet her by waving their hands; Ricky is the only one who responds.

"Hello, Mini Snooper, it is a pleasure to see you!"

Dorothy and Ricardo almost choke on their food upon hearing Ricky.

"What did you call me? You are disrespectful, but it is your mother's fault that instead of educating you, that is what she teaches you." Ines responds, clearly offended, her eyes blazing.

Dorothy does not know what to do. She is trying to hold her laughter, but at the same time, she knows that Ines is right.

"You must apologize to the lady." Ricardo tells Ricky with character, but at the same time he is about to explode with laughter.

"Why? What did I do? Isn't that her name?" Ricky answers with a confused face.

"It is clear it is not the child's fault. He did not invent it. You are disrespectful!" Ines answers angrily and leaves quickly.

Ines goes straight to the office and knocks on the door loudly. Hellen, surprised, opens the door.

"What's up, Ines? What's your emergency?"

"Please prepare the cameras because the thieves are at the market. They are having breakfast, and as usual, they will do their shopping." Ines mockingly raises both of her hands and makes the quotation sign with her fingers.

"I don't want to be near her because she mistrusts me."

Hellen runs to the security monitor to make sure the cameras are watching Dorothy's register. She then tells Ines.

"You better stay away from them. I will give you permission to come and indulge yourself in the office like a witness about the beers that were stolen last time."

Ines feels great satisfaction hearing she would be the witness. She is going to take revenge on Dorothy very soon. Hellen telephones the owner of the supermarket immediately.

"Good morning, Mr. Bob. Sorry to bother you, but I want to inform you that we are prepared with the surveillance system to have the necessary evidence when Dorothy tries to steal from us again. If you can get here in about fifteen minutes, you could be witness for this case."

Mr. Bob is a very methodical man. He is very careful not to make mistakes and to always be politically correct.

"Are you sure of what you are saying?"

"Yes, sir, I am. Also, I have Ines as witness, saying that she saw them stealing a pack of beer last time."

"Do you trust Ines?"

"Yes, Mr. Bob. She is a worker who would not invent something like that. She has my complete trust."

"I prefer to have a case of beer stolen before accusing someone and not being able to prove it later. That could be very expensive."

Hellen, in a challenging tone, answers.

"And I prefer to kick a thief out of work and not have to worry anymore if she is going to steal another case of beer. You have nothing to worry about, sir. That will not be the case here. I will have everything recorded."

Mr. Bob takes his time and then responds.

"If you're so sure, then do what you have to do. I'm almost there."

Ines knocks on the office door again, and Hellen opens the door and asks her.

"What's happening now? I told you I was going to call you."

"I just didn't know you called the police."

"I have not called anyone. Where did you get that?"

"There is a police unit in the parking lot, and I thought you called it."

"I haven't called it, but it doesn't hurt to talk to the officer."

Hellen goes out with Ines to the front of the supermarket, and they see a police car leaving. Hellen runs and signals the officer who stops. Hellen approaches him and asks him.

"Is everything okay, Officer?"

"Yes, ma'am. I just saw a cheeky guy parking in a handicap parking space and gave him his well-deserved ticket. I can't resist those cheeky ones."

Hellen takes the opportunity and tells him. "Neither do I, and that is why I want to tell you something."

The officer looks at her curiously. "What is it about?"

"I have a cashier who brings her family, including her underage son, to do their shopping. Then they go through her register and thus pass items without paying for them."

The officer responds. "If they have a child during the commission of a crime, that aggravates the situation. That is contributing to the delinquency of a minor and is heavily penalized. The state can even take the child away from them."

The officer gets out of the car and then tells her. "We better go to your office and watch the security cameras. I must also call my supervisor so that he can prepare the paperwork for the child, because if his father and mother go to jail, the state must take care of the child."

The officer, Hellen, and Ines enter the office and are surprised to see Mr. Bob and the security chief sitting in front of the security camera monitor.

Mr. Bob asks Hellen. "Why did you call the police?"

"I did not call him. He was passing through the parking lot. I just wanted to get advice from him. The officer says that involving a minor in a crime makes it a major crime, so the juvenile department must be involved."

Mr. Bob gets up from his chair, nervous.

"My god, Hellen! I told you I don't want scandals. That's not good publicity!"

Ines intervenes. "I think it is very good publicity for people to see you cannot steal here and get away with it."

"Who the hell asked you for your opinion? What are you doing in the office? Get out of here!"

Ines freezes. She had thought to ingratiate herself with Mr. Bob, but it appears she did the opposite.

Hellen tries to soften the situation and replies.

"I brought her here. She is the witness to the previous shoplifting."

The security director interrupts. "Come on and see this. They are at the register now."

Everyone is gathered around the monitor, zooming in on the image so as not to lose any detail and keeping silent.

Meanwhile, at Dorothy's cash register, Ricardo is passing the products and Ricky seems to be reading the National Geographic magazine. Ricky is on the alert and paying attention to everything that happens at the cash register. Ricardo, with his nails, has damaged the price code for the filet mignon package. Dorothy runs it through, and the scanner does not sound. She sets the price manually and marks two dollars and fifty cents. Ricky notices it but doesn't say anything and keeps reading his magazine.

Everyone in the office screams stadium-style when a goal is scored. Only Mr. Bob doesn't say anything. Hellen orders the security chief to take out the tape for the evidence and tells the officer. "Let's go and get her."

The head of security gives Hellen the security tape and sets the camera on another cash register.

Mr. Bob intervenes instantly. "Wait for them to come out to the parking lot so they will not be able to say that they intended to pay it. You wait outside, and I will wait for you in the office."

The officer, the head of security, Hellen, and Ines immediately go to the front of the store. Ines's smile goes from ear to ear. Finally, she is going to get revenge.

When Ricardo finishes passing all the products, Ricky closes his magazine, and tells Dorothy, "You were wrong on the price of the meat. That does not cost two dollars and fifty cents.

Dorothy clenches her fists and closes her eyes in anger. Ricardo snatches the magazine from him and says.

"What is wrong with you, asshole? How dare you say that!"

"I say it because I saw it. That is why I say it."

Dorothy looks to her side and sees that Cristina, the supervisory assistant, is approaching, and she quickly tells her. "Cristina, please, I need your help."

"What's wrong, Dorothy? I am in a hurry."

"It is that the price code is damaged, and when I went to put it manually, I made a mistake."

Cristina takes the package of filet mignon and asks her, "How much did you put in?"

"I put $2.50, which was the price of the previous item. I put it automatically without thinking."

"Oh my god! The day this costs $2.50, I will buy it myself every day! They say you are crazy, and I do not contradict that, but you are an honest, crazy person, and I am sure of that."

Cristina corrects the mistake and leaves.

Dorothy, with fire in her eyes, tells Ricardo.

"We are left without a penny thanks to your fucking son! Take him out of here before I kill him."

Ricardo looks at Ricky and tells him in a scolding way.

"Move, fucking asshole, move!"

"But what did I do to you?" Ricky asks.

"Fuck you! Move, move!"

Ricardo is stopped outside the supermarket and arrested by the police officer, the security chief, Hellen, and Ines. The policeman orders Ricardo to follow him to the office. Ricardo understands that they were watching him and responds.

"I do not have to go with you anywhere!

Ricky immediately pulls him by the shirt, telling him.

"Dad, my grandfather used to say that only stupid people argue with a policeman."

The policeman laughs and says. "Your son is much smarter than you."

"But my grandfather also said that there are lots of stupid policemen too."

The police officer changes his facial expression and simply tells them. "To the office. Walk, fast."

Upon their entrance into the office, Hellen tells Ines and the head of security, "You guys stay here. The officer and I will bring Dorothy back."

Ines stands defiantly, looking at Ricardo, moving her head up and down.

"See, Ricardo, the one who laughs last, laughs louder and longer."

Ricardo tells her. "You will regret this."

"Are you threatening me?" Ines turns to Mr. Bob and the security chief. "You heard him. He just threatened me!"

Ricky stands next to his father and, in his usual way of defending him, says.

"Mini Snooper, that is not a threat. My father has not threatened you."

"How dare you call me that! It's not my name. But I prefer to be called that, rather than a thief, like your mother."

Ricky, like a spring, takes a step forward, points his finger at her, and responds with a scowl.

"If I call you that, it is because everybody calls you that. And my mother is not a thief. You should immediately apologize."

Mr. Bob is impressed with Ricky, but he just says.

"Enough! I do not want to hear another word."

Hellen and the officer wait for Dorothy to finish with a customer, and then Hellen says disparagingly.

"You, close your register and follow us."

Dorothy understands that something is happening, but she doesn't say anything about it. She just closes her register and blushes with shame when she sees how everyone looks at her with accusatory eyes.

Once they enter the office, Hellen does not wait any longer, saying.

"Today is your last day here. We have you recorded when you stole us by passing merchandise and setting another price. Last time, you stole beers and were able to get away before we could stop you. This time, we were ready for you, and we have you on tape."

Dorothy points her finger at her and says, "You offend me. I have never stolen anything."

"Shameless! I have proof and witness."

Ricardo replies. "What evidence and what witness are you talking about?"

Hellen picks up the tape and says, "Here's my proof." Then points to Ines. "And here's my witness."

Ricardo replies dismissively. "Mini Snooper, and now Liar too."

The policeman takes control of the situation by saying.

"Committing a crime accompanied by a minor is a very serious offense. The kid will have to remain in the custody of the state until a judge decides otherwise. I have informed the proper authorities, and they are already on their way. You two are under arrest."

The officer takes the handcuffs off his buckle and goes to put them on Dorothy. Ricky stands in front of Dorothy, opens his arms, and says.

"You can't handcuff my mom! She hasn't done anything wrong."

The officer stops when he sees Ricky's attitude. The officer steps back.

"I don't have the heart to traumatize your child that way. But as soon as the state takes him away, you go straight to jail."

Dorothy angrily says. "I also have my witness that I have not stolen anything!"

Hellen picks up the tape and says. "Are you going to contradict this?"

"Yes. Your assistant, Cristina, is my witness."

Mr. Bob is sitting, watching what is happening. He then gets up and says. "I'll talk to Cristina. Wait here."

Mr. Bob finds Cristina doing the inventory in the back of the warehouse.

"Cristina, come here, please."

Cristina listens to the way Mr. Bob called her and is scared. Something bad must be happening, she thinks, and her name is mentioned.

"Yes, Mr. Bob. How can I help you?"

"What happened to a pack of beers and Dorothy?"

"Nothing, Mr. Bob, nothing. Dorothy once called me and told me that she had accidentally passed a pack of beer. Her husband realized when he got home that she hadn't been charged for it. He informed Dorothy, and she told me so I could charge her or the beer. I grabbed a pack of beer, then she scanned it and paid for it so inventory wasn't short. Actually, they could have kept the beers, and no one would have known, but they were honest."

"Why didn't you tell Hellen about that?"

"You are right, I should have done it, but you get used to reporting the bad and forgetting to report the good. But you can check the receipts. I think you can still see that transaction."

Mr. Bob is surprised. "Now, tell me what happened today."

Cristina, confused, replies. "What happened today? What do you mean?"

Mr. Bob realizes that Cristina does not know anything about what is happening.

"Yeah, what happened to Dorothy today?"

"Dorothy called me, and she told me that she passed a filet mignon that had a damaged price code and when entering it manually she automatically put the price of the previous item, which was $2.50. I eliminated the $2.50 charge and set the correct price for the meat. You can check the receipt. Everything should be on the tape too."

Mr. Bob feels a chill run through his entire body. He understands that he is facing a big problem. If by returning and checking the receipt everything is proven true, he could face a civil lawsuit.

"What's up, Mr. Bob? Have I made a mistake?"

"No, Cristina, only that I was not aware of this, and it is good to find out not only the bad things but also about the good things."

Mr. Bob then goes to the office, and in his mind, he only sees a civil lawsuit that will cost him dearly, plus the negative publicity that a case like this will throw at him. His path to the office seems eternal. On the way, he is approached by the butcher, who calls him.

"Mr. Bob, I need to speak with you."

Mr. Bob, who is known for being friendly, replies.

"Don't fuck with me right now! I'm not available right now for anyone."

The butcher's jaw drops. He just follows him with his eyes and goes to work.

Mr. Bob enters the office and sees Dorothy crying inconsolably as she thinks Cristina has agreed with Hellen and deep down she knows that she is guilty.

Hellen says. "As you can see, Mr. Bob, she thinks that her crocodile tears are going to soften us up."

Short-tempered, Mr. Bob responds. "Shut up and give me Dorothy's register tape."

Hellen and Ines look at each other in amazement. They have no idea what is going on. Hellen gives him the register tape, and Mr. Bob sits down to review the tape with the money. Dorothy is still crying, and Ricardo is comforting her, with Ricky standing in front of them, his arms crossed as if he were a protective guard.

About fifteen minutes later, Mr. Bob picks up the register box with the money and throws it against the wall.

"Shit!" yells Mr. Bob.

Everyone is surprised, but Hellen and Ines much more than everybody else. Mr. Bob angrily tells Hellen. "When was the beer incident?"

"Two weeks ago, Mr. Bob."

"Bring me those receipts. I want to see them now."

"Those receipts are there—"

Mr. Bob doesn't let her finish.

"I didn't ask you where the fuck are they. I told you to bring it to me!"

Now, Hellen is the one who is about to cry, and she goes out to get the receipts. Ines sees things are getting hot, so she tries to get away.

"I think they need me back in the warehouse."

"You are not going anywhere! You sit in that chair until I order you otherwise."

Ines shrugs, her arrogance gone, and she looks like a dog with its tail between its legs. Ines sits with her two hands clasped on her thighs, constantly moving them like the girl who waits for punishment from her dad. Mr. Bob tells the officer.

"Thank you very much, Officer, but you can leave. Nothing has happened here."

The confused policeman replies. "With all due respect, Mr. Bob, we saw everything that happened on the screen."

"Yes, but you did not see what happened next, and you came to premature and incorrect conclusions."

Mr. Bob tries to exclude himself from the group so as not to have any responsibility.

The officer stares at him without saying anything.

"Officer, I have told you that there will be no charge. Cancel everything and have a good day."

Ricky looks at him. "My grandfather was always right."

The officer angrily mumbles. "To hell with you and your grandfather!"

Ricardo, emboldened, asks him. "What did you say?"

"I didn't say anything. Maybe you wanted to hear something."

Mr. Bob stands up and tries to comfort Dorothy, offering her water and asking her to sit down. Hellen comes in with the receipts, handing them to Mr. Bob. Mr. Bob takes the receipts and then hands them back to her.

"At what time was the incident?"

Hellen, with a broken voice, points toward Ines and responds.

"She is the one who knows. She told me."

"What the hell is going on now? Now you don't remember the time?" Replies Mr. Bob.

Ines responds. "It was, like, 11:00 A.M."

"I don't want to see it. You check it out yourself and tell me if there is a purchase of just one pack of beers after 11:00 A.M."

Dorothy responds. "Yes, Mr. Bob I am sure there must be one around eleven forty-five, more or less. I asked Cristina to help me."

Hellen searches for the time and sees the charge for a pack of beer. Hellen turns pale, she gets up from the desk and points at Ines, saying.

"You see all the problems you have created for being a gossip instead of working?"

She then turns to Mr. Bob.

"Here it is. That is right. Here's a charge for a case of beer at 11:53 AM."

Mr. Bob is about to explode. He looks at Ines.

"You punch your card and get out of here. I don't want ever to see you around here for gossip. I do not need employees who bring problems like this! Go gossip in your neighborhood!"

Ines gets up, crying. "This is not fair!"

Ricky spontaneously says. "Mr. Bob, I have a question."

Ricardo and Dorothy close their eyes. With Ricky, it is impossible to know what he would say, and he could spoil everything.

"Is it Gossip or Mini Snooper?"

Ricardo and Dorothy are able to breathe again, but they have to force themselves to contain their laughter.

"She is a gossip, a mini snooper, a snake, and much more that I will not say out of respect for your mother."

Ines angrily slams the door while getting out of the office.

Ricky shrugs, closes his eyes with the noise, then opens them wide and exclaims.

"My god! What a temper has Mini Snooper!"

Mr. Bob tells Ricardo and Dorothy.

"Please don't leave. I need to talk to you for a few minutes."

Then Mr. Bob says to Hellen.

"Come outside with me for a moment."

Mr. Bob and Hellen leave the office, and Mr. Bob, furious, says to her.

"Five years ago, I told you to retire, and you told me that you get bored at home. This shit you've done could cost us a lawsuit. Today you are retiring. That way, you will keep your retirement from the company."

Hellen, furious and without understanding she is talking to the boss, answers.

"I have worked for thirty-five years here. You cannot do that!"

Mr. Bob takes it as a personal challenge.

"You retire or I kick you out of here, and in that case, forget about the company's retirement. I will spend less money on lawyers than what I will pay you in retirement, so for me, that is good business."

Mr. Bob turns around and goes to the office. He is a practical businessman and is terrified of the thought of a lawsuit or bad publicity. Mr. Bob walks into the office and brings some freshly made sweets that give off an exquisite smell.

"Sorry for the delay, but I want to celebrate more than apologize." Mr. Bob puts the sweets on the table and puts out several soda bottles, glasses, and napkins.

"I prefer to wait for Cristina to come. I sent for her."

Dorothy and Ricardo look at each other as if trying to guess what is happening.

Cristina enters, totally unaware of everything that has happened. She is somewhat scared and thinks that they are going to scold her. Cristina looks at Dorothy as if wanting to find out what is happening.

Mr. Bob asks.

"How many years have the two of you been working here?"

"Fifteen years." Cristina answers

"I'm turning six," Dorothy responds.

Mr. Bob gives everyone in the office a glass of soda and tells them.

"Today, thanks to an unfortunate incident, I was able to discover that among my workers, there are honest people, like those who are hardly found anymore. Hardworking and dedicated people who deserve to oversee this business. Hellen, after thirty-five years of work, decided to retire. Starting today, Cristina, you will be the new supervisor. I want you to train Dorothy as your assistant supervisor. You two will be in charge of taking the business forward. I'm counting on your cooperation, and I'm not taking no for an answer."

Mr. Bob turns to Dorothy and tells her.

"Dorothy, you can have the rest of the day off, but before you leave, you need to talk to Cristina so she can give you an idea of your training. Starting today, you will begin to earn your new salaries. So, do we toast or not?"

Mr. Bob is trying to buy Dorothy and, that way, avoid a lawsuit. Dorothy responds. "Is that I—"

Mr. Bob won't let her finish talking. "Yes, before I forget, the health insurance for you and your family is paid by the company from today, and you enter the new salary scale."

"What does that mean?" Cristina asks.

"That your salary is two dollars more than Hellen's, and Dorothy's is two dollars more than what you earned. That was scheduled for next month, but I prefer to do it now."

Mr. Bob turns to Dorothy and says. "Sorry I interrupted you. What did you want to tell me?"

"I wanted to tell you I always knew that you were a good man and even though we did not have contact, you always inspired me with great respect."

Ricky raises his hand, and everyone shuts up and looks at him.

"I see only one chocolate candy. I hope nobody else likes it."

Mr. Bob responds immediately.

"Of course, that is for you, and before you leave, Cristina will take you to the cake department so that you can choose the one you like. You've earned it by defending your mom the way you did. Your mom must be proud of you."

When they are finally alone on the way home, Dorothy looks back and sees Ricky in his usual position, like a cold statue.

"I don't know whether to beat you to death or kiss you to death, but if it hadn't been for you and your obsessed way of fucking with us, we would have been caught."

Ricky responds. "If you had done the right thing, you would not have passed that scare. I hope it will not be repeated. You will not have the need, but the temptations will still be there."

Dorothy is cold with that answer. It is not possible that a child can speak with such wisdom. She looks at her husband.

"Shit, now I am sure he is not your son. You can't beget such a thing."

Chapter 7

Five months have passed since Dorothy's promotion. The responsibility of her position has made her mature and begins to see life from another point of view. Ricardo has not changed; he is still irresponsible and deeply in love with Dorothy. Ricky has not changed either; he is still the same robot that sees everything in black-and-white. He keeps Dorothy and Ricardo on their tiptoes and guessing since they never know what he will come out with. Two important dates are approaching, Ricardo's nephew Gabriel's birthday and Dorothy's parents' fortieth wedding anniversary. Dorothy and Ricardo have not returned to their parents' house, though they maintain contact by phone. Since their last visit ended so disastrously, they decide to distance themselves so as not to worsen their relationship.

Dorothy is in the warehouse, supervising the merchandise shipment, when she receives a phone call.

"Hello, good morning. Are you Mrs. Dorothy Suarez?"

"Yes, it's me. How can I help you?"

"We are calling you from your son's school."

"What the hell has he done now?" Dorothy asks.

"Don't call me. Call his father."

"We tried to communicate with Mr. Suarez, but he did not answer."

"I'll give him the message but take my phone number out of your records."

"Madam, it is just to let you know that Ricky has won the school's principal's honor roll, and we want parents to attend the recognition ceremony."

Dorothy is silent for a moment; she is trying to understand the message since the delivery truck's noise is quite loud. She finally answers.

"I do not understand. What the heck did he do now? But if he took something from the principal, I will make sure he returns it."

The driver turns off the truck's engine, and Dorothy can hear the secretary clearly.

"Ha, ha, he has done nothing wrong. He won the principal's honor roll, and we want the parents to be at the awards ceremony. This is a very special event where the great work of the students and their parents are recognized. Please be sure to attend. It will be Friday, at 1:30 p.m."

"Don't worry, we will attend the event. You can't imagine the scare you gave me. I thought Ricky had a fight with the principal or had taken something from her."

"Ha, ha, you are right. With Ricky, you never know. He does not filter his thoughts. We already know him. Have a nice day!"

Dorothy can't help but look happy. She will take a picture of Ricky receiving the highest honor in the school. She will squeeze it in the face of her sister-in-law, who always brags about how smart her son is."

Dorothy comes home and goes to Ricky's room to break the news, but she sees that Ricky is not in his room. Dorothy is surprised, because Ricky is always in his room, studying on the computer. Dorothy decides to go to the neighbor's house to see if Ricky is there. She knocks on the door, and Mrs. Kenya opens it.

"Hi, Dorothy. Are you looking for Ricky?"

"Yes! When I didn't see him in his room, I wanted to make sure that he was here."

Kenya, with a smile, answers her.

"Please come inside. He is with Tamian in the kitchen. I prepared his favorite chocolate cake as a gift for him. Thanks to Ricky, Tamian has gotten excellent marks in the exams. That boy is a teacher! God bless him."

Dorothy can't help but feel proud of him. Twice in the same day, she has been linked to Ricky's successes. Dorothy enters the kitchen and sees Ricky with an enviable happy face. He has more chocolate on his face and shirt than in his stomach.

"My God, look what you have done to your uniform shirt! You have a fork, and you don't use it. You eat like a savage!" Dorothy scolds him, thus ending her short honeymoon with Ricky.

Ricky, with his typical way of expressing disagreement, puts his left hand behind his back, scowls, and stretching his right hand, moving his index finger from side to side, responds.

"No, no, no, not savage. The Arabs eat with their bare hands. My mom used to take me to a restaurant where we ate with our hands, and we enjoyed it a lot."

Dorothy shakes her head. "You are a lost cause. You always have an answer for everything! Stupid answer, but you do have an answer."

Dorothy looks around and asks, "Where is Tamima?"

"She doesn't feel well and is in her room. She told me that she had a headache."

Ricky, still with a piece of cake in his hand, says.

"She lies to you. She never greets me. If I show up, she goes into her room until I leave. When she sees me, she rolls her eyes, and she has never once returned my greeting."

Kenya is ashamed. She was not aware of that situation. She looks at Tamian, who avoids her gaze, and understands that what Ricky is saying is true. Kenya's eyes blaze. Once again, Ricky is the cause of a problem, and Dorothy sadly tries to calm the situation down.

"Please don't listen to Ricky. Besides, it's already late. He should go home. Come on, I have to wash that shirt."

Ricky takes his cake. "Thank you very much, Mrs. Kenya. It is delicious. Have a good night!"

Kenya does not respond, it is obvious she is furious. She just walks them to the door, says good night, and closes the door.

They have only taken three steps when they hear Kenya's cry.

"Open that door right now! When I finish pulling you around by your hair, you really are going to have a headache!"

Dorothy looks at Ricky. "Why do you have to create such a problem?"

Ricky, with his face all muddy and licking the chocolate with his tongue, trying to eat, answers.

"Kenya is my friend. I love her as if she were Nana Silvia. I don't like to be cheated on." Then he shrugs and says. "Now it is Tamima's problem. Anyway, she doesn't like me."

Dorothy tells her husband how embarrassed she was for Ricky's behavior. Ricardo says.

"I'm going to talk to him under the pretext of saying good night."

Ricardo approaches Ricky's room and hears Ricky talking. He puts his ear to the door and hears Ricky say.

"I love you very much. Have a good night. We'll talk tomorrow."

Ricardo decides to go back to his room and asks Dorothy.

"Did you know that Ricky has a phone?"

Dorothy, surprised, responds.

"What are you talking about? Who's paying for that line?"

"I don't know, but this boy has more tricks and secrets than a magician has on his chest."

******

On Sunday afternoon, Roberto and his wife, Lora, are watching television when they hear the doorbell. Roberto opens the door and sees his son; his wife, Stephany; and their two children at the door.

"Hello, Dad!" His son hugs him, and Stephany kisses him on the cheek.

Roberto looks and sees that his two grandchildren have gone past him without even saying hello. The children go to play in the yard, and the adults stay in the kitchen, talking. Lora has brewed coffee and is handing it out.

"Mom, I miss your coffee. Nobody's coffee comes close to yours."

"If you guys come more often, you wouldn't miss it that much, but you and Ricardo only call once a week to keep up appearances." Lora sarcastically answers as she sips her coffee.

"Mother, it's not fair that you compare me with Ricardo. Stephany and I are both very busy, and Ricardo and Dorothy are two lazy people with no obligations."

Roberto then looks at his father and asks him.

"Isn't that right, Dad?"

The father looks at him and, with the same sarcastic tone as his mother, answers him.

"That they are irresponsible is not a secret and has no defense. I must add, though, that Ricky calls me religiously every three days."

Those words fall like a bomb. Lora almost spits out the coffee.

"How long has that been going on? Because he has never called me. Besides, what does he have to talk about if he doesn't even know you?"

Roberto looks at his wife, then at his son and daughter-in-law, and responds.

"I'm sorry this bothers you, but he calls me to ask me how I'm doing. He tells me how he's doing at school, and he also asks me about you."

"What? He's asking about me?"

"Yes, he asks me about you. What is wrong with that?"

Roberto Jr. drinks his coffee, puts the cup down on the table, and tells his father.

"If he really is your grandson, there is nothing wrong. But his coming from the hypocritical Dorothy, God knows what is behind that!"

Roberto Sr. responds, a bit annoyed.

"You think that I'm stupid? That anyone could fool me? All I can tell you is that at least he calls me. My grandchildren passed by me today without even saying hello!"

Stephany responds. "Robert, please don't mind that. They are children and see things very differently, but I assure you that they adore you."

Lora angrily tells her husband. "I can't believe you don't see that! Since that brat appeared, that woman managed to turn you against us."

"I'm not against anyone. I just say things as they are." Roberto responds.

Stephany moves her hands as if to tell him to stop. Everyone calms down, and then she says.

"In a month is Gabriel's birthday. I really would prefer that they not show up, but we have to invite them. We have decided to celebrate it in a park so we will feel less pressure."

Roberto responds to Stephany.

"I think that if you don't want to invite them, just don't invite them. If you say Dorothy is a hypocrite, then don't act like her."

Stephany blushes. Obviously, she is offended, but she doesn't respond.

Roberto Jr. looks at his father and then at his mother.

"I think Mom is right and it is better that we leave. The children have class tomorrow, anyway."

Roberto calls the children, who are playing in the yard, and they run in.

"Grandma, I'm thirsty. Give me water."

"Yes, my love. Do you want water or juice?"

"I said water, not juice."

"Sure, my love. Right away."

The grandfather, scolding them, says.

"There is no water or juice until you learn how to ask with respect and learn how to say please!"

"What did the boy do? What flea bit you today?"

"Is it that there is not please or greeting. Is that the education they are receiving?"

Stephany angrily says. "Your grandfather is right. You are spoiled, and there will be no water or juice. We need to go home right now."

As they leave, Stephany says sarcastically. "You all are spoiled and should learn from Ricky, who is an example to follow."

Roberto pretends not to hear it to avoid any argument, but his discontent shows on his face.

******

Dorothy is working when she receives a call from her husband.

"Hello, love, I am calling to tell you that I will not be able to go to Ricky's ceremony because I am in Port Saint Lucy, doing a furniture delivery."

Dorothy takes a deep breath. "You promised your son that you would attend. He is not waiting for me but for you."

"I can't go. I'm working and I never said I will attend. Please, do your best to attend, and if you can't, he will understand."

Dorothy hangs up the phone angrily and says. "All men are a fuckup!" She turns around and realizes that she is facing Mr. Bob.

"What a way of generalizing, Dorothy. So, we're all a fuckup?"

Dorothy is embarrassed; she doesn't know what to say.

"Excuse me, Mr. Bob. I am just very angry with my husband."

"So, because of your husband we all are a fuckup?"

"No, I did not mean to offend you."

"So, I'm not a man?"

"No! My god, I would never disrespect you. It is that my husband promised his son to be at the awards ceremony for the child's 'principal honor roll.' Now he comes out with he can't make it. I am working, and now no one will be present for Ricky."

"Did your son earn the principal's honor roll?"

"Yes," Dorothy says. "He is very intelligent. He is also a grade higher than he should be for his age."

"He is a bright kid, indeed," Mr. Bob agrees. "I think you should go. It is a mother's duty after all. I give you permission."

"Thank you very much, but I don't have a car. I would be late anyway. If he had called me in advance, maybe I could go."

Mr. Bob thinks for a moment, then replies. "Then I'll take you. Let's go, quickly."

"No, Mr. Bob, you don't have to do something like that." Dorothy argues.

"Remember that I am your boss, and you are the third-in-command here. It's an order. Hurry up."

A few minutes later, Dorothy and Mr. Bob arrive at the school auditorium and hardly find a place to sit. All the children are seated in the front, and the parents in the back. After a performance by the children where they sing and dance, the school principal, Ms. Black,

LITTLE RICKY

addresses the audience, thanking for the parents' participation and cooperation in the education of the students. Then the lights go out and a spotlight is aimed at Ms. Black, who walks out of the podium and speaks.

"Today we are honored to present the principal's honor roll to a student who came from another school at the beginning of this semester. He is eight years old, and he is in the fourth grade. I did not know that he was in a higher grade than his age, so when I told him that he had to go be in third grade, he started to protest so much I had to send him home. Then I called his previous school, and they confirmed that it was true. That the boy's appetite for learning is insatiable! He went to speak with the fifth-grade teacher and asked for the course study material. In his spare time and without anyone's assistance, he studied the materials through the computer. He demanded to take the final exams corresponding to the fifth grade. We, out of curiosity, gave him the exams, which he passed with outstanding grades! Now, it is an honor for me to call Ricardo Clark to the podium!"

The audience cheers hotly.

Dorothy has no idea that Ricky has studied the fifth-grade material, much less passed the exams. Mr. Bob tells Dorothy.

"You didn't tell me your son was a genius!"

"He is very modest, and he does not like people to praise him. I help him as much as I can, but in reality, the credit goes to him, because I hardly have time to sit with him to do homework."

Ricky stands up and, with his stiff walk, marches until he reaches the podium. He stands with both arms crossed behind his back, staring at the audience. People begin to laugh as they find Ricky's attitude comical.

Ms. Black asks him. "How are you feeling today, Ricky?"

Ricky responds quickly and as if he were a robot. "Very well."

People laugh.

"Do you have someone special in the audience?"

Ricky answers again in the same way. "Dad."

People laugh louder.

Ms. Black addresses the audience and says. "The parents of our genius, please stand up."

The audience begins to applaud, and the spotlight swivels from side to side, looking for Ricky's parents. Mr. Bob sees that Dorothy does not stand up, so he tells her.

"You must stand up! You cannot do that to your son."

"I'm sorry, I can't." Dorothy replies.

Mr. Bob, seeing that Dorothy has remained seated, gets up and grabs her by the arm, trying to get her to stand up. The spotlight stops on them, and the audience sees Mr. Bob trying to get Dorothy up. The audience begins to applaud and cheer.

Ricky throws his head forward, then looks to one side, then the other, shaking his head like an owl. Dorothy is standing, and Mr. Bob is next to her. Ricky, with his left hand behind his back, his eyes puckered, and his right arm extended forward, moves his index finger from side to side in denial.

"No, no, no, that's not my dad!"

Mr. Bob sits down quickly and flushes with embarrassment. Dorothy is also embarrassed.

The audience falls silent; the silence is as if everyone thinks that Dorothy is with another man and Ricky has exposed her.

Ms. Black, trying to ease the situation, tells Ricky. "I know that he is not your dad, but who is she?"

Ricky doesn't respond; he looks upset.

Ms. Black asks him again. "But who is she?"

The third time Ms. Black asks Ricky, he responds short and fast.

"Mom."

This time no one laughs. Accusatory silence dominates the atmosphere. Mr. Bob understands that his actions and Ricky's comment have put Dorothy in an embarrassing position. He stands up and begins to walk to the podium. Everyone is quiet, including Ms. Back.

Mr. Bob then asks Ms. Black for the microphone. She doesn't know what to do. The moment is very tense, and none of this was programmed. Mr. Bob says.

"Please, I want to say a few words."

Ms. Black hands him the microphone, and Mr. Bob speaks.

"My name is Bob. I first met Ricky in a very tense situation where he showed the courage to stand in front of a uniformed police officer. He opened his arms to stop the officer and protect his mother. I want to clarify that his mother had done nothing wrong and that it was all a big misunderstanding, but Ricky's reaction and his courage to defend his mother go beyond what my words can describe. Today, when I found out that his father could not attend this event and his mother, who works for me, was working, I ordered her to come to the event. She replied that she would not arrive on time because she did not have transportation and it was already late. That's why I brought her myself. That's why she's in a supermarket uniform. I wouldn't forgive myself if none of his parents was present at an event like this."

The audience cheers for about five minutes, euphorically getting to their feet. When they finish clapping and there is silence once more, in order not to waste the occasion, Mr. Bob says.

"And as a final bonus, everyone who goes to the First Supermarket and says, 'I know Ricky,' will have a 5 percent discount."

Everyone is clapping and yelling again, "I know Ricky!"

After the ceremony, Mr. Bob decides to give Dorothy the rest of the day off and takes them to her house. Mr. Bob sees a car parked in the garage of the house and asks Dorothy.

"Whose car is that? You told me you didn't have transportation."

Ricky responds instantly. "That car belongs to the neighbor across the street. I rented the garage out to him when they told me that if I wanted internet, I would have to pay for it myself."

Mr. Bob looks at Dorothy, confused.

Dorothy closes her eyes, takes a deep breath, and says, "That's another story."

"It will be another story, but it is a true story."

Dorothy starts to scold him. "Family things are not to be disclosed in public!" She then apologizes to Mr. Bob.

"In those times we were very tight financially, and we could not pay for the internet."

Mr. Bob turns around and tells Ricky. "I congratulate you. You are brave, intelligent, and a good businessman. You are an example to follow. I hope you and I will do business one day."

Ricky is thoughtful, shakes his head, and responds.

"It could be. We will talk about it later.

Mr. Bob laughs. "Coming from you, nothing surprises me anymore."

Later, Ricardo comes home from work, picks up the mail, and finds Ricky and Dorothy in the kitchen.

"Hello, love. If you had told me that I did not have to pick you up at work, I would have avoided twenty-five minutes of traffic."

Ricky puts his glass of milk on the table and responds to his father.

"I asked her not to call you so that you understand how important communication is. You called fifteen minutes before the ceremony to say you could not attend."

"I did not call because I had no signal." Ricardo responds with character.

Ricky puts his hand on his chin and grimaces, as if he is thinking. Then he responds.

"Ha, I had no signal, the battery was dead, the phone was in the office, and there are many more that I learned from you."

Dorothy can't help but laugh.

Ricardo looks at her and throws the mail on the table. He tells her in a vindictive tone. "Look what you got in the mail. Let's see if you're going to keep laughing."

Dorothy picks up the mail and sees the invitation card for Gabriel's birthday. Her face changes instantly. She throws the card angrily.

"Shit! They already spoiled my weekend. You cannot imagine how much I would give not to go to that party!"

Ricky looks at her, shrugs his shoulders.

"You don't have to give anyone anything. Not going is enough. My grandfather used to say that you should never do what you don't want to do for others who don't appreciate it."

Ricardo puts both arms on the table and leans toward Ricky, then says in a low voice.

"Yes, but family is family. Sometimes we must do things that we don't want to do for the family."

Ricky does not respond; he just takes his glass of milk and begins to drink. Thinking that the conversation is over, Ricardo turns around and is going to walk away when he hears Ricky.

"My grandfather used to say that…"

Ricardo stops short. Every time Ricky speaks, it is like being punched in the stomach.

"The family is like a bitter syrup that sometimes we have to drink to keep our bodies healthy."

Ricardo turns around and tells him.

"I finally agree with something your grandfather said."

"What do you agree with? With what he said about family or that you are irresponsible and a liar?"

Ricardo raises his hands up. "Oh my god, give me patience!"

******

On Gabriel's birthday, Ricardo, Dorothy, and Ricky arrive at the park and see that there are a few children invited to the party. Gabriel approaches them.

"Hello, Uncle. Hello, Aunt." And without waiting for the gift to be given to him, he takes it from Ricardo's hand. Ricky takes a step to greet him and only manages to say. "Happy birthday."

Gabriel looks at him and responds. "I invited them, not you."

Stephany and her father-in-law, Roberto, come to greet them and witness Gabriel's action. Stephany takes him by the hand and tells him. "What you just said is wrong. Go play with your friends and be good."

Roberto is surprised by the little importance Stephany gives to the incident. "Don't you think Gabriel should apologize?" he asks.

"No, Roberto. They are children, and today is his birthday. I do not want to scold him today."

Roberto shakes his head and answers. "I take care of the problem right away. I do not wait till tomorrow."

"Well, I am not in a rush, so I can wait till tomorrow, and I will not beat him either." Stephany answers sharply.

When Ricky sees Roberto, he cries out in joy and runs to hug him. Roberto cannot deny that he is happy to see Ricky running toward him with open arms. Roberto waits for him with open arms and carries him. Ricky gives him a big hug and a kiss, then tells him. "I love you, Grandpa! Please don't ever leave me."

Those words hit Roberto deep in his heart, and his eyes watered. "Why are you telling me that, Ricky?"

"My two grandparents left me the same day, and they were special to me. Only you are left, and I don't have any more grandfathers."

Roberto gives him a kiss and responds. "I am not going to leave you. And don't pay attention to Gabriel. That was a stupid joke."

Ricky replies. "My grandfather told me that somebody can bother you only if you allow it."

Roberto puts Ricky on the ground, and Ricky takes out four one-hundred-dollar bills from his pocket and gives them to him.

"That's yours. Dorothy gave it to me so I could give it to you and thank you for lending it to her."

Dorothy and Roberto look at each other. Roberto sees that she is confused, but he plays along.

"Thanks, Dorothy. I'm not in a rush for the money. Are you sure about this?"

Ricky does not give her time to answer. "Of course, it is not a problem. Now she is the assistant supervisor. Now she is the third-in-command of the supermarket."

Roberto cannot believe what he hears. He cannot imagine Dorothy in a position of such responsibility.

"Congratulations, Dorothy. You have surprised me, and I mean that in a positive way."

Dorothy proudly responds. "That's right, Mr. Roberto. It took me years of dedication and sacrifice, but in the end, it paid off."

Ricky looks at her and scowls. He signals her to come lower so he can tell her a secret.

Dorothy lowers herself, and Ricky tells her in her ear. "Don't overdo it either."

Dorothy is scared, knowing that Ricky can tell everything and spoil the charm. "Love, take Ricky to the other kids, please."

Ricardo understands it is better to take Ricky away. He takes him by the hand to see the magician, who is entertaining the children.

Roberto and Dorothy are left alone. Roberto stares at Dorothy.

"I know you had no idea Ricky would give me that money. I don't know where he got it from, but I'm sure he did it so that you wouldn't look bad. That shows that he loves you and cares about you."

Dorothy is thoughtful and responds in a soft, sincere voice.

"You are totally right. I'm sure he took the money from a drawer in the kitchen where we keep cash. Thank God our financial situation has improved with my new position! And to be honest, we owe it to Ricky. That child has given us so many hard times that sometimes we feel like killing him, but at the same time, he has brought a change in our lives and then I want to kill him with kisses. If he were my son, I would be the happiest woman in the world!"

When Dorothy is speaking, Roberto begins to feel some sympathy toward Dorothy, but when he hears Dorothy saying Ricky is not her son, he feels as if a steamroller has passed over him.

"How dare you deny your son!"

Dorothy instantly changes her facial expression. "Look, Mr. Roberto, let's just leave this conversation. I know it's not going to have a good ending."

"I agree with you." Roberto answers, and they both walk toward the rest of the group. Lora has been watching Roberto from a distance. Her face shows the disgust she has when she sees her husband hugging and kissing Ricky. Lora hits her son with her elbows and signals him to look where Roberto is hugging Ricky.

"Look at your father, how tender he is with that kid. I do not know when he is going to wake up from the curse of the snake charmer and her son, the little fox." Lora is referring to Dorothy and Ricky, and she adds many more adjectives that are not pleasant at all.

Her son Roberto puts his arm around her shoulders and tells her.

"Don't you worry. One day at a time. One day he will wake up and find out his sweet dream has been his worst nightmare. Enjoy the birthday party, and if there is something you can be one hundred percent sure of, it is that my children are his grandchildren."

Dorothy and Roberto come to the table where Roberto's son and his mother are sitting. Dorothy greets them, and Roberto Jr. greets her back. Lora gets up and pretends that she is not listening. She begins to arrange the gifts so as not to return the greeting. Roberto realizes that his mother has not responded to the greeting and tries to justify her.

"Please excuse her and do not pay attention to her. I am sure she did not hear you. She's going deaf, and she doesn't want to acknowledge it."

Dorothy subtly replies. "There is nothing to excuse. As Ricky taught me, it can only bother you if you allow it to bother you."

Lora keeps her back to Dorothy but is listening very carefully to the conversation.

"Very bright and true that phrase. Your son is highly intelligent."

This way, Roberto makes sure to insinuate that Ricky is Dorothy's son and not his brother's. Roberto Sr. realizes that it is all a duel of double meaning, and he does not want to be a victim in the crossfire when Dorothy answers back.

Dorothy answers with a smile. "Yes, my son is very smart, of which I am proud. He just won the school's principal's honor roll as the best student in the whole school. He is even studying in a grade higher than his age, and he just passed the exams with excellent marks on the fifth grade, which is one more grade than he is doing now."

Dorothy opens her wallet and shows him the photos taken during the ceremony. Those words fall like a cold bucket of water to Roberto Jr. and like a hot iron on Lora's and Roberto Sr.'s butts.

Roberto looks at his mother and sees that she is as red as a tomato with rage, but since she is playing deaf, she cannot join the conversation. Roberto knows that his mother has high blood pressure and that he must intervene immediately to avoid a serious problem.

"Mom, you have been standing in the sun for a long time. Look how red you are! You must sit, rest, and drink liquid."

Lora understands that she has no other alternative; she greets Dorothy, who returns the greeting as if nothing has happened.

Roberto gives her a pill to lower her blood pressure and tells her in a low voice. "You can't take it so hard. She's going to give you a heart attack."

Roberto Sr., tired of the hypocrisy that dominates the environment, goes to where the magician is entertaining the children. Roberto puts his arm around Ricardo and tells him. "How are you doing, son?"

Ricardo, without thinking, gives his father a big hug. "I miss you, Dad."

Roberto is moved. He did not expect something like that.

"I miss you too, son. You're the one who does not visit us like before."

Ricardo shakes his head and response. "It's that lately, every time I visit you, things have not been very pleasant."

"Son, we are your parents, and we want the best for you. Maybe we have different points of view, but we do have the same goal. That is your happiness."

"I know, Dad. And don't think I don't understand. I also want you to be happy, and if our presence brings discomfort, then I try to avoid it."

Ricky pulls his grandfather by the arm and tells him.

"That magician is a liar."

"Why do you say that?"

"My grandpa told me that magic does not exist, that they are just tricks."

Roberto lifts him up so he can see from above and tells him.

"Let's see, tell me where the trick is."

Ricky answers. "You can put me down. I don't need to see from above."

Roberto puts him down and puts both hands on his shoulders and asks him. "Tell me, where is the trick? Why do you say he is a liar?"

Ricky, with his index finger, hits his grandfather three times on the head and says.

"That magician just said that he needed thirty-five dollars to pay back a friend. Since no one gave it to him, he pulled out a ten-dollar bill from behind a girl's ear, then he pulled out a twenty-dollar bill out of another boy's nose and at last he showed his bare hands, rubbed them together, and a five-dollar bill appeared out of nowhere."

Roberto shakes his head and tells him. "I think that's the answer. If money appeared out of nowhere, then that's magic!"

Ricky shakes his head and responds. "No, Grandpa. How can you believe such a lie? If he could pull money out of the children's noses, he wouldn't have to ask for money. He wouldn't be wearing torn socks. And the watch he has is not even worth five dollars!"

Roberto laughs out loud. "Brilliant, Ricky, it's a brilliant analysis! You're absolutely right!"

Roberto, still laughing, puts his hand on his son's shoulder and tells him. "This child cannot be yours. I don't give a damn what you say!"

Ricardo looks at him seriously and takes his hand off his shoulder. "That is one of the reasons that make me stay away. What you think is a joke might be an offense to me."

Roberto looks at his son, and he feels embarrassed. "Sorry, son. It was really a joke. I didn't mean to offend you."

"How would you like to be accused of being a jerk, laughed at in the face constantly, and used as a joke?"

Roberto feels even worse. "Sorry, son. I promise you that this will never happen again."

Roberto realizes that all this has happened in front of Ricky and notices that Ricky's eyes are watery.

"Grandpa, you don't think I'm your grandson either. You don't love me. If you don't want me, then I am left without grandparents!" Ricky begins to cry and hugs his father.

Ricardo carries him and hugs him. "No, son. He loves you. He didn't mean that."

Ricardo looks at his father and sees that his father is sad and with watery eyes.

"Sorry, Ricky, I didn't mean to say something like that. I love you very much! You are my favorite grandson."

"Lie, you also lie. You are like everyone else. For Dorothy, I am her son when it suits her. For grandma, I am an intruder. My cousin told me that he did not invite me to his party. My uncle did not even greet me. Only Dad accepts me as his son despite his being an irresponsible liar."

Roberto can't stop his tears from flowing, and he takes Ricky from Ricardo's arms.

"Ricky, it's me, your grandfather. I want to ask your forgiveness. If you really love me, please forgive me."

Ricky looks at him and sees that his grandfather is crying too and tells him.

"My grandpa used to say that we all make mistakes and that admitting it takes courage. So, I forgive you because I love you, but if you do it again, then you are a liar like the others."

Ricky hugs his grandfather, and Roberto hugs him affectionately. Ricardo joins the hug, and for the first time the three embrace together.

Roberto feels such a great emotion that he cannot explain. For many years, he has not hugged his son, and now thanks to Ricky, he feels that he has made peace with his son. Just as Dorothy said, Ricky has changed everyone's life.

Lora watches them from a distance, and she gets even more upset. She is arranging the gifts and starts to throw them to vent out her frustration. Dorothy pretends not to notice that her mother-in-law is fuming like a coffeepot. She takes the opportunity to indirectly add more fire to her mother-in-law.

Dorothy, in a very kind way, which is actually sarcastic, says to Lora.

"Let me help you so that you can rest a little bit."

Lora throws a package on the table and responds, almost screaming.

"I don't need your fucking help!"

"Excuse me, I didn't mean to upset you." Dorothy responds with a smile that is worse than a stab, and she sits away from the table.

Roberto Jr. witnesses everything from far away, and when he sees that Dorothy has sat away and is still smiling, he passes by her and asks.

"Are you having fun, Dorothy?"

"Yes! I love watching children play. It brings back good memories."

"Yes, children are beauties. It's a pity that some grow up to be poisonous snakes."

Dorothy looks at him and smiles.

"Yep. Not only snakes, but there are also chameleons, rats, foxes, donkeys, poisonous toads, and others."

"Your concept is interesting." Roberto mockingly replies.

"It is not a concept but a reality. When we stop being children, we become part of that social zoo where we find all kinds of animals. Where the fight for survival is as cruel as it is in the jungle."

Roberto sarcastically tells Dorothy.

"I saw what you did to Mom. Don't think I didn't realize it. You hypocritically went to offer her help, knowing that you were going to upset her. You were like a subtle, charming snake spilling your poison!"

Roberto thinks Dorothy will be offended and, even more, she will have no way of defending herself by his exposing her. But Dorothy responds with the same calm and smile, enjoying the dialogue and counterattacking with much more strength.

"Do not think that the snake is completely harmful. If it were not for the snakes, rats like you would have multiplied. In many places, they protect them to avoid rat infestations. But not only do you behave like a rat, you are also a fox and chameleon, pretending one thing when in reality you are another. You think I did not realize that your mother played deaf so as not to respond to my greeting? And then you lied to cover for her? But since you are a donkey, you were not able to understand I would notice your game. Like a venomous toad, you will leap to tell them what I have told you to create more conflict in the family. Yes, like a venomous toad."

Roberto never expected Dorothy to put him on the defensive. He is speechless. He stares at her for a while and just says. "I'm not going to ruin my son's party for you. Keep having fun. Your day is coming."

CHAPTER 8

Ricky, as usual, studies for a while when he gets home and then goes to Tamian's house to help him with his homework. Mrs. Kenya opens the door, and Ricky is a bit confused. Ricky sees that there are many boxes packed and Mrs. Kenya has been crying.

Ricky hugs her and asks her. "What happen, Nana Kenya? How can I help you?"

"Everything is fine, Ricky. Thanks for your good intention, but you can't help me." Answers Kenya between sobs.

Someone knocks on the door, and Tamian comes out to answer, while Ricky stays in the kitchen, comforting Kenya. Tamian returns and tells his mother.

"Mom, there are two men from the bank who want to talk to you."

Kenya begins to cry and goes out to meet the bank officers. Ricky follows her, holding Kenya's hand. Two men dressed in suits and with briefcases in their hands are standing in the living room.

"Madam Kenya, the bank foreclosed your house in court ten days ago and you did not leave the property. This is no longer your house. The bank offered you two thousand dollars to leave, and you have not left. We are not obligated to offer you anything, yet we did offer two thousand dollars. By law, you have ten days to reverse any foreclosure, and yours was due today at 5:00 P.M., and you did not pay the loan. I don't think that you will be able to pay now with all the court expenses added plus interest."

Ricky stands in front of the bank officer and asks him.

"How much does the lady owes?"

The man laughs and replies. "Are you going to pay for it?"

"I asked how much."

"You are going to need to break a few piggy banks to pay off her debt."

"She has stopped paying when she owed $120,000, so it'll be a few pigs."

"Can you tell me how much the total is?"

The man, out of curiosity, just to see Ricky's face when he sees the amount of the debt, answers. "Sure, Mr. Lawyer. Look."

The man opens the portfolio, takes out the papers, and shows them to him. "Here you go, Mr. Lawyer. This is the sum."

"But you said it was $120,000, and this says $182,500."

"That's right. That happens when you stop paying for more than six months."

Ricky does not respond, runs off, and screams.

"I will be right back!"

An angry Kenya responds to the bank officer.

"My company closed, and I was out of work. I have only gotten part-time jobs, that is not even enough for food."

The man responds cruelly. "Madam, the bank has offices, no heart. I am just doing my job. Please, I beg you not to complicate it."

Ricky comes back with a phone in hand and scowls, asking Kenya. "Do you have those papers?"

"Yes, they are in one of those boxes, but I don't know which one it is."

Ricky yells at Tamian. "Run, Tamian! Help me look for them. We only have three hours and forty minutes left!"

Ricky, like a madman, asks. "Where is Tamima?"

"She is in the room. What do you want her for?"

"I need her to help us find the papers."

Tamima comes out of her room and hears that Ricky is asking for her. She looks at Ricky and tells him.

"Don't be stupid. Mom already told us that it is over. Anyway, this is not your business. I'm glad at least I won't have to see your face any longer."

Kenya hears everything, but she has no strength to correct her daughter. Ricky and Tamian start opening boxes, and Kenya stops them. "What are you doing?"

Tamian looks at her mother and responds. "I don't know. Ricky told me to find some papers."

Tamima hits him on the head with an open hand.

"You do whatever he tells you to. Aren't you ashamed to be like a puppy running behind him?"

Ricky looks at her and replies. "He is my friend. He is not a puppy. You cannot understand it because you are arrogant, and you have no friends."

The bank officers are enjoying the scene. They look at each other and smile. Kenya sees Ricky is arguing with Tamima and decides to intervene.

"Enough already! I have enough problems to hear you fighting!"

"Mama, it is that Ricky is nosy. He doesn't have to come here and get into our business. He should go to his house and stop fucking with us!"

On any other occasion, Kenya would have slapped her daughter for using that phrase. But she is devastated and, in a way, feels that her daughter is right.

Kenya, with character, almost scolding Ricky, asks, "What do you want those papers for?"

"To see if it is the same amount as their papers say."

The men laugh.

Ricky squints and makes his usual gesture of reaching out his right arm and waving his finger from side to side. "No, no, no, this is not a laughing matter."

"Of course, it is the same number, Mr. Lawyer." The man answers.

Ricky looks at Kenya and asks her. "Is it true, Mrs. Kenya?"

"Yes, it is true. Now, are you satisfied, or do you need something else?" Kenya says, already upset.

Ricky goes to the bank officer and tells him, "Please show me the papers."

"What do you want the papers for? In the first place, it is none of your business, and in the second, I don't have to show it to you."

"Please show them to me," Ricky repeats, almost crying.

"I told you no, and the girl is right—fuck off!"

Ricky heads to Kenya and pleads with her. "Please, Kenya, show them to me."

Kenya suddenly remembers that the papers are not in a box but in a drawer in the kitchen. "If I show you the papers, will you promise me you will go home?"

"Yes, I promise." Ricky responds with joy.

Kenya tells her daughter.

"Tamima, take Ricky to the kitchen and show him the papers that are in the table drawer."

Tamima responds out of spite, "Let Tamian show him. I have to go to the bathroom."

Kenya feels a desire to pull her hair, but she restrains herself because she is in the presence of two strangers.

Tamian says. "Come, Ricky. I'll show you."

Ricky pulls out his phone and takes pictures of the four pages and runs out without saying anything.

The men laugh and say to Kenya. "Looks like your neighbor is not very well in the head."

"Yes, he is very strange, but he is a good kid, and very intelligent."

"Madam, the truth is that we had a lot of fun but it's time for you to tell us what you are going to do."

Kenya looks at him with tears in her eyes. The officer perceives that Kenya is in a state of weakness and pulls out the check again and puts it on a table. Then he adds three hundred dollars out his own pocket and tells her.

"This is from me. It has nothing to do with the bank. I know that your situation is tough, and this will help you. You just have to sign here."

The bank officer puts the check and the cash on the table and gives a pen to Kenya. "Sign here, please."

Kenya takes the pen, and her hands are shaking. She is trying to sign when tears fall on the form that she is about to sign. Kenya puts the pen aside.

"Sorry, I can't. I don't have the strength to do it."

The enraged officer takes the form, the check, and the money.

"You have made me waste two hours here. I have done everything possible for you, but I will not lose any sleep if you want me to throw you out on the street. At five o'clock, I will be back, putting the eviction order on the door, and there are no more offers. You will be thrown out to the street!"

Meanwhile, Ricky has gone to call his uncle. He sends him an urgent message. "Please call me. It is urgent."

Ricky's uncle is in an important meeting when he receives a message from Ricky to call him urgently. Tony excuses himself and comes out of the meeting in a hurry. Tony calls Ricky and asks.

"What's wrong, Ricky? Are you okay?"

"Yes, Uncle Tony, but you told me you would always be there for me when I needed it." Ricky says, almost crying.

Tony, nervous, thinking something has happened to Ricky, asks him.

"What did Ricardo do to you? I'm going to pick you up right now. Where are you?"

"I'm fine. I just need you to take care of a big problem for me, and you only have two hours and fifty minutes to do it."

"What are you talking about, Ricky? You scare me."

"I will send you right now a message with four photos."

Tony starts checking his messages and responds. "Yes, I got it. What the hell is this?"

"I need you to pay that bill before 5:00 P.M., or Nana Kenya loses her house!"

Tony tells him, worried, "Ricky, have you gone crazy?"

"Uncle, I beg you. Don't fail me. Can I count on you?"

Tony answers. "Ricky, that is a considerable amount. I do not have the slightest idea what you are doing. Neither do I have time to check on it. It would be a mistake to allow you to make such a blunder."

Ricky, almost crying, answers.

"Uncle, I beg you on my knees. You have to believe me. It is very important to me."

Tony answers sharply.

"No, Ricky. I am not only your uncle, but I am also in charge of your finances. It is my duty to take care of you in all the aspects of your life. I promised that to your mother. And besides, I will do it for your own good. It is not the money that matters here, it is my professional duty."

Ricky understands that his uncle is not going to help him, and he starts to cry.

"You don't understand because you are far away and I am here all by myself. That lady is like a Nana Silvia to me. She makes sure that I always have snacks when I come from school. Her son, Tamian, is like a brother to me. He gives me a ride to school every day on his bike. If they leave, I will be alone here, with no one to help me. Dad and Dorothy leave early for work and come back late, almost just to sleep. That lady has looked after me selflessly. Now she is in need. I can help her, and it would be a shame if I don't do it. By helping her, I also make my life a little easier. I have never asked for anything. That money will not bankrupt the account that Mom left me. Uncle, please help me. I beg you, please."

Tony knows that $182,500 is an insignificant amount compared to the $32 million that his mother left Ricky in a trust account managed by him. Tony understands why Ricky is in such a hurry to help Kenya, and he also realizes that by helping Kenya, he is also helping Ricky. Tony is undecided, however; his heart is telling him to help Ricky, but his business mind is telling him otherwise.

Ricky asks him. "Uncle, are you there?"

"Yes, Ricky, I am here."

"Don't fail me, please. I need you. You promised me you were going to be there for me always."

Tony is moved by Ricky's words and realizes the well-being of his nephew is more important than the money.

Tony tells him in a sweet voice.

"If it is so important to you, then I will take care of it. I will send it to my secretary to make a bank transfer, and I will send you the confirmation on a text message. If this makes you happy, it also makes me happy. I must go now. I will call you tonight. I must communicate with the secretary to take care of this wire transfer."

LITTLE RICKY

It is 4:45 P.M., and Ricky still has not received the answer from his uncle. He is sitting in the doorway of his house and is constantly hitting his right knee with his fist.

Ricky sees the men from the bank park in front of Kenya's house. He runs off to Kenya's house and knocks on the door.

Tamima opens the door and tells him.

"What the hell do you want? Mom told you not to come. Go home, gossip!"

Kenya leaves the room when she hears her daughter kicking Ricky out of the house. Kenya then sees the men entering the property with the eviction papers, and she sees Ricky turn to face the bank officers and tell them, pointing to his phone.

"Gentlemen, it is ten minutes to 5:00 p.m. You cannot enter the property unless you are invited."

The bank officer, a little annoyed, answers him.

"Listen, kid, you were funny at first, but I don't like you anymore. Now, get out of the way! I don't have time for your games."

Ricky stands in front of the two men and opens his arms.

"You cannot enter. It's still owned by Nana Kenya!"

The man takes Ricky by the arm and lifts him up and throws him aside. Kenya comes out like a beast with a broom in her hand and yells at the man.

"How dare you abuse a child! You get out of here right now, and don't come back unless you come with the police."

The enraged man yells at her.

"If you want the police, you will have it, and if you want something else, you will also have it."

The man is going to open his briefcase when he feels a push from the back that knocks him to the ground. It was DJ, the neighbor who lives across from Ricky's house. He had seen everything from his house.

"Stand up, asshole, and push me like you did to the kid."

The banker turns pale when he sees the size of the black man with gold teeth. DJ is almost fuming from his nose with fury.

"Stand up, asshole. I am going to kick your ass." DJ stands in front of him, with the man still on the ground, fearing that if he stands up, the black man is going to beat him up. The other bank officer has called the police, who are on their way in a hurry since the police dispatcher had heard the screaming over the phone.

Ricky, who is also on the ground, hears the sound of a message on his phone. He opens it in a hurry and sees the confirmation of the mortgage payment with the transfer number to the bank received at 4:55 p.m.

Ricky gives a cry that surprises everyone. He jumps like a kangaroo. He hugs Kenya, kisses her, and tells her.

"Unpack, Nana Kenya, and tell them they can't take your house from you!"

Annoyed, Kenya pushes him off and tells him. "Calm down or you are the one who is going to get hit on the head with the broom!"

At that precise moment, three police units arrive with lights and sirens. The officers come out with their guns in hand and order everyone to the ground for security reasons. The big neighbor, as he has experienced, does not have to be told twice. He throws himself to the ground and puts his hands on his neck. Kenya thinks that she does not have to lie on the ground, but an officer orders her to throw the broom and lie down. Kenya lies on the ground while she listens to the screams of her daughter Tamima.

"I told you, Mom, that boy is a curse, damn him!"

Only a bank officer and Ricky remain standing. The bank officer says, I was the one who called—"

He has not even finished the sentence when they throw him to the ground.

Ricardo and Dorothy are arriving when they see the lights of the patrol cars in front of their house. Ricardo sees that Ricky is standing in the middle of the group, and he hurries out of the car and runs to Kenya's house. An officer sees him and yells at him to stop, but Ricardo ignores the officer's orders. The officer yells at him again and, when he sees Ricardo does not stop, shoots him with the Taser. Ricardo falls to the ground and screams out in pain while he is being handcuffed. Dorothy, seeing her husband on the ground and screaming, sends herself running to his aid. She is stopped and thrown to the ground by another officer.

The officers have requested reinforcement for its being a violent call and with several suspects. Dorothy's brother is the lieutenant on duty in charge of that sector. When he hears the address of the call, he decides not to go to the scene. He does not want to see his sister. He calls the sergeant and tells him that unless it is necessary, he will not go to the scene.

At one point in front of Kenya's house, there are five people sprawled out on the ground, with several police officers who keep arriving. Only Ricky is standing like a statue with the phone held with both hands against his chest.

Sergeant Garry arrives on the scene, walks among the detainees, and sees Ricky as a little mummy among all of them. The sergeant looks at him and says, "And you—what?"

Ricky opens his scared eyes and doesn't let him finish. Like lightning, he throws himself to the ground and puts his hands on his head. It is something so spontaneous and comical that everyone laughs, except Ricardo, who is still screaming out of pain.

The sergeant stops laughing and says, "You all can sit down." Then he asks. "Who started the fight?"

The banker says. "That child was the cause of everything."

DJ says. "That is not true. He was the one who started everything. He grabbed the boy by the arm, lifted him up, and threw him to the side. Then the lady came out with the broom to defend the boy. He threatened her, and I came to defend them."

When Dorothy hears that the man had lifted Ricky by the arm and thrown him to the ground, she stands up and yells.

"How dare you touch my son!" She rushes to the man, but she is stopped by an officer, who throws her to the ground and handcuffs her.

The sergeant asks the other banker. "What happened?"

"I didn't see anything. I was on my back and heard screams, and I called you."

The sergeant looks at Ricky and tells him. "Get up and tell me what happened."

"No, thanks. I'm fine lying like this."

The sergeant has to turn his face to hide his laughter. "Tell me what happened, because I think you are the one who caused the problem."

Ricky stands up like a spring and, in his peculiar way, tells him, "No, no, no, it wasn't me. It was these two who came to take Nana Kenya's house, and Nana Kenya had until 5:00 P.M. to pay for her house. They entered at 4:50 p.m., and I told them that it was not five o'clock yet, that they did not have the right to enter because it was still private property. The rest you heard already."

The sergeant scratches his head and replies. "You're technically right. But this whole problem is absurd because the house was going to be repossessed by the bank in ten minutes."

Ricky squints again and then responds. "No, no, no, the house belongs to Nana Kenya. The men are trespassing private property. They did not let me speak."

The shocked sergeant kneels and says. "Son, there is nothing you can do. The bank has the right to repossess the property."

The bank officer says. "That's what I've been telling him all afternoon today, but neither he nor Mrs. Kenya has come to their senses."

Ricky stands in front of him and comes back with. "No, no, no, you are the one who has not wanted to listen. You have not even listened to yourself. You said she had until 5:00 P.M. to pay."

"Yes, but she did not pay. How do I make you understand that?"

"Who said she did not pay? I have the payment confirmation here."

Kenya looks at the neighbor, and the two are confused. They both are wondering what the hell is Ricky talking about.

"Where is the payment confirmation?" Sergeant Gerry asks.

Ricky gives him the phone and tells him.

"See it yourself. Here is the bank transfer number, the amount, the mortgage number, the bank to which the money was transferred, and the time received, which was at 4:55 P.M. That is five minutes before the deadline. As you can see, these gentlemen did not want to listen, and I am sure Nana Kenya does not want them in her house."

The sergeant picks up the phone and begins to read. His face changes expression, and he calls another officer to consult. The sergeant tells the bank officer.

"Look, sir, I think you will have to consult with your bank, but here it shows that the debt has been paid."

Kenya's and DJ's eyes almost pop out of their sockets. They can't believe what they have just heard.

The banker is totally confused.

"What did you say? Let me see that, please."

The sergeant gives him the phone, and the banker begins to read the message and then see the photos of the documents. He scratches his head totally confused. Ricky tells the sergeant.

"Can you take off Mom's handcuffs, please? She is calmed now."

The sergeant smiles and orders Dorothy's handcuffs to be removed, but she must remain seated. The sergeant then asks.

"Does anyone want to place charges on someone?"

Nobody responds.

"All right, everyone goes home, and I don't want any more trouble."

The banker says. "I do not understand this. This cannot be true. This must be a fraud!"

Ricky responds. "I told you that Nana Kenya was going to pay, and she paid for it. Isn't that so, Nana Kenya?"

Kenya knows that she has not paid, but just to get back at the banker, she responds.

"Yes, it is true. I had money. I did not know how to do the money transfer, and Ricky did it for me. Thank God it went through on time!"

The sergeant orders the officers to check the records of all those involved to verify that there is no pending arrest warrant.

Lieutenant Frank, Dorothy's brother, hears on the radio when the names of his sister and his brother-in-law are checked, but instead of going to the scene, he calls Sergeant Garry on the phone.

"How is the scene, Garry? Who is going to be arrested?"

Gerry replies. "Don't worry, Lieutenant, it's not worth arresting anyone. I'm sure you would have had fun. If you want to pass by, there is still time."

"No, thanks, Garry. I'm busy with papers."

Sergeant Garry orders everyone to go home.

DJ stands up, rubs Ricky's head, and says to him.

"You are my hero. When I grow up, I want to be just like you."

Kenya looks at Ricky and asks him.

"What the hell did you do?"

"I did what I had to do, and you said what you had to say. This is our secret. No one can know about this. These men will not bother you again, and you will get the title of the house in the mail."

Kenya doesn't buy Ricky's story, but she promises that she will not tell anybody.

Upon entering the house, Ricardo tells Ricky.

"Will you ever stop fucking around and causing trouble everywhere?"

"Dad, I didn't do anything."

"You never do anything! You just filled the neighborhood with police. Almost all of us went to jail, and they gave me a shock that almost killed me! They threw Dorothy to the ground, handcuffed her, and you did nothing!"

"Dad, those men were the ones who provoked everything."

"I don't want to know anything else. Where did you get that phone from?"

"It's mine, I've always had it."

"Well, you are grounded. Give me the phone."

Ricky starts crying. "No! It's not fair! I have not done anything wrong." Ricky gives the phone to his father and goes crying to his room.

Dorothy does not say a word. She agrees with her husband, then she tells Ricardo.

"You did very well. He never does anything, but everything around him catches fire. You must ask him for the phone code and check what the hell he has on that phone. I'm afraid that any day the FBI will surround the house for another of his innocent I-didn't-do-anything!"

Ricardo knocks on the door of Ricky's room. Ricky, still crying, opens it.

"What is the code of the phone?"

"Sorry, Dad, but that is private. You have no right to violate my privacy."

Ricardo angrily tells him. "You have no privacy in this house!"

Ricky responds bluntly. "No!"

"You give me the password, or you will never see this phone ever again."

"No, that is private."

Ricardo takes the belt off his pants and is about to hit Ricky when Dorothy holds his arm.

"Don't you dare hit him!"

Dorothy gets in between Ricky and her husband, covering Ricky with her body.

Ricardo keeps his arm up, keeping the belt aloft for a few seconds, and then he leaves the room, yelling at his wife.

"That's the only thing I was missing. Now you defend him and I'm the bad guy!"

Dorothy stays in the room, comforting Ricky for a few minutes, and then goes to her room.

Ricardo does not speak to his wife all night.

In next door house, Kenya also cannot sleep that night, and to that are added the continuous comments from her daughter.

"Mom, I told you that that child is evil! You ignored me and lied to the authorities, saying that you had paid the mortgage. You repeated Ricky's lie, playing along with that liar. The man from the bank was giving us $3,550 to move out, but now they won't give us anything and he will come with the police early tomorrow!"

Kenya just cries, and she says. "You are absolutely right. I was stupid and acted irresponsibly."

"Mom don't let him into the house anymore. Sooner or later, he is going to cause trouble for Tamian."

Tamian responds. "That's a lie! Ricky is my friend."

Kenya responds to her son.

"No, Tamian, your sister is right. You better cut off your friendship with that boy. Tomorrow I will wait for the bank officers to apologize, and in the afternoon, I will go out to find a place to rent."

"Mom, Ricky has always helped me in everything. When the other children made fun of me, he always defended me. And thanks to Ricky, my grades all improved!"

Tamima takes advantage of the situation and tells him.

"Yes, thanks to him, we lost the $3,500 from the bank. Thanks to him, tomorrow Mom could be facing charges for lying to the police. Thanks to him, we are the joke of the neighborhood!"

Kenya points her finger at Tamian and orders him.

"I don't want Ricky in the house anymore. The topic is not up for debate. You understand me?"

Tamian points his finger at his sister and says.

"This is all your fault. You always hated Ricky!"

Tamima takes advantage of the fact that her mother is not looking, and she sticks her tongue out to Tamian.

An enraged Tamian throws a shoe at her sister, but he misses and hits a flower vase. Kenya enters with a broom. Tamian and Tamima both run off to their rooms and close the doors almost in synchronized timing.

The next day, Ricky stands in front of Kenya's house, waiting for Tamian so they can go to school together. Tamian has always taken Ricky on his bike thus far, and Ricky then helps him with homework in the afternoon. That was a deal that they made the first day they met.

Tamima opens the door and says in a hurtful way.

"You better go. Your driver already left." Then she adds, as if an afterthought. "Ah! I almost forgot! For the time that we have left here, do not come to this house. We do not want to see your ugly White face again."

Kenya is looking out the window and sees Ricky pout and almost break into tears. But Kenya says nothing to her daughter even though she knows Tamima has been cruel to Ricky.

LITTLE RICKY

Ricky arrives ten minutes late to school because he's had to walk. When he arrives, he sees that Tamian is in the classroom, and he surmises that what Tamima said is true.

During break, Tamian walks up to Ricky and tells him.

"Ricky, you know I'm your friend. Mom and Tamima don't want you to come to the house anymore, but I still want to be your friend."

Ricky feels better. All is not lost. Both embrace like brothers, and Ricky responds.

"I am also your friend. If you need me, just tell me or go to my house. I did not think helping Nana Kenya would bring me so much trouble."

******

Two days have passed since the incident, Kenya's anxiety was growing by the minute. She couldn't sleep, and the stress was making her sick. Kenya begins to think that if the bank officer has not returned, it was because they are preparing a civil lawsuit plus the repossession of her property. Kenya will not leave the house. Once she saw a car park in front of her house and believed that the driver was a court official who was bringing her the civil lawsuit documents, her heartbeat increased so fast she thought she is having a heart attack.

In her head, Kenya constantly keeps asking herself, *My god, what am I going to do now? I don't have money to pay for a lawyer to defend me in court. How did I get carried away by a child? Who will take care of my children when I go to jail?*

******

Ricardo refuses to return the phone to him unless Ricky gives him the code, but Ricky flatly refuses. Ricky only goes to school and then locks himself in his room every day. Dorothy brings the food to the room as Ricky has said that he will not leave the room until they return the phone to him.

Exactly a week has passed since the incident. Kenya's stress is so great she has lost twelve pounds. She is convinced that with each day that goes without news from the bank, it's because the bank was preparing a bigger case against her. Kenya finally makes the decision to go to the bank to try to negotiate with them and plead for mercy.

Kenya stops in front of the bank, and she cannot control herself. She walks twice to the bank's front door but then lacks the courage to enter. Then, in an act of faith, she kneels in front of the bank and raises her hands to the sky and screams.

"Oh God, I know that I have sinned. I am sorry with all my heart, and before you I place my destiny and those of my children!"

People think she is insane when they look at her with her hands extended to the sky. Kenya is a woman of faith and fears God. She prays that God give her the strength she needs to enter the bank and put herself at the mercy of the bank executives.

Kenya rushes in and asks a representative from the bank.

"Whom can I talk to regarding a mortgage?"

The bank representative responds kindly.

"Please write your name on this sheet and write mortgage where it says reference. Also put the arrival time and wait for your name to be called."

Kenya writes the information on the paper and sits down to wait. The minutes seem like hours. Kenya constantly wipes sweat from her face, and she's had to go to the bathroom twice in the ten-minute wait. A bank officer calls her name, and Kenya gets up, scared. She looks around her and sees a police officers. She thinks he came to arrest her.

The bank officer calls her name again, and Kenya responds in a broken voice.

"It's me, sir."

"Please follow me to my office." Requests the banker.

Kenya follows him, dragging her feet. The bank officer turns and sees that Kenya is hardly walking and asks her.

"Do you feel okay, ma'am?"

Kenya recovers and draws strength from the bottom of her stomach.

"Yes, sir. thanks. I am okay."

When they're sitting in the office, the officer tells her to give him her mortgage account number.

Kenya gives him the mortgage account number, and the banker starts looking for it in the computer. Then she sees the banker start reading and jotting down something on a piece of paper.

Kenya, almost crying, tells him, "Understand me. I'm desperate."

The banker looks at her and says.

"Well, you are going to have to calm down because we are not magicians. You paid your mortgage a week ago. It takes two weeks for us to record the title of the property. It must be notarized and included in the city records. That is out of our hands."

Kenya is about to lose consciousness. Her head is spinning, her eyes want to pop out of their sockets, and she can hardly speak.

"W-what...what do you mean that the house is paid off?"

"Yes, ma'am, the house is paid. Maybe you thought you have to do more paperwork, but you are done. Congratulations!"

Kenya desperately looks around and sees the trash can. She runs to it and kneels, then begins to vomit. The frightened banker asks for help, and several employees come to aid Kenya. They help her get up and give her water.

The general manager of the bank walks into the office, concerned, and asks.

"What happened?"

"Nothing, Mr. Borton. The lady paid off her debt about ten minutes before the deadline. It seems that she thought the money did not come in on time and she had lost her house."

Mr. Borton exclaims.

"Ah! You are the lady with the incident! I want to apologize to you. I hope you understand that our officers had no way of knowing that your payment had entered ten minutes before the deadline."

As Kenya listens to Mr. Borton, she becomes convinced that Ricky has saved her house, and now she realizes how unfair she has been to him.

Kenya, like a sleepwalker, replies.

"There is nothing to forgive. Thank you very much."

She walks three steps and faints.

Chapter 9

On Sunday afternoon, Roberto shows up at his son's house. Ricardo is surprised when he opens the door and sees his father.

Ricardo hugs him tightly.

"Dad, what a surprise! What wind brought you here?"

Ricardo has always been more attached to his mother and somewhat estranged from his father.

"Son, I don't want you to be offended, but Ricky religiously calls me every three days and hasn't called me in over a week."

"Why didn't you call me and ask me? I would have told you why. But the fact that you have come here is already a great achievement that we owe to Ricky."

"Don't be jealous. I also want to see you and your wife. I know what happened on my grandson's birthday was very ugly. Later, I found out the truth about everything. I do not want things to continue to get worse."

"I am totally with you, Dad. I want only good family relations, but every time it seems more difficult. But I know you did not come to speak outside. Please come in."

Roberto enters and observes a great change in his son's house. The front of the house is clean, and inside the house looks a lot better than it used to.

"I didn't know you had such a nice car."

"It's not mine. It's the neighbor's from across the street. It's a long story. I will just tell you that Ricky rented out the parking space for $250 a month."

A surprised Roberto smiles.

"I can't believe you. Did Ricky do that?"

"Yes, believe me. We put that money in a drawer in the kitchen, and that was where he got the four hundred dollars he gave you for the air conditioning. He lied when he told you that Dorothy gave it to him to give you."

"That child is much more than one can imagine."

Roberto nods in amazement. Then he asks.

"Where is Dorothy?"

"I have to pick her up in two hours. With her new position, she now must work longer hours."

"I want to ask you a question now that we are alone. It's about something Ricky said on Gabriel's birthday that concerns me a lot."

Ricardo looks at him, confused.

"What did Ricky say?"

"Among the many things he said was that Dorothy calls him her son only when it suits her. I think that is a very strong statement. Please tell me what he meant."

Ricardo looks at him very seriously and answers with another question.

"What do you think he meant?"

Roberto, with a confused expression, shrugs his shoulders and answers him.

"I actually don't know. It may be that she is not a good mother or that she is not his mother."

"I have given you that answer many times, and you have not wanted to hear it. I do not want to go into that topic to spoil your visit."

"Sorry, son. Forget it. Where's Ricky?"

"Ricky is in his room. He is self-punishing."

"What do you mean? How does he punish himself?" Roberto asks, astonished.

"It will be better if he explains it to you, and then you tell me what you think."

Roberto knocks on Ricky's door, and Ricky doesn't respond. The third time Roberto knocks without an answer, he tells Ricky.

"It is me, your grandfather. I came to see you."

Roberto had inadvertently said grandfather, and Ricardo feels a great joy and hope pass over him.

Ricky yells and runs to open the door.

"Grandpa!"

Roberto picks him up and hugs him tightly.

"Grandpa, I missed you so much!"

"Me too. Since you haven't called me, I came to visit you."

Ricky points his finger at his father and scowls.

"He took my phone, that's why I can't call you."

"Why did he take your phone away?"

"Because I would not give him the password so he could open my phone. It's my privacy. He has no right to inspect it."

"But where did you get that phone from?"

"It's mine. My mother gave it to me and put her credit card to pay for the line."

"But you told me that your mommy died."

"Yes, she died. The card is from my grandfather's company, which still exists."

Roberto scratches his head and responds.

"I must admit that you have an answer for everything."

Then Roberto tells his son. "I can't tell you how to educate your son. I never allowed anyone to intervene with mine. But if the phone is his and he uses it responsibly, I would give it back to him. If you want to have control over his communications, to which you have the right, you give him a phone and tell him that he can't use the other one anymore."

Ricardo, annoyed, answers.

"You're siding with him indirectly."

"No, son, I just gave my opinion to you."

Roberto, out of curiosity then asks Ricky.

"What do you think, Ricky?"

"It's not my opinion what counts. It is Dad's decision. Mama gave me that phone and asked me to promise her I would not give it to anyone that I will be the only one to use it."

Roberto looks at Ricardo and says.

"Your son keeps his word. You should learn from him."

Ricardo cannot believe that his father has allied with Ricky and is attacking him.

"I'll be damned! Now I'm the bad guy." Ricardo points his finger at Ricky.

"If I give you the phone back, you have to promise me you will never take it out of your room."

Ricky, with great joy, answers. "I promise it will never leave my room."

Ricardo goes out to get the phone, and Roberto tells Ricky.

"High-five. We won!"

Ricky, with great satisfaction, high-fives his grandfather and laughs.

Ricardo returns with the phone and hands it to him. Ricky takes it and says. "Thanks, Dad."

Ricardo asks Ricky. "Can you give me the code now?"

Ricky opens his eyes wide in surprise, puts the phone behind his back, and answers. "Nope."

Roberto asks.

"What is the problem with the phone? What happened?"

Ricardo responds sarcastically.

"Nothing, Dad, nothing. I still don't know if I want to find out. I only know that thanks to Ricky and his phone, the block was filled with policemen, the next-door neighbor, the neighbor across the street, and two men that I don't know anything about. Dorothy and I ended up on the ground. It was a miracle they didn't arrest us. They Tasered and almost killed me!"

Roberto was open-mouthed and totally surprised.

"Is that true, Ricky?"

Ricky becomes scared and responds.

"Yes, it is true, but I did not do anything wrong. I had nothing to do with what happened."

Roberto, annoyed, tells him.

"Be glad it was your dad. If it were me, I would have grabbed that phone and smashed it into pieces with a hammer."

Ricky screams, frightened. He runs out in a hurry and locks himself in his room. They heard noises as if Ricky was putting furniture behind the door to block it.

Ricardo and his father laugh. Ricardo says to him.

"Dad, it isn't that I want to throw you out, but I have to go pick up Dorothy at work."

"Sure, son. I have to go home too. Say hello to Dorothy for me."

Roberto goes out to the sidewalk, and his curiosity to find out what happened leads him to knock on Kenya's house.

Kenya has spent two days trying to go see Ricky. She is so embarrassed she can't find a way to do it. Roberto knocks on Kenya's door. Kenya opens and asks.

"Good afternoon, sir. Can I help you?"

"Excuse me, I just wanted to ask you about an incident that happened a few days ago, if you don't mind?"

"If you come from the bank, you have nothing to worry about. It was all a misunderstanding."

"No, ma'am. I'm Ricky's grandfather."

When Kenya hears that Roberto is Ricky's grandfather, she hugs him and kisses him immediately. Roberto is speechless and has not been expecting such a surprise.

"That child is an angel from heaven. Thanks to him, I did not lose my home that day!"

Kenya realizes that she is hugging Roberto, and he looks scared.

"Forgive me, sir. I just couldn't contain myself. My gratitude to your grandson is greater than I can ever express. I will be indebted to him for life."

Roberto answers almost without words.

"I thought he had caused a problem?"

"No, sir, that little angel did nothing wrong. What he did was actually a miracle."

Kenya looks and sees that Ricardo and Ricky are leaving the house to pick up Dorothy. Kenya rushes out and yells to Ricardo,

"Are you going out, Mr. Ricardo?"

"Yes, we're going to pick up Dorothy."

"You can leave Ricky with me. I made a chocolate cake for him. I was planning to bring it to him later, but his grandfather is here at my house."

Ricardo sees his father standing at Kenya's door. Ricardo looks at Ricky and sees that Ricky is serious and confused about what to do. Kenya understands that Ricky is confused because Tamian has told him that she did not want him in her house anymore.

Kenya comes out and takes Ricky by the hand and tells him.

"Please come. Tamian is very sad and wants to see you."

Ricky, still distrustful, responds.

"Okay, fine, for a few minutes, and then I have to go with my grandfather."

"As you like, but please come."

Kenya holds Ricky's hand and leads him to her house.

Roberto proudly asks Ricky.

"How did you save the lady's house?"

Ricky freaks out. He knows that he must act fast before he is discovered. He winks at Kenya.

"Nana Kenya was going to lose her house that day at 5:00 p.m. She had the money but didn't know how to make a transfer. I took the foreclosure papers and made the bank transfer for her. The payment came ten minutes before the deadline, and that's why she says I saved her house. Isn't that so, Nana Kenya?"

Kenya doesn't know what to do. She remembers Ricky had asked her to keep it a secret. Ricky repeats again.

"It is true that this is what happened, Nana Kenya?"

"Yes, sir, that's what happened. If it weren't for your grandson, I would be on the street today."

Roberto, proud of Ricky, puts his right hand behind his neck and moves it from side to side, saying proudly.

"That's my grandson!"

DJ, the neighbor from across the street, comes out of his house and sees Kenya standing at her door. Roberto and Ricky are standing in front of Kenya. DJ suddenly sees that Roberto has Ricky by the neck and is shaking him back and forth. He shouts like a screaming rocket.

"Let him go, you son of a bitch, or I will kill you!"

Roberto hears the screams and turns around. He sees the impressive figure of a giant black-haired man who looks like an unbridled locomotive coming full steam toward him. The neighbor has already put both hands on the fence and jumps it like an Olympic champion. Ricky and Kenya yell at the same time.

"No, it's okay!"

DJ stops just a few feet away from Roberto, with his fists clenched and ready to hit him. Roberto almost faints. He is pale, his heart pounding, about to jump out of his chest.

"Excuse me, sir. I thought you were the stupid banker that had come back to bother her again.

What I saw from my house was that you had Ricky by the neck and were shaking him."

Roberto, almost out of breath, answers.

"Thank you very much for defending my grandson."

DJ slaps Roberto on the back in a friendly way and responds.

"Nothing to talk about, brother! Whoever touches Ricky has to deal with me."

Then he gives Roberto a handshake that shakes his entire body completely. Roberto is impressed with the size of the neighbor. DJ's friendly slap almost knocks him down, and when he shakes his hand, it has shaken his entire body. He does not want to imagine a punch from that man.

The neighbor proudly tells Roberto.

"Your grandson saved Kenya's house and solved my parking problem. He is our superhero!"

DJ grabs Ricky under the arms with two giant hands like many parents do to throw and catch a child up in the air. DJ, with his enormous strength, throws Ricky into the air, catches him, and puts him on the ground. Ricky closes his eyes and lets out a scream that scares them all and runs to his house. They only hear the door slam when he enters.

The neighbor smiles at Roberto, showing his gold teeth, and tells him.

"Your grandson is also a little strange."

Kenya slaps him in the head and says.

"Stupid animal, you threw him so high I thought he was going to hit the power line!"

* * * * * *

In two weeks, they have the fortieth anniversary celebration of Dorothy's parents' wedding to attend. Ricardo counts the days as if he has been sentenced to the electric chair. The last family encounters they had ended in disasters, and to make it even worse, there is no way to improve the situation. Ricky's relations with Kenya, meanwhile, returns to normal, and Kenya promises to keep secret that Ricky had saved her house by paying her mortgage.

Ricardo takes his wife by the hand, hugs her tightly, and tells her.

"I think the only way your parents won't attack us during their party is if the two of us stick together."

"You are right, love. Every time we part, they attack us separately. I hope this time, since there will be guests, they will behave better."

Ricardo laughs and responds. "Remember that we have Ricky. If there are no problems, he knows how to find them."

The day of the party, Ricardo, Dorothy, and Ricky arrive early to help with whatever is necessary. Dorothy has a very special cake courtesy of Mr. Bob. Ricardo is carrying an envelope with a surprise, and Ricky is holding balloons in his hands commemorating the fortieth anniversary of the wedding.

Dorothy's father, Frank, opens the door and sees his daughter holding a huge cake.

"Where is Mom?"

"She is in the kitchen. Go ahead."

Ricardo says.

"Congratulations, Frank. I hope you have many more years to celebrate this event. You are an example to me, and I hope you will give me some advice."

Frank replies sarcastically.

"In that case, I'll give you the first tip. A gentleman would not let his wife carry such a large cake when he has his hands empty."

Dorothy listens to her father, turns around, and responds.

"I want to give it to Mom myself. That's why I carry it. I'm afraid that he will drop it."

Frank laughs and pats Ricardo twice on the shoulder as he says sarcastically.

"For the record, she was the one who called you useless."

Ricardo takes a deep breath. He has tried to praise his father-in-law, but it is in vain. He only thinks that if that were the reception, he does not want to imagine the rest.

Frank stares at Ricky, who looks like a small statue holding two balloons.

"And you? Are you real, or are you made of wax?"

Ricky takes his time to respond, and then he says,

"Do I wait in the car, or do I go in?"

"Wow! What a temper! Can you take a joke?"

"My grandfather used to say that when jokes are cruel, they stop being jokes and turn into evil."

Frank opens his eyes wide in surprise.

"Excuse me, mister. I didn't mean to offend you."

"You did not bother me. My grandfather used to say that someone can bother you only if you allow it."

"Ah! Was your grandfather a philosopher?"

"No, a judge, and his father was a policeman and builder."

"How about that, a policeman and builder!"

"Yes, he started very young in the police force, and after he retired, he founded a construction company."

Frank mockingly bows to him.

"It's an honor to have a guest like you. Please go ahead."

Ricky looks at him from the side and makes a face with his mouth.

"Hmmm, look, here is your balloon."

"And what do I do with it?"

"Keep it or let it fly." Ricky, with his immutable face, answers.

Meanwhile, Sara sees her daughter carrying the cake and asks her.

"Where is your good-for-nothing—"

"Who?"

"Who else could it be? Your husband, Ricardo."

"Why did you call him that? Please, Mom, let's not start."

"I don't know why he let you carry that cake. That's not what a gentleman would do."

"I was the one who wanted to carry the cake. He wanted to, but I wouldn't let him."

"Forget it. I shouldn't get into that, and you're right. Today is not the day to try to fix what cannot be fixed."

Dorothy puts the cake on the table, puts her hands together in prayer, and begs her mother.

"Mom, I beg you, please, not today. Please!"

Ricky walks in as if he was marching, with the balloon in his hand. Sara looks at him curiously and asks Dorothy in a low voice,

"Is this going to stay with you forever?"

"Mom, what do you want me to do? Would you throw him out on the street?"

"I just can't believe he doesn't have anyone else in the world. It's your problem. If you want to be a social worker, then have fun."

"That kid was born before I met Ricardo."

"But are you sure he's Ricardo's?"

"I am not going to talk about that because in the end, I am the one who is dealing with it."

Ricky approaches Sara, gives her the balloon.

"Mrs. Sara, congratulations. I wish you many more years of health together with your husband."

"Thank you, my love. What a beautiful balloon! We are going to tie it on the chair, so it does not fly away."

Everyone, including Ricky, works in preparing for the party. About fifteen guests are expected among family and friends. It is almost 5:00 P.M., with only an hour to go before the party starts.

Dorothy, seeing that her brother, Frank, has not arrived yet, asks her mother.

"Where is Frank? Why is he late?"

"He'll be here later around 7:00 P.M."

"Why is that? I know that he does not work today. He should be here helping."

Frank Sr. is putting the beers in the fridge. He hears his daughter, stops, and responds sarcastically.

"If you had twenty officers under your command, you would understand him a little more instead of criticizing him. His work carries a lot of responsibility. He must rest to have his mind clear before he returns to work."

Dorothy understands her father, more than justifying her brother, is telling her that their jobs are far inferior to Frank's. Dorothy's parents are unaware that Dorothy is third-in-command at the supermarket now. Dorothy has not informed them since communication between them is almost nonexistent. Dorothy looks at Ricardo, who makes a sign with his hands telling her to let it pass and not respond. Ricky is watching them both. Dorothy cannot contain herself, however, she responds with the same sarcastic tone as her father.

"How interesting. I have almost ninety employees under my command and have been here since this morning. And I even have to remain accessible in case of an emergency on my day off."

Dorothy's parents look at her suspiciously. Frank responds.

"I did not know that a simple cashier had so many responsibilities."

Dorothy is about to answer, but Ricky steps forward and does it for her.

"Not a simple cashier, but the general manager assistant in the supermarket. She is the third in command, only after the owner and the general manager."

Sara asks Ricardo.

"Are you now a manager too?"

"No, Mrs. Sara, I'm still the same piece of shit you know."

Sara laughs and responds.

"I did not mean that, but if you say so, I will not argue with you."

Ricky intervenes again.

"My grandfather used to say that the loyalty and dedication of a worker to his work is more important to him than the position he holds."

Frank, a little tired of Ricky talking about his grandfather, tells him.

"Ah! Your grandfather also had ninety-five employees."

"No, he had over two thousand."

Frank laughs mockingly. He doesn't believe Ricky.

"Such a company and he left you alone and penniless."

"No, my grandparents died in an accident, and I was left alone with Mom."

"But Mom also left you penniless."

"No, she left me with Dad, and I don't want to talk about this anymore," Ricky answers sharply.

Sara, annoyed, yells at her husband.

"Frank, what the hell is wrong with you?"

Frank understands his comments have been totally off.

"I'm sorry, kid. I apologize." He puts the last of the beers in the fridge, slams the fridge door in frustration, and goes to his room. Dorothy looks at Ricardo, who is about to intervene but miraculously holds back.

Sara, embarrassed, says to Ricardo.

"Don't pay attention to him. He is getting old and stupid."

The guests then begin to arrive, and with them is Martha. She is an old friend of Sara who has a daughter the same age as Dorothy. Sara always uses Maira, Martha's daughter, as a role model for her daughter.

Martha sees Dorothy and hugs her.

"Dorothy, how are you? It has been so long since I have seen you. I always ask your mother about you. She always answers the same way and, in reality, never says anything!"

Dorothy kisses her and responds.

"It is because there is not much to say. How is Maira?"

Martha, with a prepotent tone, responds.

"Well, you know, she graduated from marine biology six years ago, and she is currently pursuing her doctor's degree. It's a shame you dropped out of school and didn't finish high school. You could be studying with her, and she could have helped with the thesis. You know a university diploma is a key that opens many doors. Otherwise, you are destined to third-class jobs!"

Dorothy bites her lip to keep from answering her. Sara tries to intervene to avoid anyone being upset. She knows that Martha is very reckless. Dorothy is not a girl any longer and, at any moment, would put a stop to Martha's insinuations.

Sara asks Martha. "Guess what my son, Frank, gave me?"

"I don't know, but I am sure it must be something interesting."

"Yes! He gave me a German sewing machine."

"Since when you sew?"

"I do some things from time to time. Most of the time I make alterations."

Ricky walks over with a cupcake in hand and asks Dorothy.

"Can I eat this?"

Martha sees Ricky and covers her mouth as if she has seen a ghost.

"My god, how well you had hidden this kid! No wonder you never went back to school. The father surely did not take part on this. You did it all by yourself. He is a replica of you!"

Dorothy turns red and is about to explode. Instead of changing the subject, Martha continues with her recklessness.

"But your husband is not the father of that child. How old is he?"

Ricky responds in his usual cold and blunt way.

"You are wrong, madam. Her husband is my father, and I am eight years old."

"Well, if you say so and you are happy with it, I have nothing to say. You are very cute, did you know?"

"My grandfather used to say that the beauty of a person is inside, and I have never seen inside myself."

Martha tells Dorothy in her ironic way.

"Dorothy, the devil knows more from being old than for being a devil. I have known you since you were a little girl. You are like a daughter to me."

Dorothy tries to change the conversation and responds to her.

"I am not sure I understand what you mean."

Ricky instantly responds.

"She meant to say that she is older than the devil and that is why she knows everything."

Martha turns burnt red. She does not like what Ricky has said. Sara and Dorothy have to make an effort not to laugh.

Martha looks at Ricky, and with a serious face, she tells him.

"Elderly people must be respected no matter how old they are. It may be that your mother did not educate you and that's why it is not entirely your fault, but you must learn that respect is the basis of peace."

Sara gets nervous. The situation is getting out of control, and she tries once more to calm things down.

"Martha, why didn't your daughter come? I thought she would come with you."

"She is studying to give her PHD thesis. She has no time to party. She says that time should not be wasted and those who do end up marginalized by society."

Dorothy shakes her head from side to side and takes a deep breath, trying to contain herself and not tell her to go to hell.

"Sorry, my dear, if this bothers you. I have to tell you the truth to wake you up. You are still young. You can go back to your studies, be someone in life, and leave the neighborhood you live in. I give you a mother's advice: listen to me and open your mind."

Ricky is standing with the cake in his hand, waiting for permission to eat and, at the same time, listening carefully to the conversation.

"What's wrong with our neighborhood?" asks Ricky.

Dorothy doesn't let him finish, almost yelling at him, "I told you to go eat that cake! Go with your dad now!"

Ricky looks scared, and he realizes that he better go to his father.

Dorothy tells Martha in a slow but serious tone, "I heard that you have two grandchildren."

Martha nods proudly. "I do have two beautiful grandchildren."

"I understand she never married."

"Yes. Unfortunately, today's men do not assume their responsibilities."

"Is she working now?"

"No. After her graduation, she could not find work. It is very difficult to find work in such a specialized area of education, but now she is working on her doctorate degree to be more qualified when looking for work."

Dorothy puts her left hand on her waist, and with the right hand, she scratches her head. Then, in a mocking way she tells her.

"Let me see if I understand what you say. Maira is an eternal student who has never worked. She is living off her parents and in the process, she has had two children, one of African descent and the other of Asian descent, but she has no husband. She does not live in a marginalized area as I do because she still lives with you in a parasitic way."

Dorothy pauses a bit and gives the final punch.

"Just as you gave me advice as a mother, I want to give you advice as a daughter. Tell her that instead of studying marine biology, she should have studied international relations, because her talent is in the procreation of different races. And finally, tell her what you meant is to open her mind, not her legs."

An enraged Martha replies.

"I don't slap you only out of respect to your mother. I hope I don't ever see your face again. I'm sorry, Sara, but I'm leaving. I never thought your daughter would disrespect me in such a way."

Sara angrily orders Dorothy to apologize to Martha immediately. Dorothy, with the same temperament as her mother, answers her.

"She has been provoking me from the beginning and you didn't stop her. Nothing I have said is a lie, nor do I have to retract it. It is obvious that it bothers you more what people say about your friend's daughter than when it's about your own daughter. I don't care if she stays, but if I'm the one who bothers you, tell me and we'll go right now."

Sara is surprised. She did not expect her daughter to rebel that way. But she knows deep down Dorothy has put up a lot with Martha's provocations. Sara takes Martha by the hand and tells her,

"Please don't go. I will have a talk with her and put her in her place, but let's not spoil the party."

"I'm sorry, Sara. You know to me you are like a sister, but she is your daughter and the one who must go is me. Our friendship is not going to be ruined by a spoiled and disrespectful girl, believe me. I feel sorry for you having such a daughter."

Dorothy puts both hands on her waist now, looks at her mother, and asks her with fire in her eyes.

"Are you going to answer her, or do I have to?"

Sara understands that her daughter has reached her limits, and her friend Martha is continuing to provoke Dorothy. Sara looks at Martha and sadly tells her.

"I think you're right. You'd better go, and we'll talk another day."

Ricardo, Frank Sr., and Frank Jr. are talking on the patio when Ricky comes eating the cupcake. Ricky stands next to his father, and Ricardo puts his hand on Ricky's shoulder.

Frank Jr. asks Ricardo in a mocking way.

"What happened a few days ago that the police had to go to your neighbor's house on an emergency call?"

Ricardo responds without any malice.

"That was terrible. It was a misunderstanding that almost ended very badly. How do you know? Who told you?"

"I heard the call on the police radio. That's why I know it was at your neighbors' house. I also heard that you were Tasered."

Ricardo throws his head back and raises his eyebrows.

"Oh! That was terrible. But who told you?"

Frank answers with a smile.

"When the officers verified the criminal record of all who were involved, and I heard your names. That Taser is terrible. I know it because during the certification, we went through that."

Ricky responds. "Yes, it's terrible. Dad was screaming very loudly. The policeman was holding the Taser in his hand, and two cables were sticking out of the Taser stock into my dad's back. It seemed as if the policeman was fishing, and Dad was a fish out of water."

Frank and his father laughed, but Ricardo did not.

Frank Jr. points his finger at Ricky.

"That was for not stopping when the officer ordered it."

"Dad thought I was in danger and ran to protect me."

"Yes, but he did not obey the order of the officer, and now you see the result."

Ricardo responds, a bit annoyed.

"If I believe that my family is in danger, I will do it a thousand times more."

Ricky is staring at Frank without blinking. Frank looks at him, and when he sees Ricky staring at him without saying anything, he asks him.

"Do you want to tell me something?"

"Yes, I want to ask you something."

"Fine, ask. You have my full attention."

"If you knew we were all involved, why didn't you show up to the scene?"

"Because I'm a lieutenant. I'm not an officer. I have sergeants and officers who respond to calls, and then they report back to me."

"My grandfather would not agree with you."

"Don't tell me your grandfather was a policeman?"

"Yes, he was a police captain, and he said that many times he had to pull the ears of lazy lieutenants because they did not go to the scene of an emergency calls. What surprises me the most is that you knew that your sister was involved and yet you did not care to stop by to check up on her. I don't think anyone would have Tasered you."

Frank Sr. changes his expression, clearly looking annoyed now.

"Why did you not go to check on your sister?"

Frank sees that his father is upset because Ricky has unmasked him. Frank does not respond and only makes signs with his hands as if to say that what happened was not important. Frank Sr. asks him even louder.

"I asked you a question: Why didn't you go check on your sister? Dammit!"

Frank lowers his head and answers.

"It was my mistake. I am sorry."

Frank then angrily turns around to go inside, and he looks at Ricky, muttering. "Gossip bastard!"

Ricardo, offended, gets in his way.

"What did you call my son? Let's see if you have the balls to repeat it again."

Frank Sr. quickly gets in the way pushing the two of them off each other and tells them.

"You better respect my house. There is no one more macho than me here. If someone wants to fight, let's start with me."

Ricardo takes a step back and responds.

"It was not my intention to disrespect you or your house."

Frank Jr. is standing in a defiant way. His father asks him.

"Do you want to fight? You better disappear before I slap you right here in front of everybody."

Frank knows that his father will not think twice to slap him in front of everybody and goes inside the house.

During the photo session, Frank Sr. asks the photographer to take a photo of them with their two children. Then Dorothy calls Ricardo to join them for one more photo. Ricardo takes Ricky by the hand, and they stand next to Dorothy. When Frank Jr. sees that Ricardo and Ricky are going to join the photo, he steps aside. Dorothy does not realize that her brother is not in the photo, because they are on Sara's side.

After a while, Frank calls his son aside and asks him.

"Why did you step out of the photo with your sister?"

"No, I was in the photo with her, but I didn't want to be in when she called her tribe. My sister has become White trash. She is married to a wet ass, and now they have added a little bastard to the tribe. He is a son of who knows who. Are you going to deny you called them that yourself?"

Frank could not answer him back since he himself had said several times his daughter had turned into White trash and that her husband was a wet ass.

At the end of the party, Dorothy helps her mother in the kitchen while Ricardo and Ricky help Frank Sr. gather the chairs from the patio. Frank Jr. has been sitting in the kitchen, talking on the phone the whole time. When Ricardo, Frank, and Ricky end up in the patio, they enter the kitchen. Ricardo says.

"Now that the two of you are together, and before we forget, we want to give you our gift for your ruby wedding anniversary."

Ricardo takes out of his pocket an envelope and hands it to Frank and his wife, Sara. Frank opens the envelope curiously and sees it is a cruise for two. Frank nods in acceptance, saying.

"Thanks! This is a surprise! Whose idea, was it?"

Sara can't stand her curiosity and asks.

"What is it? Tell me, please."

"It is a cruise through the Riviera Maya."

Sara kisses Dorothy and totally ignores Ricardo.

"The cake was enough. You should not have spent so much!"

"It's nothing. The cake is a gift from Mr. Bob, my boss. That's why Ricardo and I decided to give you something that you could enjoy together."

Frank Jr. mockingly asks Dorothy.

"Is that the cruise you canceled, and now you are giving it to Dad?"

"You are wrong. This one is better because it is a new ship. In addition, it is a gift for both to enjoy, to rest and have fun. It is not like the gift that you gave to Mom to make alterations in your uniforms."

Frank stands up, annoyed.

"Mama has always wanted a sewing machine."

"Sure. Dad was crazy about a sewing machine too." Dorothy responds angrily.

Frank, more than offended, feeling exposed, tries to counterattack in a quite offensive way.

"I know Mr. Bob. He is an old millionaire widower who does not do or give anything if he does not receive something in return. I doubt that that cake was a gift."

Ricardo stands up and confronts him.

"What do you mean? Say it at once if you are a man!"

Frank, defiantly looking into Ricardo's eyes, responds.

"I have only said what I know and see.

Ricardo is breathing heavily, the veins on his neck looking like they are about to explode.

Frank, seeing that he has Ricardo enraged, in a mocking way, spreads his arms with the palms open, then answers.

"If there is something I do not know, tell me."

Ricardo is going to raise his hand when Ricky, like a lightning bolt, comes in front of him and, with his typical way of squinting and pointing an accusatory finger, says to Frank.

"My grandfather used to say that family is not chosen, that God gives them to us to love and defend them, not to harm them or try to destroy them."

Frank is surprised by Ricky's attitude.

"Where did you get the idea I want to hurt or destroy my sister?"

Ricky, in the same mocking way that Frank used, responds to him by saying.

"I have only said what I know and see. If there is something else, tell me."

Ricky's tease is so comical and timely that Sara and her husband burst out laughing. Frank, however, turns red. The roles have changed. Now it is Frank who is about to explode.

Ricky continues.

"My grandfather also said, 'You must treat everyone fairly and with respect, because you never know from whom you might need in the future.'"

Frank responds hurtfully.

"I don't think I'll need anything from a supermarket cashier or a furniture deliveryman. I eat in restaurants, and my apartment is already furnished."

Dorothy, still offended, yells at Ricardo and Ricky.

"The party is over! Everyone home!"

Ricardo answers. "You are right. It would be better if we go home."

Dorothy and Ricardo have already taken a few steps toward the door when Dorothy realizes that Ricky is still standing in front of Frank with his arms open and his fingers spread out, moving up and down, as if he was moving his wings to flight.

Dorothy grabs him by the collar of his suit and gives him a pull that almost lifts him up.

"I said home! Or are you deaf?"

Ricky, surprised, exclaims.

"Wow! What a temper this lady has!"

This time everyone laughs, except Frank, who is standing in the same place as if were turned into a statue.

CHAPTER 10

Dorothy returns home after a gynecologist's appointment. Ricardo and Dorothy have tried to conceive a child for almost a year to no avail. Ricardo notices the sad face of his wife and hugs her, trying to comfort her.

"What is happening, dear? Why are you like this?"

"The doctor has told me that the only way for me to have a child is through in vitro fertilization, and my insurance does not cover it. He told me that because I am high-risk. I cannot work for those nine months. It costs a fortune, and without working, it is impossible!"

Dorothy, enraged, to vent her frustration, yells at her husband.

"It is not fair! There are women who bear children like rats. There are those who abandon their children. There are even those who kill them! I want to have a child and I am denied!"

Dorothy cries inconsolably in the arms of her husband. Ricardo caresses her and, with a soft voice, tells her.

"We will have our children. God will not abandon us."

******

Ricky's uncle Tony keeps talking to Ricky every other day. Tony calls Ricky one day and says.

"I have good news for you."

"What's up, Uncle?"

"You may not remember, but Grandpa started a project to build a resort on Cayo Samaná in the Bahamas. It is on a small island located in the center of the Bahamas. Grandpa wanted to do the project as a gift for your mommy and me, but his sudden death put a stop everything. Now, after several years, yesterday I received a call from the Bahamian government telling me our project, together with the US International Construction, has been selected. I must leave for Nassau to make the final presentation. Your mom must be very happy, because that was her dream too. You will be the owner of her part. I am sure that Grandpa and your mom were doing something from up there to make this come true. I will keep you informed, and I will continue calling you as always. I love you very much, my crazy little chick!"

"Me too. I miss you so much!"

******

Albert Infante is the owner of the US company International Construction, based in Boston. He is of medium height, and heavy, wearing thick glasses. He is known for talking down to his employees. He is also known for his relentless way of negotiating. He uses all kinds of legal and nonlegal tactics to get the contracts. Gilbert Roy is Albert strongman. Gilbert is a retired Boston police detective in his sixties, of whom there are rumors of involvement with organized crime.

Albert is in his office on the tenth floor, which has large glass walls overlooking the city. His secretary and the accountant are giving him a report when Gilbert knocks on the door.

"Come in, Gilbert. It is time for you to show up."

Gilbert walks in, greets them warmly, and replies that he is busy on his Manhattan errand. Albert responds immediately, saying.

"Forget about that project. We have other priorities now."

Albert tells the secretary and accountant.

"I need to speak to Gilbert alone for a moment. We will continue at another time."

Once they are alone, Gilbert sits down, crosses his legs, and leans back.

"Oh! This must be very important for you if you've decided to put the Manhattan project aside."

"Yes, it is. I received a call from the Bahamian government; they want to continue with the Cayo Samaná project."

Gilbert is surprised. "I thought that project was dead?"

"So did I, but the new government thinks differently. We are competing with a Florida company. The owner of the company died, and his grandson is the one who currently represents it. My contact in the Bahamian government informed me that they have an ecological project, and that surpasses us in everything. The only way to beat them is if he leaves the negotiating table. You have twenty-four hours to bring me all the information on this Tony Clark to see what his weak points are. I will wait for you here tomorrow at 1:00 P.M."

Gilbert stands up and responds.

"How many generations of this Tony do you want me to find out?"

Albert stands up and walks over to a painting on the wall.

"This is personal to me. The old man who founded that company in Florida, someone named William Clark, won a contract from my father about thirty years ago. My father ignored me and played fair, so he lost the contract. That was the only contract we have ever lost."

Albert, looking at the painting, adds.

"I will show you, Father, I was right. This will be for you."

Then he turns to Gilbert and tells him.

"Find out how many generations it takes until you see a weak point to attack."

"Consider it done. Tomorrow I will not only have the information but also the plan to completely remove it from the negotiation."

The next day, Gilbert shows up at Albert's office with a briefcase full of documents. Albert is alone with Gilbert in the office. He has been waiting for him all morning.

"What have you got for me? I hope it is good because the amount of money you charged me with is exaggerated."

Gilbert is tall, gray-haired, always dressed flawlessly, and his presence inspires respect.

"The sum is justified when I tell you the plan to get rid of Tony not just from this contract but for good."

Albert leans back in his chair with a smile.

"Well, if that is so, I do not mind the payment. Now, explain to me what you have and what is the plan.'

Gilbert puts the briefcase on the table, starts pulling out documents.

"As you will see, Tony Clark is not the grandson of Mr. William Clark. He is the adopted son of William Clark's son. His real name is Tony Martinelly. He was adopted when he was a troubled teenager. The Clarks gave him an education. He became a lawyer, and he has been working at the company since graduation. Tony has been faithful to his new family and has proven to be a true steward of great vision. When Mr. William and his son died in a car accident, Virginia Clark, who had an out-of-wedlock son, and Tony were left with the company. Virginia died of cancer, and only Tony Clark and Ricky, Virginia's son, remain. For some mysterious reason, Tony took the boy to live with his biological father. The boy lives in a marginalized area, virtually in poverty."

Albert, clearly annoyed, replies.

"And for that fairy tale I have paid you thirty thousand dollars?" What the fuck is wrong with you? I don't need to know that shit! That does not help me at all!"

"No, sir, this information is like finding a diamond."

Albert punches the table.

"Well, polish the diamond, because what I see is a piece of glass. I have only one week to negotiate this, and I want Tony out of the game."

"He will be, sir, but I need thirty thousand more."

Albert takes the briefcase and throws it against the wall.

"How dare you ask me for thirty thousand dollars more! Do you think I am an idiot?"

Gilbert stands up and, visibly angry, tells Albert.

"You calm down! You don't talk to me like that. I am a professional, and if I tell you that Tony will go down, that is how it will be. Where you see a fairy tale, I see a solution to all problems. But it will be an operation that must be performed by professionals, not cheap pickpockets!"

Albert sits down and, still not very convinced, tells Gilbert.

"Explain yourself, and make sure what you say is true."

Gilbert picks up the briefcase, puts the documents inside, and responds.

"I can reimburse your thirty thousand dollars and it's all over, but if you want to continue, it's thirty thousand dollars more, and not one more threat. Now, say what you want to do."

Albert has never treated Gilbert that way. He understands that Gilbert is not just any employee and that he is not afraid of him. Albert takes a deep breath; he is desperate and has no other alternative.

"Okay, I'll listen to your plan."

Gilbert stares at him and replies.

"If you want to hear the ending of the fairy tale, it's thirty thousand dollars."

Albert responds in a lower tone.

"We have known each other for many years and have always worked without any problem."

"That is true, but you have never disrespected me until now, and just because I work for you does not mean that I am your employee. You hire me because you know that I solve problems that nobody else can."

Albert goes to write a check, and Gilbert stops him.

"I cannot pay the people that I must hire in checks. It must be cash."

Albert gets up, kicks the desk, and opens the safe. Albert takes out the cash and puts it in front of Gilbert.

"Here you go. Now finish the fucking story."

Gilbert, to show that he is the one in control, takes his time putting the money inside the briefcase, and when he finishes, he leans back, crosses his legs.

"It is very simple. There are only two Clarks left in the family, Tony Clark and Virginia Clark's son. If Virginia Clark's son disappears, Tony will become the sole heir to the fortune."

Albert, to the point of exploding, asks.

"And what the hell do I care if this guy gets richer than what he is now?"

"That will not happen because we will make it look as if Tony wanted to get rid of him to take what belongs to his nephew. This way, he will be under investigation or in prison. When I kidnap the child that will bring in the FBI, since it is a kidnapping case. We can't recruit just any idiot. Tony will abandon the negotiations and return to Florida to look for his nephew, and if he does not do so, he will increase suspicions of his being involved, so the FBI will most likely bring him to Florida for investigation."

Albert slaps the table.

"Fantastic! Excellent! Forgive my previous attitude. You deserve all my respect! Do you have the people for that job?"

Gilbert grins wickedly.

"That's the most difficult, because I need people who are smart enough not to get caught and stupid enough not to realize that we are going to give them away."

Albert is surprised, extends his arm, and puts his hand in the air to stop him.

"Wait, wait, wait. Are we going to give them away? Have you gone crazy?"

"Yes, but we will make them believe that they are working for Tony. When they get caught, they will try to negotiate a lower sentence by delivering Tony to the authorities."

Albert gets up from his chair, slowly walks over to the safe, and takes out ten thousand dollars, handing it to Gilbert. Gilbert looks at him suspiciously; he does not understand why Albert is giving him more money.

"What is this money for?"

"It's a bonus for you. You've earned it with your cool plan. If you need anything else, let me know. I need you to get started on it as soon as possible."

Gilbert takes the money and tells him.

"Remember, you cannot talk to me about this over the phone. I will be in Miami, in charge of the operation. You will stay informed through the news." Gilbert says goodbye to Albert and reminds him once again not to use the phone.

Two days later, Gilbert, through his contacts in the underworld, meets with two Colombians in a Miami Beach restaurant.

Gilbert wears a tropical shirt and dark glasses. They are sitting at the tables outside the restaurant, enjoying the view. The two candidates chosen by Gilbert appear at the restaurant separately. The first is Francisco Robledo, of medium height, black hair, and few words. He is a paramilitary drug trafficker who has entered the country three years ago through the Mexican border and moved from state-to-state committing crime. The second is Alex Cuervo, tall, white skin, black hair, and wearing prescription glasses. Alex is an ex-guerrilla drug trafficker who has a scar on the left side of his neck from a bullet that almost killed him. His specialty is kidnapping and extortion.

Gilbert introduces himself under the name Thomas and has them believe that he works for Tony. Once the three of them are seated at the table, Gilbert asks the candidates.

"Do you know each other?"

They both look at each other and answer. "No, Mr. Thomas."

"I am very glad to know that. The less you know about your past, the easier the operation will be. The boss who is going to pay you wants both of you to leave Florida when it is over and not keep in touch with each other. The work is very simple. You will pick up a child from school and take care of him for a week. You will receive fifteen thousand dollars at the beginning, and fifteen after the job is completed."

Alex takes a sip of his drink and tells Gilbert.

"Mr. Thomas, I want it to be clear to you that I do not kill children. If this operation has that purpose, you can forget about me right now."

"No one has said the child will die. We will only guard him for a week, that's all. Do you think you can handle that?"

"Yes, Mr. Thomas. I have no problem with that. And forgive me, but I have been traumatized. I have seen many children die at the hands of the paramilitaries in my country. Something like that is totally out of the question."

Gilbert is concerned, his two best prospects could damage the operation for a political issue.

"The first thing I ask you is not to talk about your past. That you are going to do a job and never see each other again. I think that is not so much to ask for thirty thousand dollars."

Robledo responds with great cynicism. "Mr. Thomas do not worry. I will not be the one who brings problems. I assure you that I can do the job professionally with this guerrilla man or with any other bandit as long as he respects me. You can count on me for whatever it is, and if you give me fifteen thousand more, I will kill the child, the child's mother. And this guerrilla man? I will kill him for free."

Alex, with his stone-cold face and without blinking, answers.

"Mr. Thomas, from my part everything is clear. I do not see why we cannot work together. My goal is to do the job and not talk stupidities."

Gilbert, in other circumstances, would have fired them both, but he does not have time to contact other prospects. So, he decides to continue with them. Gilbert puts his right hand on his chin and stares at the two Colombians. The Colombians are serious and do not say a word. Glances are exchanged between the three, as if each one is trying to find out what they are thinking.

Gilbert breaks the silence and tells them.

"I have no problem giving you the job. However, I want it to be very clear that if Mr. Tony Clark pays you that amount of money for this simple job, he will not mind paying someone else to keep you safe six feet underground forever if you fail. Don't mess it up because whoever plays with fire always gets burned. Do we agree?"

Robledo responds.

"I have no problem. It is only one week."

Alex responds in the same way, and Gilbert feels relief. His operation was on the verge of failure before starting.

Gilbert pulls out a notebook and tells them.

"You will do everything exactly as I tell you. You cannot deviate from the plan."

He turns to Alex.

"Alex, you will go to school and pick up the kid at dismissal time."

Gilbert gives him a picture of Ricky and tells him.

"Remember his face. You will tell him that his uncle Tony sent you. Make sure you tell him that Tony sent you, otherwise, he won't go with you."

Then he tells Robledo.

"You will be the driver. You will take them to this address, and in the glove compartment, there will be a remote control to open the garage. Once you enter the garage, close it immediately. One of you will stay with the child inside the house, and the other will wait outside. A fumigation company will then come to tent the house. The company will install signs on the property that say, "Beware of poison gas," to keep the neighbors away. This will make them think it is poison, and nobody will get close to the house. Whoever stays outside will leave with the fumigation company and return in the afternoon with a marked private security unit and stay outside overnight. At dawn, the roles are exchanged. You will be on duty outside and the other stay inside with the child. On the third day, the company will remove the tent and you will move to another residence. Everything else remains the same. When the company removes the tent for the second time, we will sedate the child and leave him at a bus stop. You must be extremely careful because this will be a high-profile case and the FBI will be involved. There can be no fingerprints or DNA. Remember that your skin is at stake. Any questions?"

They both respond without looking at each other. "No, Mr. Thomas."

Gilbert pulls out his phone and puts it on the table. He calls Albert and puts the phone on speaker. Gilbert has changed Albert's profile photo to Tony's. His goal is for the Colombians to see Tony's photo when he calls Gilbert.

When Albert answers the call, Gilbert instantly tells him.

"Hello, Mr. Tony. I want to tell you that the recruits are ready to execute the project. Do you have something else to add?"

Albert responds. "No, Mr. Thomas. Just warn them that I won't forgive them if you fail me."

"I don't see why you should worry, Mr. Tony. They are two professionals."

Gilbert hangs up the phone.

"Well, everything is approved by Mr. Tony. Let's have lunch; I invite you both."

The Colombians do not waste any time and ask for the most expensive in the menu, running a bill up to $325.25. Gilbert does not want to take out his credit card to prevent the Colombians from seeing his real name. Gilbert has only $330 in cash. He puts it on the table and tells the waiter.

"I'll pay for the food, and they will take care of the tip."

The waiter takes the money and responds. "Thank you very much, sir."

Gilbert gets up and leaves without saying goodbye. The Colombians stare at each other, wondering who is going to pay for the tip. Alex asks the waiter.

"How much is the tip?"

"Usually, it's fifteen percent of the bill, sir."

"How much is the bill?" Robledo asks.

"That's $325 dollars, sir."

"That is almost fifty dollars, boy!" Yells Robledo.

"Tell me, what the hell did you do to earn fifty dollars in an hour?" Alex says mockingly.

Robledo gets up and, in a threatening way, tells the waiter.

"In my town we kick the waiter in the ass as a tip. Tell me, how much is the bill again? I will be glad to give you a generous tip."

The frightened young waiter takes a step back and responds.

"It is not mandatory to tip. Have a good afternoon."

The next day, Robledo and Alex are parked outside the school, waiting for Ricky to come out. They see Ricky riding on the back of Tamian's bike. Alex stops in the middle of the sidewalk, and Tamian brakes to avoid hitting him. Alex tells Ricky.

"I need you to come with me."

"I don't go with strangers. Neither do I talk to them."

"I'm not a stranger. Your uncle Tony sent me to look for you. It is an emergency. After you see your uncle, I will return you home."

Ricky is surprised when Alex mentions his uncle Tony by his name.

"Why didn't he come or send someone I know?"

"Your uncle must go to the Bahamas this afternoon, and he doesn't have time. It must be something very important for him to send me so urgently."

Ricky gets off the bike and says to Tamian.

"Go ahead and I'll be back later."

Tamian, confused, asks him.

"Who is your uncle Tony?"

"I'll tell you about it later, but don't tell anyone I went to see Uncle Tony."

Alex and Robledo carry out the plan. They have Ricky chained one leg to a bedpost, giving him only a few feet of movement. Robledo is in charge of taking care of him the first day. Ricky does not stop talking and demanding his release. Robledo, tired of listening to Ricky, takes duct tape and covers his mouth.

Later that evening, Dorothy and Ricardo arrive from work and realize that Ricky is not there. They think he is at Kenya's house since sometimes he has stayed until seven thirty. Ricardo, hugging his wife, tells her.

"What do you think if we take advantage Ricky is not here to order a baby?"

Ricardo and his wife enter the room and undress each other as fast as they can. They make passionate love, always thinking that Ricky could spoil it at any moment. Both are exhausted after a long day at work and spending what little energy they have left making love. Ricardo and Dorothy are lying down, facing the ceiling, holding hands. Dorothy looks at her watch and sees that it is 7:30 p.m. and she hasn't heard Ricky yet.

"Love, don't you think it's kind of late for Ricky to be bothering the neighbors?"

"No. He must be in his room. I am sure that he came home, and we did not hear him."

Ricardo gets out of bed and goes to check on his son. He knocks on the door, and having heard no answer, he opens it and sees that Ricky is not there.

Ricardo closes the door, returns to his room, and tells his wife.

"This kid wants me to punish him again. I have told him he should be home by six thirty the latest!"

Ricardo puts on his clothes, and Dorothy acts with complete indifference.

"I couldn't care less if he lives at Kenya's house. When was the last time we had a moment of intimacy? He is always there to fuck everything up at the right time!"

Ricardo does not answer and goes out to look for Ricky. Ricardo knocks on the door, and Kenya looks at him with curiosity. She is used to having Ricky in the afternoons, but he has not shown up today. Ricardo, a little annoyed, tells Kenya.

"Forgive me, Mrs. Kenya, but Ricky needs to come home. It's already 8:45 p.m., and don't wait for him for a week. He's grounded. I warned him he should be home when we come home from work."

Kenya puts her hand on her heart, and her eyes widen.

"Oh my god! Please, Ricardo, do not play like that. Tell me that you are joking!"

"This is no joke. Tell Ricky to come out immediately." Ricardo responds firmly.

"Tamian told me Ricky ran off with a man after school."

Ricardo turns pale and gives a cry that comes from his soul.

"What did you say? Where is Tamian?"

Kenya calls Tamian and starts crying uncontrollably. Tamian shows up, scared to see his mother crying. Kenya tells her son.

"Tamian, tell Mr. Ricardo what happened this afternoon."

Tamian, scared, thinking that he is in trouble, begins to speak between sobs.

"We were coming home, and a man came between us and took Ricky away in a silver car."

"But what did he tell him? Ricky doesn't go with strangers. Tell me the details."

Tamian remembers that Ricky asked him not to say anything about his uncle Tony, so he tells them.

"The man told him he had to show him something and that someone would bring it back."

Kenya slaps Tamian over the head twice.

"Stupid jerk, why would you keep something like that from us?"

Tamian runs to his room crying and screaming.

"I didn't know anything!"

Kenya picks up the phone and calls the police immediately. The call goes on the air, and the sergeant responds to the call with the reporting officer. The sergeant calls the lieutenant, as it is required by protocol, but knowing that Frank does not want contact with his sister, he calls him on his cell phone.

"Frank, you should stop by."

Frank answers him. "If it is the house where we had that incident where my sister was involved, I prefer to stay away from there."

"Frank, we are talking about a possible kidnapping of a minor."

"Tell me, Ramos, are we talking about the lady's son?"

"No, he is the same boy who caused the incident, your sister's stepson."

"I will stay away even more now. Bring me the report as soon as you have it completed. That kid is such a troublemaker that we would have some peace if he disappeared for a while."

The sergeant is very close to Frank, but he sees that things are going in the wrong direction. He wants to distance himself but, at the same time, try to make his friend Frank reconsider his position.

"Lieutenant, you should stop by the scene."

"Sergeant, I think I'm the one giving the orders here. Or am I wrong?"

The sergeant does not respond and just hangs up the phone on him.

Meanwhile, Dorothy has the dinner ready in the kitchen, waiting for them to return. She steps outside of the house and sees two police cars parked in front of Kenya's house and the front-door neighbor talking with one of the officers.

Dorothy closes the door and exclaimes.

LITTLE RICKY

"Shit! What has this demon done now? I am not going over there so that they throw me to the ground like last time."

Dorothy starts to watch television, waiting for them to return. When she sees that it is almost ten o'clock and Ricardo has not returned, she decides to go see what has happened. When Dorothy opens the door, she sees Kenya crying and Ricardo hugging her with watery eyes.

"They kidnapped him, love, they kidnapped him!"

Dorothy, totally confused, exclaims.

"How did they kidnap him? Who the fuck is going to kidnap Ricky?"

Ricardo answers between sobs.

"There are many sick people on the loose. There are sexual predators, organ traffickers, sex traffickers where children are sold. Whatever it was, I assure you that it is not good at all."

Dorothy bursts into tears and feels guilty for not paying attention to what is happening.

Sergeant Ramos tries to comfort her.

"Calm down, ma'am, we're already setting an Amber Alert. That's an alert that goes out on all Florida phones with your son's information. Tomorrow early we will check all the security cameras, and we will continue searching everywhere."

Dorothy asks the sergeant.

"Is Lieutenant Frank on duty today?"

"Yes, ma'am, he is on duty."

"Is he informed of the situation?"

"Yes, ma'am, he is aware of the situation."

Dorothy calls Frank's cell phone, and Frank doesn't answer her. Dorothy then asks the sergeant.

"Can I use your cell phone?"

"Who do you want to call?"

"I need to call Lieutenant Frank."

"But didn't you just call him?"

"Yes, but he did not answer me. I am sure that if I call him from your phone he will answer."

The sergeant does not want to get involved. But he also knows if he does not allow her to use his phone, it will look like he is covering up for Frank.

"I will give you the phone only if you promise me you will not involve me in your family problems."

Dorothy calls Frank, and Frank responds instantly.

"What's happening, Ramos?"

"Why didn't you answer my call?"

"I did not hear it."

"And how did you immediately respond to his number?"

"What? Did you want me not to hear it either?'

"Are you aware of what is happening?"

"Yes. Sergeant Ramos informed me and is making the report."

"Are you not going to stop by here?"

"It is not necessary. He is a professional, and I will take care of passing all the information out to the detectives in the morning."

Dorothy can't contain her anger and yells at him.

"You are a shithead! Who the fuck do you think you are? You are a stupid, spoiled asshole!"

Frank separates the phone from his ear and puts it in front of him as if he were talking on the police radio, blows her a kiss, and responds.

"Happy Easter to you too baby."

Frank is in his girlfriend's apartment, which is located out of the city. He puts the phone on the bedside table and says.

"I couldn't care less if that little asshole disappears for a while."

Frank's girlfriend is a young woman named Yurisleidy, a girl who has arrived on a raft from Cuba two years earlier. Yurisleidy has on a very sexy robe. She stands in front of him and asks him,

"What happened, dear? Take off your uniform. I'm going to take away that angry face of yours."

Frank spends at least two hours every night at Yurisleidy's apartment. Frank puts his hands on her shoulders, makes her kneel, and tells her.

"I don't think today is a good idea for me to take off my uniform, but you can entertain yourself for a while."

Yurisleidy, at the young age of twenty-five, has traveled more miles than the space shuttle. She opens Frank's zipper and gives him oral sex.

Back at Kenya's, an independent reporter who listens to the emergency frequency channels is the first to arrive. He is the kind of reporter who will sell his report or video to the highest bidder. The reporter speaks with everyone on the scene and then shows up early at the police station to interview the chief of police regarding the kidnapping. The reporter sees the chief of police arriving and shoves the microphone and camera in his face, taking the chief by surprise.

"Excuse me, Chief. What steps are you taking to investigate the abduction of the eight-year-old boy that occurred yesterday at 1:30 P.M. when he was leaving school?"

The chief's jaw drops. He has no idea of such news. The journalist, like a shark who has smelled blood, realizes that the chief has no idea what he is talking about.

"Do you mean a child was kidnapped in your city almost twenty-four hours ago and your department has not informed you of anything?"

The chief's face changes color. When this report comes out on the television channels, he will be the center of everyone's joke for the day.

"Yes, I am informed. I was on the way to a meeting about the case to make decisions and plans for going forward."

The reporter knows he won the lottery and wants to make the most of it.

"Can you tell me the name of the child and his description, so our viewers are alerted?"

"Sorry, it is an ongoing investigation. I can't give you any more information." The chief turns to leave, but the journalist gives the chief the last thrust, a thrust from which he will not recover.

"Sorry, Chief, but this is not a criminal investigation where no information can be disclosed. This is an investigation of the kidnapping of an innocent eight-year-old, where information must be disclosed immediately because every second counts and the life of an innocent is in danger."

The enraged chief turns around to answer, but his blank face gives him away. There is nothing he can think or say. He just stares at the reporter.

The reporter savors his moment of fame at the chief's expense and says in a consoling tone.

"You don't need to respond. It is obvious that your department has not informed you of this yet. It is your fault that no procedures are in place for a case like this and they have not been implemented or even started. Your procedures need to be updated. I have gathered enough information, which I will be glad to put at your disposal if you require it."

The chief is slow to respond. He is about to explode from the sudden rise in his blood pressure but holds back. He responds calmly.

"I thank you for your collaboration, and I assure you that this will be my priority."

Sergeant Ramos finds out what has happened in front of the station between the journalist and the police chief. Ramos immediately calls Frank, who looks at his phone and sees that Ramos is calling him, but he decides not to answer him. Frank is angry at him for almost ordering him to show up on the scene and then lending his phone to Dorothy so she can call him.

The chief walks into his office, and without saying good morning. He orders the secretary to call the shift captain and the lieutenant who was working the night shift to his office immediately. The concerned secretary sees that the chief is in an extremely bad mood and proceeds to communicate the message to the captain and then to Frank.

"Lieutenant, the chief wants to see you in his office right now."

Frank, without giving it any importance, answers.

"I am checking the reports from last night to close the shift. As soon as I finish, I will go to his office."

"Lieutenant, this is an order. Delegate that to a sergeant and come immediately.'

"What is going on? What is the rush?"

"I have no idea, but he is fuming through his nose. I have never seen him so angry."

Sergeant Ramos walks into Frank's office, and Frank tells him.

"I need you to close the shift. The chief wants to see me at the office."

"Yes, I will close the shift, but I have to tell you something."

Frank looks at him, confused, when he sees the concern on Ramos's face.

Ramos tells him in a low voice.

"I called you several times this morning, and you didn't answer me."

Frank answers. "I had the phone muted by mistake. You should have called me on the radio."

Ramos is a little annoyed and replies.

"I was calling to help my friend Frank, not the lieutenant. I was calling you to tell you that a reporter this morning caught the chief by surprise when he entered the station and made him look like an ass in front of the camera."

"What do I have to do with it, Sergeant?"

"Oh! Is that the way you want it to be? So let me tell you, Lieutenant, that everything is related to yesterday's kidnapping. You and I have known each other from the academy. I knew you were arrogant, but I never thought you were stupid. Now, go see how you can fix that mess and keep me out of it. From now on, you are on your own. I am warning you."

Frank's face changes instantly, and the arrogance disappears. Concern is visible on his face. Frank is number 1 on the promotion list for captain, and something like this will surely disqualify him.

Frank walks into the chief's office and sees the captain sitting down. Frank enters and sits next to the captain. The two are facing the chief.

The captain asks the chief.

"Can you tell me what's going on? We are both here now."

The chief, pointing a finger at the captain, tells him.

"What is the protocol when a child is abducted? And I do not mean that the father or the mother took him."

The captain has no idea what has happened. He looks at Frank, seeking an answer, but Frank's face is one of terror.

"Chief, the protocol to follow is that both the sector sergeant and the lieutenant on duty must go to the scene. An Amber Alert must also be sent. That way, the child's and the suspects' information is on the phones of all Florida residents. All superiors in the chain of command must be informed, including the FBI, as they have jurisdiction on kidnapping cases."

The chief asks the lieutenant. "Is that correct, Lieutenant?"

"Yes, Chief, that's our protocol."

"Did you know that an eight-year-old boy was kidnapped yesterday after leaving school?

The amazed captain responds.

"No, no, no, I don't know anything about it. What are you talking about?"

"And you, Lieutenant? Do you have something to say?"

"Chief, the captain doesn't know because the call came in at 8:15 P.M. He was off duty."

The captain, to save his skin, responds.

"That is not an excuse. They call me for thousands of stupid things after hours. How can you not call me about something like that?"

The chief tells the captain.

"In that case, you are not at fault, because the chain broke before reaching you."

The chief angrily tells the lieutenant.

"I want a detailed report from the starting point when this call went out to the end of the call. I want the names of all the participants and actions taken by each one."

The chief points to Frank and tells him.

"You have made me look like an ass in front of a reporter's camera, and everyone must be laughing at me on television. It will even be more serious if something happens to that child because of your incompetence. Leave my presence and don't come back until the report is finished."

Frank leaves the office and begins to think how he can work his way out of such a problem. He writes a long report where he tries to save himself, no matter who he would harm. Frank shows up at the chief's office with the report and puts it on his desk. The chief takes the report, puts it aside, and says.

"I want to hear your version before I read the report."

Frank convincingly begins to relate his version.

"Chief, I begin by admitting I am partly to blame for not listening to the call when it came on the air. Sergeant Ramos was in charge of taking a detailed report and alerting the corresponding authorities. The fact that he has not contacted me on the radio does not mean we have been indifferent to the case."

The chief opens the folder with the report, takes out the CD with the recordings of the communications related to the call, and asks him, "Is there any communication between you and Sergeant Ramos about this call?"

"No, Chief. You can verify it, but I'm sure Sergeant Ramos was not aware of this. Sergeant Ramos is a professional, and a mistake can be made by anyone. Unfortunately, that reporter was looking for a story and took advantage of this to find his five minutes of fame. We should not punish a sergeant who has an impeccable record for an unfortunate incident. I ask you to let me take care of the matter internally and I give you my word that an incident like this will never be repeated."

Frank takes a deep breath. He feels great relief when he sees the chief putting the folder aside and hears him say.

"You can leave. I have finished with you."

Frank thinks that the chief has concluded the incident and is about to leave when the chief tells him.

"I want you to bring me Officer Ramos."

Frank freezes. He feels chills down his spine.

"You mean Sergeant Ramos?"

"No, you heard me correctly, Lieutenant. I said Officer Ramos."

"Chief, Sergeant Ramos went home. His shift ended three hours ago."

The chief raises his tone.

"Lieutenant, what part do you not understand when I tell you that I want Officer Ramos in my office?"

"I understand perfectly, Chief, but if I call him, we will have to pay him overtime. You know that we are trying to eliminate unnecessary expenses."

"Since when are you the one who determines how to spend the budget? Bring me Officer Ramos! And you better start thinking about promoting a new sergeant."

Frank tries to hide his nervousness.

"Chief, please do it for me. Don't demote Ramos. He has many years of service, with an impeccable record. This will be viewed as an abusive punishment by the officers and will be a serious blow to the morale of the department."

Frank has managed to convince the chief that he is not at fault in the incident. The chief, in a lower tone, answers.

"I understand you, Frank. You and Ramos are friends from the academy and have always worked together. It is natural that you cover each other's backs. I admire your loyalty and friendship, but there is no going back. I want the two of you here before twelve noon."

Frank tries one last time.

"Tell me, Chief, what can I do to change your mind? I accept the responsibility and punishment that you deem necessary. I am a single man. My financial needs are not as high as those of Ramos, who has a family, and they are expecting a baby."

"You can't do anything, Frank. I really admire the value you give to friendship, but only Ramos and a miracle can make me change my mind. Don't talk about it anymore before I get mad at you too."

Frank calls Ramos and tells him. "The chief wants to see you in his office before twelve noon."

Ramos has just gone to bed, and he takes a few seconds to assimilate the news.

"Listen to me, Ramos. The chief wants you in his office before twelve noon."

"Shit! I told you, Frank, but you don't listen. Tell me what's going on!"

"You know it better than I do. That son of a bitch reporter humiliated him, and now he wants to take it out on someone. It will pass. I took responsibility for the matter and asked him to punish me. He keeps fucking around with it and wants to talk to you. The best thing for you to do is act sorry, and he will get over it. If he gives us a week's suspension, you will win, because you will have a week of vacation and I promise to pay for it out of my pocket. I am the guilty one, but as I told you, that idiot has his ego hurt. When you get to the station, call me and I will come in with you to calm down that idiot."

Two hours later, Frank and Ramos enter the chief's office. They both sit across from the chief, and Frank tells the chief.

"Please let me say a few words before you begin."

The chief leans back in the chair. He crosses his arms and responds to him.

"Go ahead, Lieutenant. Say what you need to say so you don't interrupt later."

"I just want to say that as the shift commander when the events occurred, I take responsibility once again and ask that Sergeant Ramos be excluded from all blame. I did not listen to the call, and that is a fault on my part. I have known Ramos since the beginning of my career and am a witness of his professionalism. Do not take my word, his record speaks for itself. He has never had a warning, has been an officer of integrity, and is an example for all."

When Frank finishes, the chief nods in approval and admiration at the same time.

"Excellent, Lieutenant. You should be a defense attorney."

The chief pulls out the CD from the folder and tells Ramos.

"I listened to all the transmissions of this call, and as the lieutenant says, at no time you inform him of the kidnapping. I can understand that someone, for whatever reason, may not hear a call, but being on the scene and not communicating to your superior what is happening in a case like this is a fault beyond the ordinary. Because of you, I am the joke of the entire county. I have seen my face on television on four local channels, so it means I have surely appeared on many more at the state level, and it may even be national. Because of you, I will have to answer the mayor, as this has become political. Your friend has tried in every way to intervene for you. I congratulate you for having friends like him, but I already told your friend to find your replacement. You are suspended for two weeks without pay, and you will return as an officer. If you have anything to say in your defense, say so now or shut up forever."

Ramos is pale, looking at Frank and the chief alternately, waiting for Frank to say something. Frank is speechless. Ramos understands that if he does not defend himself, his demotion is imminent. He has no alternative but to defend himself.

"Yes, Chief, I have a lot to say. I will begin by saying that it is true, I did not contact Lieutenant Frank through the police frequency. But I did call him on his cell phone and inform him of the seriousness of the case."

The chief is surprised and asks him.

"Why did you call the lieutenant on his cell phone instead of using our radio frequency?"

"I did it because the lieutenant does not want to get involved in calls concerning his sister. We had an emergency call a while ago where he was contacted, and he did not go to the scene. That call was not routine. It was a call where there was use of force, and the Taser gun was used. I also want to add that not only did I call him, but his sister called him as well. He refused to respond to the scene.'

The chief has turned red. His eyes are blazing.

"Is it true, what Ramos says?"

"Technically, yes, but I want to explain. I avoided attending the scene where my sister is involved so that it does not look like a conflict of interest or favoritism."

"Where were you when all this happened?"

"I was in the office, working on the quarterly reports."

"You have lied to my face, betrayed your friend, and tried to blame him to save yourself. Give me your phone."

"Chief, what do you want my phone for? I admit that it is true that he called me."

"That phone is not yours. It belongs to the city. I don't need a warrant to check your calls. Give me your phone. Get out! You are suspended until further notice!"

Frank stands up, gives the chief the phone, and leaves without being able to look Ramos in the eyes.

Ramos, thinking that he would also be disciplined, tells the chief.

"I am sorry for everything that happened, and I accept my share of responsibility."

The chief looks at him seriously and responds.

"Your mistake has been not knowing how to choose your friends. I hope you learn that in your work, friendship is not a defense for not following protocol. I'm going to check the lieutenant's phone to verify the calls. In the future, keep in mind that our communication is on the radio, not by phone. You can leave now."

Ramos, confused, without knowing if he is under suspension, asks.

"What will happen to me? Am I suspended?"

"If I told you to go, it is because you're still Sergeant Ramos. Now, walk away, unless you have something else to say."

"No, Chief, that was all from me."

The next day, Ricky's photo appears in all the news, along with surveillance videos showing ex-guerrilla Alex Cuervo, who is seen with Ricky entering a car. It is a vehicle that has been reported stolen. Detectives go to extraordinary lengths to compile surveillance videos and are able to follow the car from the school exit to the highway that leads to the Florida Keys. Gilbert has another car ready on the side of the road in an isolated area where they will make the vehicle exchange and return to Miami. Because no cameras are located at the exchange point, detectives do not know Ricky's final whereabouts or the vehicle in which he was transported. The lab practically tears the vehicle to pieces and only finds Ricky's fingerprints and DNA.

The FBI joins the case and immediately understands that there are professionals involved. The news adds sensation to the case when according to the media the city of Miami police lieutenant on duty when the incident was reported is the kid's uncle. Instead of worrying about his nephew, he did not inform his superiors. The tabloid media practically lists Frank as a suspect.

Two days after the kidnapping, and without having had any progress in the investigation or contact with the kidnappers, the chief calls Frank at his office. Frank walks in and sees the chief next to the sergeant in charge of the department's internal affairs.

Frank sits down and cordially says.

"Good morning, Chief. Good morning, Sergeant Gary."

The chief doesn't answer him; he just opens the folder and says.

"You are an embarrassment to the department. Internal affairs obtained a detailed report of your cell phone communications. This shows not only that you lied in the report, saying that you were at the station when the kidnapping call came out, but you have left the city every night and gone to a home in South Miami, where you spent almost the entire shift answering from your mobile. We traced your calls. It took us to a young woman named Yurisleidy, who confirmed that she has a romantic relation with you and that you visit her almost every night. In other words, the department pays you a salary for you to be fucking! This is not an incident. The records show that you have been doing the same for more than four months."

Frank cannot answer. He has deflated in the chair and looks like a Salvador Dalí painting, resembling the picture of the melted clock.

Frank, with almost no force in his voice, says.

"Chief, you are absolutely right. I deserve suspension or demotion. It is very hard when you have to learn from mistakes, but I will face it and get over it. Never in your life will you hear anything negative about me or my performance at work."

The chief responds.

"You are damn right about that because you are fired from the department! You are lucky we will not ask for those four months' salary back. You already have enough with the loss of your job and retirement. Get your identification and everything that belongs to the department together. An internal affairs officer will pick it up tomorrow. That's it, and as you said at the beginning, have a nice day."

Sergeant Gary and Frank leave the chief's office. Frank angrily tells Gary, "That old son of a bitch is acting like he's an example for everyone to look up to! I have heard stories about him when he was an officer. I am going to contact the union lawyer, and I am going to get my job back. My mistake is not serious enough for them to fire me from the department."

Gary stops and looks at Frank in bewilderment.

"What's up, Gary? Do you think I won't win this case?"

Gary answers sharply, "If you fight the case, you will go to jail."

"What makes you get such an idea, Gary?"

"Listen, asshole. The officer who interviewed your bitch is Officer Oliva. He is the same one you screwed up his sergeant promotion. That Yurisleidy said that she got to know you one night when she was driving drunk, and you stopped her. You parked her car and took her to her house, and since that night, you have been sleeping with her. She also said once, she was stopped for speeding seventy-five miles per hour in a thirty-mile-per-hour zone. She called you, and you made the ticket disappear. All that is recorded, and I omitted it so that you would not be imprisoned."

Frank lowers his head and realizes that his career has come to an end in a dishonorable way.

Chapter 11

On the third day, the kidnapping is on the news all over the country. The FBI has taken the case as a priority based on the great publicity given by the press. The FBI appoints J. Ocano, one of their best investigators, to work on the case. Ocano decides to start from the beginning, so he interviews Tamian again since he was the last person to see Ricky.

Ocano sits at the table with Tamian and Kenya and begins by telling him. "You were the last to see Ricky. Tell me everything from the beginning, and do not omit anything, because what may not be important to you may be the key to finding Ricky."

Tamian freaks out. He knows that he has omitted that the kidnapper has mentioned the name of a certain Tony and that he is supposedly Ricky's uncle.

Ocano sees that Tamian is nervous and does not look him in the eye, constantly avoiding his gaze. Ocano says to Tamian. "Please go to your room. I need to talk to your mother."

Tamian leaves, and Ocano tells Kenya. "Your son knows something that he is not telling us about. Do you have any idea what is happening here?"

Kenya responds. "No, and I doubt my son is involved in this."

Ocano leans back in his chair and responds in a low voice. "I am not accusing him of being involved, but I'll have to push him a bit to get to the bottom of this. I need your understanding. This is a very delicate matter, and that child's life is in danger."

Kenya springs up from her chair. She is visibly upset. Ocano thinks that Kenya has been offended and will not let the detective pressure Tamian. Before he can explain, however, Kenya yells the name of her son.

"Tamian! Come here immediately!"

Tamian leaves the room with wide-open eyes. The scream from his mother makes him very nervous. He understands he has no choice but to say what he has been hiding. Kenya orders Tamian to sit at the table again.

Ocano is used to questioning adults, but the interrogation of a minor has totally different protocols. He takes the time to question the minor without frightening him in front of his mother. Kenya, seeing that Ocano is going around the point and has not just asked any questions, slaps the table, which scares even Ocano.

Kenya stands up and, with her imposing size and tells Tamian.

"Tell me right now what you did not say last time, or I'm going to rip your head off, right here in front of the police!"

Ocano is surprised, and Tamian petrified. Tamian, between sobs and trembling with fear, answers.

"I didn't say it before because Ricky asked me not to tell anyone, but the man who came up told him that he was coming from his uncle Tony. That he would take him to see his uncle and then return him to his house."

"Who is that Uncle Tony?"

"I don't know. Ricky had never mentioned him, but it must be true, because Ricky got worried when he heard that his uncle Tony needed him. He asked me not to tell anyone."

"Could you recognize that person if we show you a photo?"

"Yes, sir."

"What language does that person speak?"

"He speaks English, but he had a Latino accent. I also remember that he has a scar on the left side of his neck."

"Anything else?"

"No, that's all, sir."

Kenya sends Tamian to his room again and tells Ocano.

"I have something to tell you. It is not related, but I think you should know."

Ocano is surprised. He thinks that there is something else in reference to the case, immediately sits down, and takes out his notebook.

Kenya tells him.

"It's about Ricky. But not about the kidnapping case."

Ocano closes his notebook and answers.

"I do not understand the relation of one thing with the other."

Kenya quietly tells him.

"That child is not an ordinary child. He is a mystery, and I get chills when I think about him."

Ocano sees that Kenya is very worried and tears are beginning to flow from her eyes.

"What is going on, ma'am? Tell me at once."

"He lives next door. You see, the house where he lives is in worse condition than ours. He lives with his dad and his stepmother. They are working-class people, like everyone else in our neighborhood."

Ocano answers. "I already took that into account. The kidnappers have not asked for a ransom because they are poor, and the kidnappers have not communicated to ask for anything. This case tends to be child trafficking, organ trafficking, or perhaps a sexual predator."

"You are wrong, Detective. I told you he is a mystery. My house was foreclosed by the bank and Ricky paid the debt. He saved my house, and it was $182,500."

Ocano laughs and responds.

"Ma'am, please, this is a serious investigation."

Kenya looks at him angrily.

"Do you think I am joking? Would you like me to bring you the papers so that you can convince yourself?"

Kenya gets up from the table and goes to her room and brings the documents that prove that her house was foreclosed. Kenya gives him the documents.

"Convince yourself if you do not want to believe me. If there is something you can be sure of, it is that I do not have that kind of money."

Ocano's jaw drops. He quickly opens his notebook.

"Tell me everything, slowly, from the beginning. But if that child has that amount of money, how come he lives in those conditions? An eight-year-old child cannot make a bank transaction without the collaboration of an adult. That does not make sense."

Kenya shrugs. "I don't know, and I think his parents don't know either that he has money. He made me promise that I wouldn't tell anyone."

"What do you know about that guy named Tony?"

"Nothing, sir. I have never heard of him. I thought he had no other family. When his mother died, his mother's lawyers handed him over to his father."

Ocano shakes his head from side to side. "Oh my god! This is a time bomb. Please do not discuss this with anyone. Keep it a secret."

Ocano leaves Kenya's house and goes straight to Ricky's house. There are many things that don't make sense, and after Tamian's and Kenya's testimonies, it will be like starting from scratch. Ocano is received by Ricardo, who opens the door, and Ocano shows him his identification.

"Good evening. I'm the FBI agent in charge of your son's case."

Ricardo does not let him finish and interrupts him nervously.

"Give me good news, please. It can't be that you don't have a single clue."

Dorothy immediately joins, and the three sit in the kitchen. Ocano looks around and sees that Ricardo's standard of living does not match a son who can afford to give away $182,500.

"I want to ask you a few questions, and I need you to tell me everything. Even the things that you think are irrelevant to the case or unimportant."

After a slight pause, he continues. "Are you Ricky's father?"

"Yes, sir." Ricardo responds firmly.

"That is what he says." Dorothy responds.

Ocano is confused. The case is becoming more and more entangled.

"What do you mean by that?"

Dorothy, stressed, responds.

"That child was brought here by two men who claimed to be the lawyers of Ricky's late mother. They had official documents from the state of Florida where they gave Ricky's custody to my husband. My husband has never done a DNA test. I am not sure he is his son."

Ocano becomes more and more confused, but he continues his interrogation without mentioning what Kenya has told him. Ocano asks Ricardo.

"How did you end up with this child?"

"I had a relation with Ricky's mother nine years ago. It is true she told me she was pregnant, but I did not believe her. I refused to accept responsibility for the child. She never contacted me again. I only went to her house once and only met her father. They had a lot of money, but I am not interested in money. I am happy with the way I live. I received a certified letter from Ricky's mother where she asked me to pick him up because she was going on a trip. I ignored the letter because I thought she was going to Europe or elsewhere. I didn't think it meant that she was dying."

Ocano asks. "If she had told you she was dying, would you have gone?"

Ricardo thinks for a few seconds and answers.

"No, I don't think I would have gone, but when they brought Ricky to me, it was something that cannot be explained. It can only be felt. I felt tied to him from the first moment I saw him. I recognize we do not resemble each other physically or in any other way, but I feel he is part of me. The fact that two strangers brought him to me doesn't mean anything to me. A doctor is an unknown person to you, but he brings your son into the world and then hands him into your arms. You have never seen the doctor or the baby. But moment you see that baby, even though he does not resemble you or anyone else, creates a spiritual bond that is so strong you would give your life for that baby from the first time you see him."

Ocano tries not to get carried away by emotions and responds to him, saying.

"I understand and I agree with you. I want you to understand that to be efficient in my work, I must put my emotions aside and be totally practical."

After a slight pause, he asks.

"Did you ask Ricky's mother for money?"

"No! Never."

"Did she or any of her family members offer you money?"

Ricardo, offended, responds.

LITTLE RICKY

"One moment, detective. Are you investigating the kidnapping, or are you investigating me? I have never received or asked for a penny from those people. When they brought Ricky to me, I decided to go and find out if it was true that she had died. It is a closed community, and they didn't let me in. They didn't give me any information."

Ocano stands up and says. "I need to see Ricky's room."

Ricardo and Dorothy take Ocano to Ricky's room. Ocano begins to observe the room. It is a humble room, but very orderly. In fact, too orderly for an eight-year-old boy. He is struck by the fact he doesn't see toys anywhere.

Ocano asks Dorothy. "Why is this room so orderly?"

"Because he keeps it that way. He does not like us to go into his room."

"Where are his toys?"

"He came without toys, has never asked for toys, and we have never seen him play with anything."

Ocano decides to start asking deeper questions.

"Don't you think it's strange for an eight-year-old to behave that way?"

Ricardo shrugs his shoulders and responds.

"I know it's strange, but we are all different."

"Do you know Tony?"

"Yes, I know two Tonys."

"Is any of them related to your child?"

"No, they are coworkers."

"Does Ricky have any more family than you?"

"That's what the lawyers who brought him told us. That's what Ricky says, and that's all I know. If you know anything different, please tell me."

Dorothy becomes suspicious and interrupts.

"I have my suspicions."

"What do you suspect, ma'am?"

"He has a phone that he keeps hidden. I have heard him several times speaking to someone at night. We demanded that he give us the phone's code, and he refused to do so."

"Whom does he talk to? What does he say?"

"I don't know, and he speaks so softly I couldn't understand a thing."

"Who pays for that line?"

"I give him fifty dollars every month, he gives it to Kenya, and she pays for the line."

"Are you sure of that?"

"That was what he told me, and I believe it, because Kenya would do anything for Ricky after he saved her house."

"How did he save her house when the bank foreclosed it?" Ocano pretends to know nothing and asks him, "How does he pay the debt?"

Ricardo and Dorothy look at Ocano in disenchantment. Dorothy asks, sarcastically.

"Are you kidding? How is Ricky going to pay Kenya's debt? Where the hell is an eight-year-old going to get that kind of money? What Ricky did was transfer the money that Kenya had to the bank doing the foreclosure because she didn't know how to do it. That transfer came ten minutes before the deadline, and that's the reason why Kenya did not lose the house."

Ocano decides not to say anything about Kenya's comments. He only asks for the phone to check it, in the hope of finding a clue. Ocano oversees the team made up of detectives from the city of Miami, Miami-Dade County, and the state of Florida. They all met at the county police station. Ocano starts asking for reports.

Detective Vargas puts Tony's photo on the board and says.

"On his mother's side, Ricky only has one uncle, who is not related by blood. He was adopted by Ricky's grandfather. He had an extensive criminal record when he was a minor, but after the adoption, he kept clean and graduated in law and business administration. He worked from an early age in the family business, starting from the bottom. After he graduated, his adoptive grandfather raised him to the company board of directors, where he was the right hand of his grandfather. When his father and his adoptive grandfather died in an accident, he assumed the presidency of the company. According to my reports, he has conducted himself as if he were a blood member and not an adopted one. He wanted Ricky's mother to give him legal custody, but she did not want to. The Clark family's fortune is valued at nine hundred million dollars. Only Tony and Ricky remain as heirs."

Miami-Dade County detective Matos oversees the investigation of Ricardo's and Dorothy's family. He stands up and says.

"My investigation reveals that Ricky has been the source of disagreement within Ricardo's family. His kidnapping is not a great concern to them except for Ricardo's father, who seems to be affected. With Dorothy's family, the indifference is even greater. The only interesting point is that Dorothy's brother is a lieutenant who was fired from the department for his poor performance during this call, but we have nothing strong enough to implicate him in the kidnapping."

Florida State detective Philbrick says.

"I have court orders to wiretap Ricardo's, Dorothy's, Kenya's, and Tony's phones, as you asked me to. The information we got from Ricky's phone is as follows: Ricky uses that phone only to communicate with Tony on Tuesday and Thursday nights always, from 8:00 P.M. to 8:30 P.M. Except once that he used it three times in the afternoon two months ago to call Tony asking for a wire transfer to stop a foreclosure."

Ocano takes the report and says.

"Let us analyze the following. Who would benefit from this?"

"Kenya has already received $182,500. I do not think she has the means or the intelligence for an operation like this."

"Ricardo would benefit more with Ricky alive than dead. I do not think he knows or cares about Ricky's fortune. If he were an ambitious person, he would have married Ricky's mother instead of Dorothy."

"I see no benefit for Dorothy. She has not been a loving mother, and neither has she been a horrible stepmother. The only benefit to her would be to have her husband only for herself but does not amount to such a risk.

"Tonyn is the only one who would inherit everything if Ricky disappeared. He has a criminal record, so he is not a saint. Kenya's mortgage was paid for by the Clarks' construction company. If Ricky, at the age of eight years, is powerful enough to order Tony to pay $182,500, that gives you an idea of the power that Ricky has. Imagine when Ricky gets to be an adult. In other words, he eliminates the monster before it grows. Here we have a clear motive. With Ricky out of the picture, the fortune would pass completely to Tony's hands. Finally, the kidnapping conveniently occurs when Tony is out of the country, giving him the perfect alibi.":

"Tomorrow we will travel to the Bahamas and question Tony. We will probably bring him back as a precaution. He will not be under arrest, but he will not be able to leave the country."

******

Meanwhile, Ricky is still in the room, chained by the ankle to a bedpost. He can only move about three feet around the bed. Alex walks in to replace Robledo and sees that Ricky's mouth is covered with duct tape.

"How dare you commit such a crime!" Alex removes the tape from Ricky's mouth.

"You are all the same! You torture innocent people just for fun!"

Robledo looks at him in amazement.

"Weren't you the ones who bombed a church full of civilians with propane tanks and killed men, women, and children?"

Annoyed, Alex responds.

"That was a tactical, error for which we apologized."

Robledo sarcastically responds.

"Oh, it was a mistake. You already convinced me. I covered his mouth because I could not take any more of his grandfather's shit. No matter what I say, he comes back with, "My grandfather used to say." That kid is a pain in the ass."

It was Alex's turn to have custody of Ricky. Alex looks at Ricky and tells him.

"Not all men are the same even though they sometimes do the same thing together. Sometimes the end justifies the means."

Ricky thanks him and asks for water.

Alex tells Robledo. "How can you have this child without giving him water? Our job is to take care of him and not torture him."

Robledo responds angrily.

"Fuck you! Paramilitary exists because of the crimes that you committed. Now you want to cover it up with cheap and deceptive philosophies!"

Alex gives Ricky water and says.

"Never compare me to this man. You are too young to understand the difference between a reactionary right-wing philosophy and a progressive left philosophy based on equality and human rights."

Alex sits in an armchair, takes out a book, and begins to read.

"What are you reading?" Ricky asks.

"It is a masterpiece written by Karl Marx. It is called "Das Kapital." This book is like the proletariat's bible. Here he unmasks the cruel and savage capitalism that thrives on the work and the ignorance of the people."

"Is that about socialism and communism?"

Alex looks at him, surprised. He didn't expect an eight-year-old to know about socialism or communism.

"Exactly, socialism is the first phase of the construction of communism."

"My grandfather used to say that in theory, socialism is a beauty."

"Your grandfather was an intelligent person if he could see that. Then he should have told you that it is paradise come true."

"No, he said that in reality, it doesn't work. Wherever that system has been implemented, people emigrated to somewhere else, seeking a better future. Nobody flees from paradise. Cubans jumped into the sea, and many drowned to get away from that paradise. My father's family escaped from that paradise."

"What do you know about life? You do not even know what poverty is!"

"My grandfather used to say, if our system is so bad, why do so many people come from all over the world, looking for opportunities to improve their lives? The vast majority flees from a socialist paradise. Nothing there belongs to anyone, and everything belongs to the people in power. He said that in those systems, the rulers use the people as excuses to perpetuate themselves in power. The Castros took over the island, Ortega seized Nicaragua, Chávez died in power and passed the throne to another who does not let it go. In North Korea, they are going for the third generation, passing power in the family, and that is the same in every country that system takes over. Do you want that for your country?"

Alex gets up and angrily tosses the book aside. "How can somebody poison a child like that? It is a pity how you can express yourself so nicely and are politically blind."

"My grandfather used to say that anyone who is young and is not enthusiastic about socialist ideas has no heart."

Alex looks at him, puzzled. "At least I agree with your grandfather on that."

"At what age did you begin to admire that system?" Ricky asks.

"From an early age, I became aware of social injustices and began to fight for what I believe in."

"And how old are you now?"

"I am forty-five years old, and I will keep fighting until my strength is exhausted."

"But my grandfather's complete sentence was, 'Whoever was not enthusiastic about socialist ideas as a young man did not have a heart, but if he became an adult and continued to be enthusiastic about those ideas, he still has a heart, but he does not have a brain.'"

Alex stands furious in front of Ricky and yells at him,

"Fuck you, fuck your mother, and fuck your grandfather!"

He takes the duct tape and goes to cover Ricky's mouth. Ricky, shaking his head, trying to avoid the tape, says.

"Socialism has not taken power yet and there goes the freedom of expression!"

******

Ocano shows up with two Bahamian policemen at the hotel where Tony is staying. Tony is leaving his room on the way to the preliminary project meeting when he is intercepted by Ocano and the Bahamian police.

"Good morning, Mr. Anthony Clark."

Tony is surprised because they have called him by his full name.

"Good morning, gentlemen."

"We need to talk to you."

Tony has no idea what has happened, but he knows that in an hour he has an important meeting.

"I will be glad to talk with you after I have my meeting with the minister of finance, which starts in an hour. I will be at your disposal as soon as I finish."

Ocano pulls his ID out, shows it to him, and tells him.

"I'm very sorry, but you will have to join us. You need to make a call to postpone the meeting. I'm afraid you won't be able to make it today."

Tony asks him. "Am I under arrest?"

"No, we are working on a case, and we need your help."

"Then you will have my full cooperation as soon as I finish. If you can tell me what this is about, maybe I can help you on something."

"Yes, of course."

Then Ocano asks. "When was the last time you spoke to Ricky?"

When Tony hears the question, he pales. He feels a chill down his spine that almost takes his breath away.

"What happened to Ricky?" Tony asks, terrified.

Ocano does not know what to think. Maybe Tony is a good actor. He continues to treat him as a suspect.

"You have not answered my question."

"I talked to him five days before I came to the Bahamas. Tell me what happened?"

"Ricky was kidnapped when leaving school."

Tony slowly steps aside and sits in on a chair that was in the hall. He puts his elbows on his knees and covers his face with his hands.

"It is all my fault. I should not have given him to his stupid father. He did not want him, and I'm sure he's glad he got rid of him. May God forgive me. I told you, Virginia, to leave him to me, but you, as always, made me do what you want!"

Ocano takes out some photos taken from the school security cameras and asks Tony.

"Do you know this man?"

Tony looks at the photo and replies.

"No, I've never seen him before."

"Is there somebody else besides Ricky in the Clark family who can claim the fortune?"

Tony gets up, furious, and pushes Ocano, who is taken by surprise and falls to the ground.

"What are you implying, you son of a bitch?"

The police officers immediately immobilize Tony and put handcuffs on him.

Ocano gets up and asks the police to release him, that he needs to question him. The police officer responds.

"You can question him at the station, but we don't allow these things on our island."

Ocano has no choice but to go to the police station to continue the interrogation.

Tony is visibly concerned, but Ocano is firm in his suspicion. Tony tells Ocano the whole story about why he gave Ricky to Ricardo.

Ocano listens carefully and takes notes, then asks him.

"Does Ricardo know you are Ricky's uncle?"

"I don't know. If Ricky hasn't told him, he shouldn't know."

"Does Ricardo know of the Clark fortune?"

"I do not know."

"Finally, I want you to tell me, who are the people who are entitled to the Clark fortune?"

Tony, with tears in his eyes, answers, "Ricky and I."

Ocano comes out of the interrogation room and tells the Bahamas sergeant on duty.

"It would be much better if you guys released him, so we could monitor him. He might lead us somewhere."

The sergeant responds.

"We can only release him if you do not press charges against him."

Ocano responds immediately.

"In that case, you can release him immediately. I will not press charges against him."

The officers release Tony, and Ocano sets out to follow him. Tony takes a taxi and tells the driver.

"Take me to the Nassau Hotel."

Ocano is being assisted by a Bahamian detective. His plan is to follow Tony to see if he is meeting with someone. They keep a safe distance so as not to be noticed, but a truck gets in the way, completely covering the taxi.

Tony, in despair, tells the driver.

"Change of plans. Take me to the airport."

The taxi driver turns and heads to the airport. Ocano cannot see Tony's taxi turn because the truck is blocking it completely. A few seconds later, the detective passes the truck. He realizes the taxi has disappeared.

Ocano, disappointed, says. "Oh no! We lost him."

The detective smiles, parks his vehicle, and responds,

"Don't worry, I can find him."

Ocano sarcastically replies. "I think parking the car won't help much."

The detective takes his radio and communicates with the police station. He asks them to contact the taxi dispatcher and ask where taxi 425 is heading. One minute later, the detective is informed that taxi 425 is heading to the Nassau Hotel. The detective shakes his head and says.

"They are all the same."

Ocano asks impatiently. "What's going on?"

"Nothing. The taxi is heading toward the Nassau Hotel. Seeing that Tony is not a local, the taxi driver is taking him on a much longer route to charge him more money. We also have people here who are not very honest."

Ocano asks the detective to go to the Nassau Hotel and wait for Tony to arrive.

Tony arrives at the airport and goes to buy a ticket for the next flight to Miami. The airline representative tells him, "Sir, the next flight leaves in an hour, but it's totally sold out. I only have seats for the 7:00 p.m. if you want."

Tony looks around and sees the passengers waiting to board the next flight.

Tony asks the young woman.

"If I get someone to sell me their seat, will you change the boarding pass to my name?"

"Yes, sir, I have no problem helping you with that."

Tony thanks the young woman and heads over to the passengers who were waiting to board the plane.

"Please listen. I have an emergency. I need to leave on the next flight to Miami. I offer one thousand dollars and an extra one hundred dollars to have dinner at the restaurant while waiting for the next flight at 7:00 p.m. to whoever give me his or her place"

A young man immediately gets up, says.

"Show me the money, and I'll give you, my seat."

Tony responds.

"Give me your ticket and I will give you the money."

The young man is happy. He has earned $1,100 just for waiting a few hours.

Ocano tells the detective. "I think something is not right. I understand that the driver could drive around for fifteen more minutes, but not an hour."

The detective responds. "You read my mind. Something is not right."

The detective calls again. He asks the dispatcher to ask the driver of taxi 425 where he took the passenger that he was supposed to take to the Nassau Hotel.

Ten minutes later, the detective receives a call to his cell phone.

"Hello. Detective Morris, please."

"It's me. Who is this?"

"I am the driver of taxi 425. What do you want to know?"

"You picked up a passenger in front of the police station. Where did you take him?"

"He told me to take him to the Nassau Hotel. When we were stopped at the traffic light, he suddenly told me that he had changed his mind and asked me to take him to the airport."

"Did he talk to someone on the phone?"

"Yes, sir. He told me that his phone had a dead battery and asked me if he could use my phone."

"Did someone pick him up at the airport?"

LITTLE RICKY

"No, sir."

The detective hangs up the phone, and Ocano asks him.

"Tell me what's going on."

"He wants to escape. He knew we were following him, and he took advantage that the truck was blocking our view to go straight to the airport. On the way, instead of using his phone, he used the driver's phone in case we were intercepting his calls. What do you want to do now?"

Ocano screams angrily.

"Shit! Let's go to the station immediately! We must put out an arrest warrant on him."

The Nassau Hotel is close to the police station, so in just five minutes, Ocano and Morris passed all the information to the airport to prevent Tony from leaving. Ocano receives a call from the police sergeant at the airport.

"Detective Ocano?"

"Yes, it is me."

"It is to inform you your subject took off on a Bahamas Air flight fifteen minutes ago, with destination to the city of Miami."

"Perfect! Thanks." Ocano calls the FBI office and requests Tony's arrest upon arrival at the airport.

* * * * * *

Albert Infante, the president of the US International Construction has achieved his goal. Tony has not shown up for the negotiation with the economy minister for the construction of the Cayo Samaná project. What will be his surprise when Walter, the minister of economy, decides to wait one more day to give Tony the opportunity to present his project. Albert telephones Gilbert, who is in Miami, supervising the kidnapping.

"Hi, Gilbert! How is everything?"

"Well, sir, everything is fine."

"That stupid Walter, the minister, decided to postpone the meeting one more day because he thinks that Tony didn't show up due to a personal problem."

Gilbert, surprised, asks him.

"What about Bill? He is the vice minister, and he has been paid quite a bit to promote the project."

"Bill is behaving well, and thanks to him and his contacts in the police, I found out that Tony was arrested and later released. He is flying to Miami on a Bahamas Air flight and will be arrested upon arrival at the airport. I need you to leak this information anonymously to the press so that there is a big scandal when he gets there. I doubt that the minister wants to commit to a person who is involved in a kidnapping."

Gilbert responds.

"Okay, but as soon as you have that contract signed, let me know. This has taken a dimension beyond what was expected. We must get rid of this kid as soon as possible."

******

Tony arrives at the airport and is stopped by an FBI agent and two police officers. The big news is that there are thirty reporters, who take the agents by surprise, surrounding them with their microphones and cameras, bombarding Tony with questions.

"Is it true that you kidnapped your nephew for the sole purpose of making him vanish to keep the fortune to yourself?"

"How do you plead to the charges against you?"

"Is that the way you pay the family that took you in and gave you a home and an education?"

"Where were you trying to escape to when you were discovered?"

The officers do not let Tony answer any questions; they remove him from the scene and transport him to the county jail.

The news is all over local and national T.V. stations. The case has reached a publicity level not seen before. Gilbert sends the newspaper to Albert, who gives it to Bill to show the minister.

Bill shows up at the finance minister's office and gives him the newspaper with a picture of Tony being arrested and surrounded by reporters. The minister is caught by surprise. He has a highly positive opinion of Tony.

Bill pushes one more time. "Mr. Minister, I think, after this, there is no need to keep waiting for Tony."

Walter becomes suspicious about Bill. He notices that Bill has shown an interest in Albert's project. Walter takes the newspaper and asks him.

"Bill, where did you get this newspaper? It is today's edition. How did you get it so fast?"

Bill is paralyzed. He did not expect such questions. He has no idea that he is being investigated for receiving bribes from foreign contractors. With this, Walter reaffirms his suspicions that Albert is bribing Bill. He has asked himself on more than one occasion why his vice minister is always favoring Albert's project when Tony's project surpasses Albert's in all aspects.

Walter stays quiet for a while and then responds.

"You're right, this doesn't help at all, but today we can't decide. I have an unscheduled meeting with the president. Tomorrow, we will meet again. Tell Mr. Albert that you will tell him the time later."

When Walter sees the expression on Bill's face, he becomes convinced one hundred percent something is wrong. Walter goes straight to the Economic Crime Investigation Office to speak with Detective Carter, who oversees Bill's investigation. They both manage to gather enough evidence to convince a judge to issue an order to tap the vice minister's phone.

Meanwhile, in Miami, Ricardo and Dorothy have aged ten years in just five days. The house feels empty without Ricky. Dorothy realizes Ricky has given meaning to their lives, that he has forced them to become responsible adults. The reporters do not leave the block, and the police have maintained a unit in front of the house. It was almost impossible for them to leave the house without being harassed by reporters.

Ricardo and Dorothy are leaving for work when a reporter asks Dorothy.

"Do you think Ricky's uncle is behind the kidnapping?"

Dorothy answers bluntly.

"I just found out that Ricky has an uncle. That uncle came here and told us that Ricky has no living relative. He not only abandoned

Ricky but also threatened my husband to send him to jail if he would not take him. Yes, I do believe that he is behind the kidnapping since he is the only one that would benefit from Ricky's disappearance. He has offered a reward of fifteen million dollars because he knows that no one will be able to collect it. If they were real kidnappers, they would have asked for a ransom. It means that the objective is to get rid of Ricky. If he had really loved him as he says, he would never have delivered him as he did. He practically forced us to receive him. So let him rot in jail!"

Dorothy inadvertently has expressed her feelings, and she is crying before the cameras, showing how important Ricky is in their life.

The reporter responds.

"There is another theory that nobody has expressed yet, but it is also logical."

Ricardo tells him.

"Say it, please. Every idea is welcome, no matter how far-fetched it may seem."

The reporter looks at him and says nothing.

"Say it. I want to know. That theory could be the correct one."

The reporter says.

"All right if you insist. Ricky and Tony are the only legal heirs to the fortune."

Ricardo, disappointed, responds.

"We already know that. It is nothing new."

"If Ricky disappears and Tony receives the death penalty, then it would clear the way for you to claim the fortune as Ricky's biological father. Isn't that why you never had a DNA test? Because if you are not the biological father, then you would have no legal claim."

Ricardo yells and lunges at the journalist.

"You son of a bitch! I'm going to break your neck!"

Thanks to the intervention of the officer guarding the house, a tragedy is avoided, but the news spreads like wildfire.

Ocano is furious. He does not understand how the news of Tony's arrest has been leaked and the reporters could have arrived before the officers. Ocano meets again with his detectives.

"Gentlemen, I hope that you have something to contribute, because I am going crazy. Nothing makes sense, and time continues to pass."

Detective Matos answers. "I thought you had your man with the Tony arrest."

Ocano shakes his head and responds.

"Tony is the one who comes closest to being guilty, but at the same time, there are many things that do not match. Whoever leaked the information that Tony would be arrested upon arrival in Miami not only has infiltrated the police but also has an interest in destroying Tony. Tony refuses a lawyer and insists on his innocence. He has offered a fifteen-million-dollar reward for information leading to Ricky's release. If he had wanted to escape, he would have hired a yacht to take him out instead of going to the airport. The person who flees hides and does not make himself visible. I have seventy-two hours to charge him, or I have to let him go."

"How are you going to let him go? That would be like setting off a bomb."

"It is worse to take him to trial on circumstantial evidence. He will be acquitted, and then we cannot prosecute him again, even if we find the necessary evidence."

******

Robledo enters to replace Alex and tells him.

"Do you know that Tony is offering fifteen million dollars to any person who give any information leading to Ricky's whereabout."

Alex, thinking they work for Tony, responds.

"I know, and I think it's a good move on his part, so no one will think he's behind it."

"No wonder you were a guerrilla. You don't see beyond your nose. This is the chance to win us fifteen million!"

"How?"

"I have everything planned. We go to a park and kidnap a parent with his child. We give him the choice between turning in Ricky and making a million dollars or having his son killed. He will receive the reward, but he will have to give us fourteen million. It is a great opportunity for the parent to make a million and save his son. We make seven million each. It is a win-win situation for everybody."

Alex tells Robledo with concern.

"It does not sound bad. This is so hot that I'm about to disappear and abandon it all. These gringos are not idiots, and the more time passes, the closer they get to us. I would rather make seven million than thirty thousand. Ricky looks weak. He has stopped eating and talking. I didn't cover his mouth because he did not speak or get out of bed. I tried to get him to eat something because the last thing we need is for him to get sick."

"Don't worry, hunger will make him eat. If not, I will force him to eat."

Gilbert tries to contact Alex and Robledo to tell them that they will have to extend the kidnapping for three more days. Albert doesn't want to release Ricky until he has the project approved. When not receiving a response from Alex and Robledo, Gilbert starts to worry. He decides to check on them, since a fifteen-million reward is enough reason for a betrayal.

Alex and Robledo hear a noise at the door, draw their weapons, hide, and prepare to shoot.

Gilbert announces himself before appearing to avoid being shot, and thanks to that he saves his life. He has been among bandits all his life. He has a sixth sense that has allowed him to survive. Gilbert knows the juicy reward offered by Tony can jeopardize the operation.

"Hello, guys. I have tried to communicate with you, but none of you has answered the phone."

Robledo answers.

"Excuse me, Mr. Thomas, but we have decided not to carry phones. This case has gotten out of control, and the phone can give up our location."

Alex intervenes. "Are you coming to take the child?"

Gilbert, just by looking at them and seeing that neither of them will make eye contact with him, understands that they are plotting to hand over Ricky to collect the reward. Gilbert sits down, trying to pretend that he doesn't know what is going on.

"You are right. That is why from today onward, the three of us will watch the kid. I will be with him and one of you all the time. We have to extend the kidnapping for two or three more days. The fumigation company will tell us tomorrow where we should move."

Robledo and Alex look at each other suspiciously.

"You told us it was six days. Longer is riskier."

"I get it, but Tony is the one making the decisions. You will be rewarded with five thousand dollars for each extra day.

******

Meanwhile in the Bahamas, Bill is in his office when his secretary calls him.

"Mr. Vice Minister, you have a call on line 4 from Minister Walter." Walter had twice canceled the meeting with Albert, hoping Albert will react and put pressure on the vice minister.

"Good morning, Mr. Minister, how can I help you?"

"I need you to contact Albert and tell him that it will take about three days for us to meet. The president is changing his mind and does not know whether to build or make it a protected area for the local fauna."

Bill is scared; he has already received a large sum of money and he had promised Albert that his project would be approved.

"Mr. Minister, where did the president get such an idea? We have put a lot of time on this project. I understand that giving Tony the contract would give us a bad reputation. We have Mr. Albert's project, which has been on the island for a week and has invested a lot of money in this."

"I understand you, Bill, and I agree with you, but it is not my decision."

Desperate, Bill tries to convince the minister. "Please, Walter. You put me in a compromising position."

"Why? I do not understand."

"It is that when Tony left, Mr. Albert decided to leave too, and it was not easy to convince him to stay. I did it because this project is a great investment for our country, and we should not let it go. If I tell him we continue to delay in making a decision, I fear that we will lose him too, and then we will have nothing. Walter, you and I don't need this project, but the people on that island do."

"I understand, Bill. Just contact him and let him decide what he wants to do."

Bill hangs up the phone and leans back in his chair with his hands on his head, takes a deep breath, and says.

"Damn it, I can't be beaten by some fucking turtles to ruin my business!"

Bill leaves his office and drives off to talk without being interrupted or overheard.

"Hello, Mr. Albert."

"Hi, Bill, thanks for calling. I do not know if you have realized that I am not a tourist here. This was not what you promised me."

"I know, Mr. Albert. We have to wait a few more days."

"What the fuck are you talking about? You first told me I had to get Tony out of the way, and I did. Do you know how much an operation like that costs me? Not to mention the danger involved on it! Gilbert gave you more money than you can make in two years for you to give me shit. You fix that problem at any cost and remember that if Gilbert can make a child disappear in the United States and neither the FBI nor all the police departments can find him, then I don't think they will find you or your children if you don't fix this."

"You don't have to be like that, Mr. Albert. It will take me longer, but I'll do it. Remember that your project has no competition. I just have to tell the press that the minister prefers the welfare of the turtles rather than feeding the citizens."

"Get your act together, Bill, because if your minister prefers to feed the turtles, I am going to feed your ass to the sharks."

Albert throws down the phone furiously. He is used to having no opposition and everyone lowering their heads when he speaks.

Carter calls Walter right away and tells him.

"Your idea was fantastic. His phone call to Albert confirms that Vice Minister Bill has been taking bribes from the contractors and Mr. Albert is one of them. But there is more. This case has ramifications to a criminal case in the United States. Detective Morris was accompanying an FBI detective working the case."

Walter, surprised, responds.

"You can't imagine how glad I am to know that. Have you contacted the FBI detective yet?"

"No. You are the first person to know. I am going to prepare an arrest warrant for the vice minister, and then I will contact the FBI detective."

"No, Carter, contact the detective first. Remember that there is an innocent person in prison, and then we arrest Bill."

"You are right, Minister, so I will."

Chapter 12

Robledo and Gilbert are inside the new residence that serves as their hideout, waiting for Alex, who has gone out to buy food. The presence of Gilbert, who they know as Mr. Thomas, is evidence that plans have changed. They think that Gilbert wants to turn in Ricky to collect the reward before they do. Alex contacts a friend to coordinate Ricky's delivery.

"Hello, Orlando. It is me, Alex. I need to meet you at the Havana restaurant. You must go alone and bring me a narcotic strong enough to put two horses to sleep."

"Oh! Alex, you haven't changed. When do you want it?"

"For yesterday. Your first payment is five hundred dollars. When I explain the job, you will see that you could retire completely after this."

"I will be there in half an hour."

Orlando is a man in his fifties, very tall and thin. His hair is long and tied up with a rubber band at the back. He had participated with the guerrillas in Colombia and was the chemist who ran the clandestine laboratories where cocaine was produced. Orlando arrives at the restaurant and sees Alex waiting in the parking lot. He gets out of his car and gets into Alex's car.

"I thought you were going to take me out to lunch."

"No time for that. Did you bring what I asked for?"

"Yes, and I also brought you a syringe in case you have to inject it into a sealed drink."

"You are the best in your class. That's why I always keep your phone number."

Orlando shows Alex the bag with the narcotic and tells him.

"Give me my five hundred dollars and take your bag."

Alex hands him five one-hundred-dollar bills, and Orlando's eyes sparkle.

"Listen, Orlando. We are a good team, but this has come to an end. We cannot continue with that kidnapped child. The plan to follow is that in forty minutes you will go to the police and say you saw a strange movement in front of a tented house, and you heard a child screaming inside. Then you will claim the reward and we will split 50 percent each."

Alex has his cell phone in hand and has video recorded everything.

Alex plays the recording back to Orlando and tells him.

"As you can hear and see in this recording, it is as if you took part in the kidnapping from the beginning. If you don't give me my share, I will send this to the police, they will arrest you, and they will take your money, so don't try to screw me, because you are the one who is going to get screwed. I might not get any money, but I will be free somewhere in the world."

Orlando laughs and replies.

"You are a son of a bitch, but I will not miss this opportunity for anything in the world. Give me the address."

Alex gives him a paper and tells him.

"Here is the address. You have to wait about forty minutes to make sure they are well asleep, and I have left the house."

Orlando takes the address and then injects the narcotic through the cap to the two water bottles and tells Alex.

"This is tasteless. They will fall asleep in five minutes and be asleep for a minimum of fifteen hours."

Meanwhile, at the hideout, Gilbert tells Robledo.

"We must make this child eat. We cannot allow him to get sick."

"Mr. Thomas, we've tried, but I will have to force him."

Gilbert responds.

"The problem is that you have not given him something he likes. I have a peanut butter and jelly sandwich. Kids love that."

Alex arrives with the food, and Gilbert asks suspiciously.

"Why did you take so long?"

Alex responds without hesitation.

"Mr. Thomas today has not been a good day. First, they gave me the wrong food order and I had to wait for them to cook again. When I got to the corner, I saw that there was an accident, and the police were making the report. I had to keep driving around until they left. I did not want to risk being seen walking into a tented house."

Gilbert does not press the issue anymore and begins to eat with Robledo.

Alex asks Robledo. "Did the kid eat anything?"

"No, he still does not want to eat."

Alex takes the opportunity to try to feed Ricky and wait for the narcotic to take effect. Gilbert throws Alex a bag and says.

"Give him that sandwich. The kids love that, and we have to make him eat something."

After two minutes and seeing that Alex has not been able to make Ricky eat, Robledo gets up, takes the sandwich, and tells Alex.

"Let me show you how to feed a child. You'll see how he opens his mouth and eats the whole sandwich."

Alex steps aside and responds. "He will not open his mouth."

Robledo grabs the sandwich in his left hand and holds it in front of Ricky's mouth.

"Look what I brought you. It is delicious."

Ricky is lying on the bed looking straight at Robledo's face.

Robledo quickly squeezes Ricky's testicles with his right hand. Ricky lets out a yell of pain, opening his mouth wide open. Robledo pushes the whole sandwich into his mouth and covers Ricky's mouth with his left hand, so he won't spit it out.

Gilbert laughs and says.

"Your child pedagogy is very effective."

"You're an animal! How can you do that to a child?" Alex yells at Robledo.

After about thirty seconds, Robledo releases him and sees that he has forced Ricky to swallow a piece of the sandwich.

"You can rest now. I made him eat a little. Isn't that what you wanted?"

"That was child abuse! The kid will refuse eating from now on. I myself lost my appetite."

Robledo laughs. "Great! I'll eat yours if you don't want it."

The narcotic begins to take effect, and Robledo and Gilbert fall fast asleep.

Robledo is lying down on a couch. Alex takes Robledo's arm and places it about ten inches above his eyes, then he lets go of the arm. He sees Robledo's arm falls freely, hitting Robledo's face. This gives him the certainty that he is drugged. Alex repeats the same with Gilbert to make sure that Gilbert is also drugged.

When Alex stands in front of Ricky, he sees that Ricky is having a seizure. Alex remembers that after Robledo forced him to eat the sandwich, Ricky screamed.

"I can't eat that—I am allergic to peanut!"

Terrified, Alex carries Ricky to dump him on the street, hoping someone finds him. He knows that if Ricky dies, there is no ransom money but a possible death penalty. Alex puts Ricky in the front seat to make it easier to get rid of him.

Meanwhile, Orlando, savoring the thought of ransom money, sees a police car with its lights on approaching at high speed. He stands in the middle of the street with both arms up. The officer has to apply the brakes to avoid hitting Orlando. The officer gets out of the car, angry.

"Are you stupid, or do you want to get killed? Don't you see I am going on an emergency call?"

"Excuse me, Officer, but I think what I am going to tell you is also an emergency. A block from here there is a tented house. When I passed by the front of the house, I saw a suspicious man hiding in the house. I thought he was a thief who was trying to break in to steal, but I heard a cry inside the house, and I'm sure it was a kid's cry."

The officer immediately communicates the message to the police station and several units are dispatched to that address in an emergency mode.

Ocano is in a meeting with the detectives working in the case and tells them.

"I want to inform you I have decided to release Tony. It has been seventy-two hours since his arrest. I think it is better to keep it under surveillance to see if we find something worthwhile."

Miami-Dade police captain Jordan opens the door and says.

"We have information on a possible hiding place for the kidnappers. Several units have already been sent to close a perimeter before proceeding."

He then approaches Ocano and tells him.

"You have a phone call from a Bahamian detective named Morris. He says that it is very important."

Ocano, very reluctant, went to answer the call.

"Hello, this is Agent Ocano."

"Agent Ocano, this is Detective Morris."

"Hi, Morris. How can I help you?"

Morris jokingly replies.

"I have something for you to listen to, but I need you to sit down first."

"Listen, Morris, I do not have time for jokes. I am letting free Tony. I can't keep him any longer. This is a disaster. Tony offered a fifteen-million reward, and the calls are pouring in, but we got nothing."

Morris insists again.

"Sit down. I will play something for you that will make your day."

Ocano, just to get rid of him, tells him.

"Okay, I already sat down. Let's hear it."

Morris tells him.

"We were investigating the vice minister of economy on suspicion of receiving bribes, and we got a court order to tap his phone."

Ocano, a little angry, replies.

"I'm sorry, Morris, but I have enough problems here to be interested in yours."

"It may be that this recording will help you with your problems."

Morris plays the recording.

"What the fuck are you talking about? You first told me to get Tony out of the way, and I did. Do you know how much an operation like that costs me? Not to mention the danger involved on it! Gilbert gave you more money than you can make in two years for you to give me shit. You fix that problem at any cost and remember that if Gilbert can make a child disappear in the United States and neither the FBI nor all police

LITTLE RICKY

departments can find him, then I don't think they can find you or your children if you don't fix this."

When Ocano finishes listening to the recording, he sits down, takes a deep breath, and says.

"Let me hear it again. This time I am sitting down for real."

Morris plays the recording again and tells him.

"I wanted you to listen to it first. Now I'm going to arrest the vice minister."

"No, please, that can alert Albert and he can flee. You better wait for me, and we arrest the two of them together."

"It will be a pleasure. We will make him believe he will have the final meeting with the minister to close the contract, and then we arrest them both."

******

Alex drives through the streets, looking for a place dark enough so that no one would see him and yet crowded enough, so they will find Ricky. Alex stops at the red light at an interception, looks to the right, and sees a bus stop with a booth. The street is dark, so he thinks no one will be able to distinguish him. He looks and sees no one around. He hastily gets out of the car, opens the passenger door, and carries Ricky to the bus stop bench. Alex doesn't notice a homeless man lying down on the bus bench covered with a dark blanket.

The homeless man sees Alex running toward him. He freaks out, stands up, and screams.

Alex, frightened by the cry of the homeless man, throws Ricky to the ground, and runs to his car.

He tries to flee at maximum speed running the red light at the interception. When he enters the intersection, he gets hit by a car that is coming at full speed, trying to beat the light change. Alex's car overturns about four times and ends up against the light pole. The intersection, which seemed empty, is immediately filled with people that have heard the crash and cries of the homeless asking for help for Ricky.

The police have set a perimeter around the block from the house where Gilbert and Robledo are sleeping. A special command uses caution to enter the residence. They are wearing gas masks and riot gear due to the seriousness of the call. They rush in at the command of the team leader to surprise anybody inside. They find Gilbert and Robledo asleep inside the house. Sergeant Fernandez, who is in charge of the command, thinks they are dead, since they don't react to all the screaming and yelling of the officers while entering the house. The sergeant is reporting on the radio that there are two dead subjects due to poison gas inhalation when an officer interrupts him and tells him.

"No, Sergeant, they are not dead. They are sleeping. They have vital signs."

After clearing the house, Sergeant Fernández communicates with the station and reports that they have not found Ricky. There are two suspects who are apparently drugged inside the residence.

The command makes a final search of the residence, and Sergeant Fernández finds Ricky's schoolbooks on the bed. An immediate search is done all around the perimeter area, while Gilbert and Robledo are placed under arrest.

Ricky is transported to Jackson Memorial Hospital in an ambulance. No one recognizes him. He is malnourished, dehydrated, and almost deformed due to the allergic reaction he has to peanuts.

Roberto, Ricardo's father, is the only one who has expressed solidarity with his son Ricardo.

Roberto invites Ricardo and Dorothy to have lunch at his house. Lora, Ricardo's mother, objects, but in the end, she agrees to avoid fighting with her husband. Lora begs her son Roberto to come with his wife and children so she will not be alone with Dorothy and Ricardo. Roberto Jr. agrees not to leave her mother alone and to defend her in case Dorothy argues with her.

The Suarez family is complete. Everyone is sitting at the table. Ricardo said only a few words, and Dorothy had not even spoken with her husband. Lora glances at her eldest son, Roberto, and his wife, then she moves her head and sticks out her tongue in a mocking way. Ricardo and Dorothy barely taste the food. The anguish can be seen on their faces. Lora gets up from the table and goes to the kitchen. Her son Roberto Jr. and his wife follow her with the excuse of helping her.

Roberto Sr. takes his son's hand and tells him.

"God won't let something bad happen to Ricky. Have faith in God."

Ricardo, with tears in his eyes, answers him.

"Dad, it's been seven days, and there is not a single clue."

Dorothy breaks down in tears and hugs her husband.

Lora, from the kitchen, looks at them and tells her son.

"I'm not happy that something bad has happened to the kid, but it is pathetic to see your brother crying for someone else's child and the other scoundrel crying as if she loved her child."

The television is on, and suddenly the programming is interrupted by breaking news.

"News flash: Miami Police just arrested two suspects in connection with Ricky's kidnapping. The suspects were found in a South Miami home. Both were drugged, and Ricky's belongings were found inside the home. The child is still missing. This morning, Anthony Clark, uncle of the kidnapped child, was released after spending seventy-two hours in custody in the county jail."

Ricardo and Dorothy run toward the TV and are jumping with joy, which turns to tears when they hear that Ricky is still missing. Roberto Sr. hugs them and tries to console them.

Lora tells her son and her daughter-in-law.

"I can't stand seeing your father acting like that. He was always the one who fought the most with your brother, and he couldn't even hear her name mentioned."

Ricardo becomes furious when he hears that Tony has been released.

"It cannot be that they let out that murderer! That crook doesn't know that his freedom is actually his death sentence, because when I find him, I will kill him."

Lora listens to her son and understands that Ricardo is serious. She leaves the kitchen and goes straight to her son.

"How are you going to do such a thing? What are you going to solve with that? Are you going to ruin your life for her son? That is the only thing I am missing. Put on your big-boy pants once and for all!"

Lora is out of control. She is about to have a heart attack. Roberto Jr. and his wife close their eyes, waiting for Dorothy's response to such an attack, but Dorothy does not respond. It's as if she has not heard Lora's insults.

Roberto yells at his wife. "Shut up, Lora!"

Lora responds in anger.

"I am not going to shut up. I am not going to let my son ruin his life for this. If you allow it, you will have that on your conscience!"

"Shut the hell up!" Roberto yells furiously.

Everybody is silent when they hear the programming being interrupted again.

"We interrupt our regular programs for last-minute information. A child was abandoned last night by a suspect who tried to flee the scene, causing a serious accident, where the suspect lost his life. The child is White, seven to nine years old, and in an induced coma due to his critical condition.

The minor's face is unrecognizable due to strong allergic reaction to peanuts that were found in his stomach. Anyone with information related to this case is asked to call the police."

At first, Ricardo and Dorothy screamed with joy, but then they fall silent, thinking that Ricky is not allergic. Everyone has remained silent. Only Roberto and Lora are staring at each other with tears on their eyes. Lora looks up, raises both hands, and says, crying.

"Forgive me, God."

Lora faints and falls to the ground. Everyone rushes to help her and does not understand what is happening.

Ricardo and his brother see their father crying inconsolably and their mother fainting after asking for forgiveness. They do not know what to do.

"What's up, Dad? What's going on?"

"Son, it is that your mother is super allergic to peanuts. You do not know it because we have never bought anything that has peanuts to prevent her from consuming it by mistake or in case you were allergic too. Let us run to the hospital. That…that boy is Ricky!"

LITTLE RICKY

Lora comes to herself and, crying, apologizes to her son and Dorothy. Dorothy does not respond. It's as if she were in another world after the news that Ricky is in a critical condition.

Lora grabs Ricardo by the hands and tells him.

"Son, Ricky needs you. We need you. Promise me that you will not do something crazy and try to do justice on your own."

"I'm sorry, Mother, but I can't promise you that. If Ricky dies, I'll kill that son of a bitch!"

Roberto takes Ricardo by the shoulders and shakes him.

"Your mother is right. You can't do something like that."

"I'm sorry, Dad, but I know you would do the same in my place."

The television program is interrupted again.

"We once again interrupt our regular programming due to a news flash. The FBI has just arrested the mastermind behind Ricky's kidnapping in Nassau, Bahamas, the wealthy builder Albert Infante, who paid Gilbert Roy, his company security director, to carry out the kidnapping. Gilbert and another Colombian suspect named Robledo Albizu are in custody at the county jail. The whereabouts of the kidnapped child is not yet known, but with the arrest of these three individuals, the authorities are confident that his release will soon be achieved."

Roberto tells his son.

"And you wanted to kill that man."

Ricardo, almost out of breath and about to faint, answers.

"The one that's going to kill somebody is that television if you don't turn it off."

The entire Suarez family rushes to the hospital. Two police officers and a doctor are at the front of the hallway. They are next to the entrance of Ricky's room. One of the officers sees them coming in a hurry and stops them.

"Sorry, you cannot pass. This is a restricted area."

Lora stands in front of him and defiantly responds.

"Of course, I can come in. My grandson is there. He is the child that was kidnapped and was abandoned last night. We found it out on television because not one of you had the decency to let us know! He suffers from a peanut allergy like me. I am his grandmother!"

Ricardo, Dorothy, and Roberto look at one another, surprised with Lora's attitude. She has become a model grandmother in an instant. Lora turns around and sees Ricardo, Dorothy, and her husband silently staring at her, and tells them firmly.

"What the hell is wrong with you? Why are you looking at me like that? Yes, my grandson. Does anyone have a problem with that?"

The officer asks. "Are you Mr. Ricardo Suarez?"

"Yes, Officer."

"We tried to reach you earlier, but you didn't answer the phone."

"Yes, we have it off. The press is driving us crazy with their calls."

"The officer assigned to your house said that you left early, and that was why we were unable to communicate with you."

Lora interrupts again.

"Son, that's already water under the bridge. Here we are, and that is what counts. I want to see my grandson."

The doctor tells her in a calm voice.

"Madam, calm down, please. The child is in critical condition.

We have stabilized him with an induced coma. It would be nice if any of you could recognize him."

Ricardo responds.

"Of course, Officer, I can recognize him."

Lora says, "I'll go with you."

The doctor stops her.

"Sorry, ma'am, but only one person can go in."

Ricardo enters with the doctor. Lora hugs Dorothy and starts to cry while saying.

"Oh God, save our Ricky!"

Dorothy pats Lora on the back, trying to comfort her while she looks at Roberto, shaking her head, wondering, who would have told me this three hours ago?

After about fifteen minutes, Ricardo exits the room with tears in his eyes. Desperate, Dorothy asks.

"How did he look? Tell us something, for God's sake!"

"He is not Ricky."

"How is it not him?" Dorothy screams.

"He is a White boy with black hair. His face is so swollen I cannot recognize him. He has blue eyes like Ricky but does not have Ricky's clothes. I wish he were Ricky, but he is not."

Dorothy and Ricardo hugged each other, crying. Roberto hugs them both, trying to comfort each other.

"Don't lose faith, son. God won't let anything bad happen to Ricky."

Lora angrily says.

"Your dad always said you were an asshole, and I always defended you, but I must admit he is right. Of course, he's Ricky!"

"Didn't you listen? He has black hair and does not wear Ricky's clothes!"

Lora angrily answers.

"You are really stupid. They dyed his hair and dressed him in other clothes so he would not be recognized by anyone that might see him!"

The officer is surprised. "The lady is right. You should work as a detective, ma'am."

The doctor shakes his head and says.

"No wonder no one has responded to the case. We must do a DNA test to make sure."

The doctor asks Dorothy.

"Ma'am, would you give us a DNA sample?"

Lora interrupts. "She is not the child's mother. My son Ricardo will give you the DNA sample. Go ahead, get moving. We will wait for the result right here."

Lora has taken charge of the situation and is giving orders everywhere.

After giving the DNA samples, Ricardo joins the family in a hospital waiting room. Television begins to cover Tony's release. A reporter asks him.

"Do you feel hurt by the accusations made against you by Mr. Ricardo Suarez?"

"Not at all. On the contrary, I feel happy."

The reporter, confused, responds.

"I don't get it. How can someone accuse of a horrible crime, and you are happy?"

"It is because he really believed I had committed the crime. I saw the sincerity in his eyes. I understood Ricky really mattered to him as a father loves his son. I begged my sister many times before she died to leave Ricky with me, but she refused. She wanted Ricky to have a father and a family. She said if Ricky did not know his father and stayed only with me, then if I were gone for some reason, he would be left alone in the world. By reuniting Ricky with his father, she made sure that Ricky would have a father and an uncle who would watch over him. My sister must be happy in heaven, and I have faith we will rescue Ricky. That man and that woman had no idea about Ricky's fortune. There was no show of interest of any kind involved from their side."

Lora looks at Ricardo, who is open-mouthed and visibly embarrassed.

"How dare you slander that man like that! Shame on you. I always told you that you should never talk about anyone if you do not have absolute proof of what you are saying!"

Roberto stands up and tells his wife.

"I think it is better that you leave this subject alone. You are not going to come out very well. You also have quite an apology to make and need to ask to be forgiven."

The doctor and the police officer show up in the waiting room and tell Ricardo.

"You can go home. DNA results won't be ready in at least twenty-four hours."

"Thank you, but we will not move from here until the kid recovers."

Dorothy asks the officer.

"Can you tell me if Lieutenant Clark works tonight?"

"No, ma'am, not tonight or the next."

"I didn't know he was on vacation. He is my brother. We don't communicate very often."

"I believe you, ma'am, because your brother was kicked out of the department last week."

Dorothy and Ricardo are surprised by the news.

"That was on the news. Didn't you see it?"

Meanwhile, at the Miami-Dade County Jail Hospital, Robledo opens his eyes after nineteen hours of sleep. They have him under medical observation. Robledo looks around, sees a police officer sitting at the door of the room, sees that he is handcuffed to the bed, and says.

"Fuck! Who would be the son of a bitch who sold me?"

Ocano enters the room and tells him.

"Good morning, Mr. Robledo. I hope you have rested long enough for you to tell me your story, or do you want a lawyer?"

"No, I don't need a lawyer. I haven't done anything wrong, no matter how it looks. It is fate that made a bad move on me."

"Well, explain it to me so that I can understand it. First, sign here that I have read you your Miranda rights and you are voluntarily giving us your statement."

Robledo, seeking sympathy and knowing the judicial system, responds without hesitation.

"Of course, I will sign. I have nothing to hide."

Robledo signs and begins to testify.

"I admit that I am a cheap thief and that it has gotten me into this problem. I was following the extermination companies. I would wait until the second day so that the chemicals are no longer lethal. Then I go to see what they left outside around the house that I could take. I collect all kinds of recycling material that I can later sell. I knew that house was on the second day, so I passed by. I heard two men arguing inside the house and a kid crying. I remembered about the famous kidnapping and the reward. I decided to enter and saw two men. One had a Colombian accent, and the other was an Anglo. The Colombian said they had to kill me because I was a witness, and they could not take that risk. I was very scared when I heard him say, *"Mr. Thomas, we can't take any chances. I will kill him."*

"Then Mr. Thomas said that he did not make the decisions. that only Mr. Tony could give the order. Mr. Thomas got on the phone with Mr. Tony, who said that he didn't want dead people. They covered my face with a gas mask and gassed me. I don't remember anything else until I woke up."

Robledo thinks that Tony is actually the person behind the kidnapping and that his story will get him out of the trouble he is in.

"Did you anytime see Tony?"

"No, I only saw the photo of him on Mr. Thomas's phone when he called him to inform him that I had discovered them."

Ocano takes out four photographs including Tony, Albert, and two other people.

"Which of these is Tony?"

Robledo immediately points to Tony. "This is him. I remember it clearly because my life was in his hands."

Ocano gets up and says.

"Very well, that's all."

"What do you mean that is it? Are you going to lock me up? I am innocent!"

Ocano shows him the photo of Gilbert and tells him.

"I hope you will give me a more credible version when I return, because according to your Mr. Thomas, things are very different."

Robledo pales when he sees Gilbert's photo. Now he is sure that Alex is the traitor. He has no idea what has happened or what Gilbert's story is.

Ocano goes to see Gilbert next. He is older, and so the drugs have had much more effect on him. He has just woken up.

When Gilbert opens his eyes, he knows he is under arrest. Gilbert calls the officer guarding him and tells him.

"I know my rights, and I need to call my lawyer. I will not speak to anyone until I know what is happening and what my charges are."

Ocano has kept them separate so that neither of them knows the other's version. While Gilbert is talking with his lawyer, Ocano takes the opportunity to question Albert.

Ocano allows him to listen to the recording where he incriminates himself with kidnapping during the bribery.

Albert has prepared a story for him and begins to testify.

"I asked Gilbert to go to Miami and look for anything we could use against Tony to win the contract. I admit that it is unethical, but it is not illegal. I promised him a two-hundred-thousand-dollar bonus if he won me the contract. I knew my project was inferior and

I needed a miracle to win the contract. I never thought Gilbert would do something like that. I never would have approved of it or told him to do it. Gilbert, in his ambition and with his unscrupulousness, acted on his own accord. When I found out what was happening, I wanted to report it. I decided to first use the situation to intimidate the vice minister and pressure him to get the contract. My intention was to report it immediately."

Ocano gets up and tells him.

"I'm glad your lawyer is here because I just spoke with Gilbert. We negotiated a reduced sentence, and his story is totally different. He says that he has the necessary proof to verify his version. Take time with your lawyer and rearrange the story. I will return tomorrow at the same time."

Albert begins to have palpitations. He believes Gilbert has gone ahead and handed him over on a silver platter. Albert has to be rushed to the hospital, suffering from heart failure.

Ocano returns to question Gilbert and sits across from Gilbert and his attorney.

"What do you want to know?" Gilbert asks.

"No, I did not come to ask anything. I just want to hear your version of what happened."

The lawyer interrupts. "That is a trap. That way, he can give more information than you ask for."

"Does it mean that your client intends to lie?"

"My client has never lied, nor does he intend to lie."

"So, I don't see why you are scared. Nobody is jailed for telling the truth."

"We are not going to fall into this game. You ask, and he answers."

"Very well. What were you doing inside the house where the child was kidnapped?"

Gilbert feels trapped; the question is forcing him to make a story.

"I have worked for Albert for many years. I know he has no limits, but I never thought he would do something like that."

"What did Albert do?" Ocano asks, undeterred.

"I knew that he was competing against Anthony Clark in a big project in the Bahamas. He proposed that I kidnap Tony's nephew so they would implicate him and arrest him. I flatly refused, and he accused me of being disloyal and a coward. He fired me from work and told me never to come back to his company. Then I realized that Albert was actually the one behind the kidnapping."

"Why didn't you say anything to the authorities?"

"I am a detective. I know the business. I have been solving a case when you were probably at the academy. I wanted to make sure I was correct. I used my underworld contacts to get the information on the kidnappers and tracked them down."

"If you already knew who they were and where they were, why didn't you tell us?"

"That was my mistake. I was carried away by the glory of solving the case of the century all by myself. I didn't do it for the reward. I entered the house and saw the boy tied to the bed. The kidnapper was seated in front of him. I drew my gun and ordered him to kneel with his hands on his head. The adrenaline rush was so great that I didn't realize there was another kidnapper, and suddenly I felt the barrel of a gun behind my head. He ordered me to get down on my knees and drop the gun. Then he put a tissue over my nose, and the next thing I remember, I woke up in the hospital."

Ocano stands up and tells him. "That is a very good story. I congratulate you. It is a pity that Mr. Albert asked first if he could cooperate to obtain a reduced sentence and says that he has evidence that shows the opposite. I think he is ahead of you."

Gilbert feels like a train has just run him over. He knows that Albert would sell his mother to save himself. His face pales, and despite maintaining control, he cannot help but sweat as if he were inside a sauna. Ocano says.

"I have one more question."

The lawyer realizes that Gilbert is totally out of his mind and he needs to reorganize his defense.

"My client will not answer any more questions for today."

"Too bad, because the answer to this question is the only one that can get you out of this mess."

Gilbert desperately says.

"Ask. I will answer."

Ocano takes out Gilbert's phone and dials Mr. Albert's number.

"Can you explain this to me? Why when I dialed Mr. Albert's number Tony's picture appears on your phone?"

Gilbert's jaw drops. He can't answer.

Ocano tells Gilbert.

"You put that photo in your phone before you bought the plane ticket to Miami. You have been in Miami for more than a week. That doesn't match what you just told me."

Gilbert responds.

"My lawyer was very clear to you. I am not going to answer any more questions for today."

* * * * * *

Early in the morning, Frank and Sara appear in the waiting room, where Ricardo, Dorothy, Lora, and Roberto have been since the day before. Sara hugs her daughter and, worried about her, tells her.

"My child, we are worried about you. You do not answer the phone, and you look terrible."

Frank hugs her and tells her.

"Sweetheart, we never thought that this child represented that much to you."

Dorothy, with tears in her eyes, answers them.

"I didn't know it either. He means much more than I imagined. If that child is dies, I think I'll die too."

The waiting room door opens again, and Tony enters with his driver. He is, as usual, very well dressed, and everyone goes silent when they see him enter. There is a moment of uncertainty. They look at each other as if trying to guess what will happen because there have been so many accusations made by Ricardo and Dorothy against Tony. The least they expected is that Tony would demand an apology.

Tony says. "Good morning, everybody."

No one answers. Tony's presence is impressive by itself.

Ricardo stands in front of him, and everyone is waiting for what will happen. Dorothy is shaking, and her father tries to calm her down. Ricardo calmly stares at him in the style of a poker player trying to guess his opponent's cards. Tony, undeterred, tells him.

"Tell me what you have to say, but I prefer you to be sincere."

Ricardo, embarrassed, answers him.

"Everything I said about you in front of the cameras and microphones for several days was said because I believed it and I would say it again if I continued to believe it. I even swore to my parents that I would kill you, even if I had to spend the rest of my life in jail or die while trying. I am assuming responsibility for everything I did, and now, convinced of your innocence, I apologize, and I swear that I will also do it in front of the cameras if they give me a chance. I know I deserve a slap. And do not hold back. I am here to receive it."

Tony responds. "What I want to give you is a big hug, if you will allow me."

Ricardo is surprised but relieved at the same time. Tony and Ricardo hug each other, and Dorothy runs to hug Tony and apologize for her insults.

Tony, with a giant smile, answers her.

"Each one of your insults was a great joy for me. Just knowing that my Ricky could count on someone if I went missing took a great weight off my shoulders. I owe all that to the great vision of my sister, with whom I disagreed and argued many times."

Tony, worried, asks Ricardo.

"What can you tell me about the boy? Was he confirmed to be Ricky?"

Lora interrupts. "Of course, he is Ricky! I know my grandson."

Roberto firmly tells her.

"Can you shut up for once? They are not talking to you. It will be known only when they have the test results."

Ricardo responds with concern.

"The child I saw is unrecognizable, had black hair, and was not wearing his clothes. I cannot guarantee it one hundred percent."

Sara, seeing the anxiety on the face of her daughter, approaches the policeman standing at the door of the intensive care corridor and asks him.

"Could you let my daughter in for a moment to see her son?"

The officer answers sharply.

"No, ma'am, I can't. Only the doctor gives permission."

Sara returns to the group and tells her husband.

"I don't know what that policeman thinks. I asked him the favor of letting Dorothy in to see the child, and he treated me like garbage. I wrote down his name to give to Frank. I would love to see his face when she finds out that my son is Lieutenant Frank Smith."

Dorothy's father takes it as an insult and tells his wife.

"You wait here. I am going to talk to him, and you will see how this is fixed right now."

Dorothy holds her father by the arm and tells him.

"Please don't do it. You better talk to your son first."

"He is very busy. It has been more than a week since we have not seen him. Yesterday he told me that he has too much work and has been very busy."

Dorothy does not want to tell her parents her brother was kicked out of the department, and so she only responds.

"Exactly, he does not need any more headaches."

It is eleven in the morning, and everyone is still in the waiting room. Tony tells his driver to go to the cafeteria and bring seven coffees with milk and guava cakes for everyone.

Frank looks at Tony curiously and asks him.

"Are you Cuban?"

"No, I am Italian. Why?"

"That is Cuban custom. They love coffee with milk and guava pastries."

Tony shakes his head and responds.

"I'm not Cuban, but I love it."

Tony tells the driver again.

"Just bring six. The gentleman here doesn't like it."

Frank instantly responds.

"No, no, I didn't mean that. I just asked if you were Cuban."

Lora, in a strong and shocking tone, says.

"Hey, kid, bring eight! In case the doctor wants, or someone will take a second."

Twenty minutes later, the driver enters with two trays, bringing coffee and cakes, followed by the doctor. Everyone forgets about coffee and cakes and surrounds the doctor.

"What news do you have, Doctor?" Dorothy asks desperately.

"I have good news and bad news. Which one do you want first?"

"I prefer the bad first."

"The child remains in critical condition, but stable, thanks to the induced coma." The doctor shifts slightly. "The good news is that the DNA results confirm he is Ricky."

There are loud shouts of joy in the room. The police and hospital security came running to the waiting room thinking there is fight going on. They all hug one another as if they have always been great friends. Ricky, with his misfortune, has managed to unite two families, including his uncle. Something that none of them would have ever thought off.

The doctor asks for silence and adds.

"With this result, the kidnapping of Ricky is closed. We also know the suspect who died in the accident after abandoning Ricky was one of the kidnappers. Now I need you to give me your medical history so that I can better understand what is happening with the child."

Lora tells the doctor.

"Ask me. He inherited all my allergy problems."

The Suarez family and the Smith family, along with Tony, celebrate the news of Ricky's freedom, toasting coffee with milk and guava cupcakes. When the doctor finishes asking Lora the medical questions, she tells the doctor.

"No, wait, I asked for an extra cup of coffee and a cupcake."

Lora asks her husband.

"Please, Roberto, give the doctor the extra coffee and the guava cake that is on the table."

Roberto looks and doesn't see any extra coffee or cake. Lora, with her high-pitched voice, says.

"Who the hell ate the extra cake that was on the table?"

Frank, ashamed, responds.

"It was me. I thought nobody wanted it."

News about Ricky spreads immediately, and suddenly, the room is filled with reporters. Ricardo and Dorothy take the opportunity to publicly apologize to Tony. Photos of the two families and Tony hugging one another make national news, as do photos of Albert, Gilbert, Alex, and Robledo, who have been implicated in the kidnapping.

******

Ocano receives a surprise call from a witness. He picks up the phone and asks.

"Hello, this is Detective Ocano. Who is this?"

"Hello, Detective. I was the waiter who attended those individuals the day before the kidnapping. They had lunch at my father's restaurant. I was the one that served their table. When they finished their lunch, they made fun of me and threatened to beat me up. I felt powerless and abused. I kept the security tape from the security cameras we have installed outside. These tapes are high-quality since we have had many incidents where customers try to flee without paying."

Ocano could not be happier. That is the icing on the cake. The review of the tapes in the FBI lab is able to reveal even the photo of Tony when Gilbert puts the phone on the table to make the Colombians believe Tony is in charge of the kidnapping. The time on the tape is the same as when Gilbert's phone records list the call to Albert's phone.

******

The Suarez and Smiths get to know one another and interact during that difficult time for both of their sons. They are able to understand that the pain of a child is transmitted to the parents in the same way, regardless of ethnic origin. A friendship grows in two days that have been wasted for more than five years. Lora finds in Sara a friend as gossipy as her Hialeah Spanish friends, only that she don't speak Spanish. Frank finds in Roberto a friend with whom he shares many things in common, such as a love for fishing and a past in the United States Armed Forces. They both had served in the Army and participated in the Vietnam War. Both families have converted that waiting room into a second home, where they take turns to cook and share their food. Ones prepared by Lora, and again prepared by Sara. Tony has also made friends with both families but had to travel to the Bahamas to sign the Cayo Samaná project contract.

The doctor enters the waiting room, and as usual he is surrounded by everyone. The barrage of questions does not take long. The doctor patiently answers them.

"Ricky has been responding favorably, and we have moved him from the intensive care unit to another room where you all will be able to see him. We will begin to reduce his medications to end his coma. We do not know how long it will take for him to react and what the consequences will be after he emerges from the induced coma. He must be kept under strict observation. We have the advantage that Ricky is a strong, healthy child, and with God's favor, this nightmare will be history very soon."

The next day, they are all gathered in the room. The mood has changed. There is no longer the constant crying and uncertainty. It becomes a gathering between old friends telling one another stories from the past while they wait for Ricky to wake up. Each couple recounts the moment they met their soul mate, and at the same time each parent tells how they were opposed to that relationship and thanks God they have been wrong in everything.

Suddenly, they hear a babble and they run toward Ricky's bed. They surround him and see that he has opened his eyes. At that very moment, two men enter the room. It is Tony and Frank Jr., who, for the first time, have taken the courage to go see his sister. Tony and Frank are scared to see everyone crying and saying.

"Ricky, Ricky, look at us! Listen!"

Ricky comes to himself with all lucidity, takes Dorothy's hand, and that of his father. Everyone is silent while Ricky looks at everyone carefully. Ricky sees that Dorothy and Ricardo have grown remarkably old.

Ricky asks them. "What has happened to you?"

Dorothy responds.

"A hundred years have passed in a week of not knowing about you or your whereabouts."

Ricky, with a smile, gives everyone a great relief as they silently listen to his answer.

"I was with Mommy. She came to look for me and took me for a walk through a very beautiful place. There was a large garden loaded with flowers and a stream. We sat in the shade under a large tree. There were many rabbits and many birds. Nana Silvia brought food and cookies. We sat down to have a picnic on a rainbow-colored blanket. Grandpa and Papa Grandpa came with drinks and fruits. Papa Grandpa as always, scolded Grandpa, and Grandpa scolded Mommy, Mommy scolded me, and Nana Silvia scolded us all. Mommy told me that I should call you Mommy and that she thanks you for taking care of me. Papa Grandpa and Grandpa thank Grandfather Roberto for taking care of me and taking me out to the park."

Ricardo asks him. "What did they tell you about me?"

"They said the same old thing, that you are a disaster, but that they are happy you did what you should have done from the beginning."

Ricky sees Tony and gives a cry of joy and extends his arms.

"Uncle! They all send you kisses! Mommy thanks you for having fulfilled her will."

Tony, with tears in his eyes, answers him.

"I am the one who must thank her, and if you see Papa Grandpa again, you tell him his dream of Cayo Samaná project came true yesterday. Half of that is yours. I know you will not spend that money, because you came out to be as stingy as your grandpa and your mother."

******

Three months later, life had changed for all of them. Ricky returned to his mansion, where he lived before with his mother and his grandparents, but this time with Dorothy as Mom and Ricardo as Dad. Kenya and Tamian live with them. Kenya took the place of Nana Silvia, and she delighted everyone with her great culinary talent. Tamian assumed the place of the brother that Ricky never had to play with. Tamima refused to move with her mother and went to live with her grandmother in Georgia. Tony, as a good businessman, entered a partnership with Mr. Bob. They bought the adjacent shopping center to his supermarket and replaced it with a hardware and furniture store. His commercial motto was, "Ricky Has It." Ricardo was in charge of the hardware and furniture store. Dorothy and Mr. Bob oversee the supermarket.

Frank Jr. applied for many police department, but he was rejected due to his dishonorable discharge from the Miami Police Department. His situation was critical, and his arrogance vanished.

Frank, desperate, and as a last resort, shows up in Ricky's mansion to ask for help from his sister, and Kenya opens the door.

"Good morning, lady. Can I speak to Dorothy, please?"

"They just left. They always have breakfast at the supermarket cafeteria on the weekend."

Frank thanks Kenya and heads again toward Miami to speak to his sister. While driving back to Miami, he keeps praying to God his vehicle will not run out of gas since he is driving on an empty tank and has not a single penny left. Ironically, the only job he could find was delivering patio furniture for a small company. His salary is not enough to cover the mortgage and high maintenance of his Miami Beach apartment. He could barely cover his basic necessities.

Frank runs out of gas two blocks from the supermarket. He parks his vehicle and continues walking until he gets to the supermarket cafeteria. He is sweating, pale, and sad.

"Hi, Frank! What a surprise to see you here!" Ricardo tells him.

"Can I join you?" asks Frank.

"Sure. Bring a chair over and join us for breakfast." Dorothy answers.

Frank is tired and hungry, but those are secondary problems. He must forget about his pride and ask for help from the one he has always put down. Frank does not order anything to eat. He keeps moving in the chair as if the chair was on fire. He tries to find the words to ask his sister for help, but he cannot seem to find them.

Dorothy looks at him and tells him.

"Speak, Frank. What do you need?"

Frank, clearly ashamed, responds.

"I am in a critical situation. I need a job. If you could help me, I would be eternally grateful to you!"

Dorothy does not answer. She looks at Ricardo, who is as astonished as her. They both keep silent. It is hard to believe that the one that once said that he did not need anything from a supermarket cashier or from a furniture deliveryman since he only eats at restaurants and his apartment is fully furnished is now asking for help.

After a while, and since neither of them answer, Frank gets up and starts to walk away.

Ricky asks. "Where are you going, Uncle Frank?"

Frank is paralyzed. He never expected Ricky to be the one to call him back, needless to say, he has called him Uncle. Frank turns around and sees Ricky in his usual way, squinting his eyes and pointing his finger at Dorothy and Ricardo.

"No, no, no, you never abandon your family. He is your brother, regardless of how stupid, arrogant, etc. he might be. My grandfather used to say that we all make mistakes but that we all have the right to a second chance."

He then turns to Frank. "I am sure that they can find a job for you, and if they don't, Uncle Tony will give you one."

This time Dorothy and Ricardo are the ones who are ashamed. Ricardo gets up and shakes Frank's hands.

"I am sorry, Frank. Ricky is absolutely right—"

Ricky will not let him finish.

"What am I right about? That he is stupid and arrogant or that—"

Ricardo will not let him finish too.

"Shut up! You are about to ruin all the good you did."

Dorothy can't help laughing. She gets up and hugs her brother.

"Please sit down and have breakfast. I could see that you are starving."

Franks replies. "You are right. I am starving!"

Ricky grabs his plate with both hands and pulls it toward him.

"Uncle Frank, I saw the way you looked at my plate. No, no, no, you get your own!"

Frank, with tears in his eyes, responds.

"Ricky, you are right. I have been stupid and arrogant. I had to hit bottom to realize that I have done many things I truly regret now. I never thought I could be penniless and even run out of gas on the way here."

Dorothy, surprised, asks him. "Where is your car?"

"I ran out of gas two blocks from here, and I do not have a penny in my pocket."

Ricky says.

"Don't worry, Uncle Frank. I will lend you a dollar for gas."

Dorothy looks at him.

"My god! You are the stingiest person I've ever met. What can you buy with a dollar? You did not think twice to pay $128,000 for Kenya's house, and you are going to give only one dollar to Frank, and as a loan?"

Ricky puts on a serious face.

"Yep, but who was going to give the snacks if Nana Kenya would lose her house? You must understand that money is very hard to get these days. But you are right, I would lend him two dollars."

They all laugh, and Tamian says.

"How can you be so stingy, Ricky?"

Ricky points at him and answers, playfully.

"You shut up. Don't think that I forgot you asked me for twenty-five cents when I met you and you still have not paid it back."

Frank joins them for breakfast. While he is eating with them, he cannot take away the picture in his head of Ricky pointing at him with his finger and saying.

"My grandfather used to say, 'Treat everybody fair and with respect, because you never know from whom you might need something in the future.'"

Frank Jr. became the head of security for Ricky Has It, and ironically, the ones he called White trash and wet ass are the ones who, by giving him a job, prevented the bank from foreclosing his Miami Beach apartment. Ricky did not want to get rid of his father's old house in Miami, so he rented it to DJ for the yearly real state tax and the commitment to keep it the same way as it was. When Tony hears the story about how Ricky's neighbor DJ has defended Ricky, he gives him a job as the family driver. Kenya rented her house and, with that money, opened an account to pay for Tamian's college.

On Ricky's birthday, a big party is organized in the courtyard of the mansion. All the Suarez, the Smiths, and many more guests surround the large chocolate cake. Dorothy is going to light a large candle in the shape of the number 9 to represent Ricky's ninth birthday. Dorothy, before lighting the candle, tells him.

"You have to think of a wish, and then you blow the candle to make the wish come true."

Dorothy lights the candle, and simultaneously, Ricky blows it out.

"Why did you do that? Now your wish will not be fulfilled."

"No, Mommy, my wish came true already. I have a family again."

THE END.

www.ingramcontent.com/pod-product-compliance
Lightning Source LLC
LaVergne TN
LVHW091636070526
838199LV00044B/1095